BEAU POOK PROPOSES

Beau Pook Proposes lays bare the jungle of the used car trade and the ruthless operators standing behind their gleaming bangers. Anything but a woman's world, yet Pook enters it in partnership with his great-aunt Dot, a lady born before the motor car was invented, determined to make good in the nation's toughest mart.

We pity them as the victims of the notorious Tax Man con game, then marvel at Aunt Dot's inspired counter-move against the Robbin' Hoods of auto-ville.

But this story is not all power struggle on the forecourts of Britain. Pook tells of his unrequited love for the beautiful Wanda Wells, and how in his despair he wrote to Nurse Dawn of *Family Help* magazine, and how Nurse Dawn came to his side by return of post to begin a love affair to melt the heart of any franchise dealer—wherein Pook becomes engaged to Nurse Dawn's glamorous sister, Gipsy Rosa with the Crystal Ball.

A poignant novel for all men who love cars and for all women who love ugly, muscle-bound men who love cars.

Pook says beauty is only sin-deep anyway.

Peter Pook titles
In the order in which they were originally published

Banking on Form
Pook in Boots
Pook in Business
Pook Sahib
Bwana Pook
Professor Pook
Banker Pook Confesses
Pook at College
Pook's Tender Years
Pook and Partners
Playboy Pook
Pook's Class War
Pook's Tale of Woo
Pook's Eastern Promise
Beau Pook Proposes
Pook's Tours
The Teacher's Hand-Pook
Gigolo Pook
Pook's Love Nest
Pook's China Doll
Pook's Curiosity Shop
Marine Pook Esquire
Pook's Viking Virgins

BEAU POOK PROPOSES

PETER POOK

EMISSARY PUBLISHING
P.O. Box 33, Bicester, OX26 4ZZ, UK.

First published in Great Britain 1973 by
Robert Hale Ltd.

First published in paperback 1996 by
Emissary Publishing, P.O. Box 33, Bicester, Oxon., OX26 4ZZ, UK.
Reprinted 2000

This edition published 2007

British Library Cataloguing-in-Publication Data.
A catalogue record for this book is available from the British Library.

ISBN-10: 1-874490-64-3
ISBN-13: 978-1-874490-64-7

Front Cover Illustration: Richie Perrott

Produced by Manuscript ReSearch (Book Producers)
P.O. Box 33, Bicester, OX26 4ZZ, UK
Tel: 01869 323447 Fax: 01869 322552
Printed and bound by MWL Print Group Ltd., South Wales

ONE

My Auntie Dot—or Aunt Dottie as we called her during her more trying phase—was not really my aunt but my great-aunt. She was extremely secretive about her age, always parrying my investigations into our family history by observing that she was born in the year dot or shortly after, having narrowly missed the Flood owing to her mother's delayed pregnancy.

But the fact which held me in awe about her longevity was that her grandmother had danced with the Prince Regent at a ball in celebration of the Battle of Waterloo. Aunt Dot constantly referred to the Prince Regent as Prinny, as if she herself knew him intimately.

"When I was a little girl my Gran often told me how she had danced with Prinny at the Assembly Rooms in Bath," she said, adjusting her indoor hat. Aunt Dot's indoor hat was only a mini-hat, secured by elastic round her bun like a modern party novelty, serving no useful purpose as far as I could see, except to observe the Victorian rule that one always wore some form of head cover, even in bed.

"How much did it cost to get in the Assembly Rooms, Aunt Dot?" I inquired. "It's one-and-sixpence at the Cudford Assembly Rooms." I seemed always to have been a mercenary child. At the early age of three I discovered how adults were taken by my white curls and blue eyes, often patting my head and giving me sweets money. I encouraged such generosity by gazing up at them with the blue eyes stretched beyond their natural aperture, plus a simpering smile that developed into what I imagined to be an engaging chuckle of goo, goo, goo, goo, till a tiny bubble appeared on my lips. I found this most effective, even with strangers at bus stops. If my relations were sitting down I made no bones about it but simply went across and dumped my head on their laps for fondling. Should they not respond I got hold of their hands and placed them on my curly pate, gurgling and bubbling to indicate it was sweetie time.

"One did not pay to enter the Assembly Rooms, Peter," my aunt replied, taking up the local paper to check the Deaths column. "One received an invitation from Beau Brummell."

"Was he the brother of Bo-Peep? Ha, ha, ha, ha!" I laughed to let my aunt know I had cracked another joke. I considered myself an extremely witty child, though often misunderstood by humourless adults. For example, my Headmaster, Dr Windebank, when he pulled me up for a hole in my shirt at school. I promptly told him it was an Airtex shirt, whereupon, instead of laughing inordinately, he took me into his study and caned me for impudence. Likewise in the Royal Marines one Monday morning when I tried to cheer up Sergeant Canyon by pointing out that he had such a long face today that he should have a wheel fitted to his chin. Instead of chuckling he hit me in the mouth and broke a tooth.

Above all, I learned not to joke with girls because they slapped your face and then cried for you. It was most discouraging to make jokes which produced tears from one's audience, like the dreadful night I kissed Hilda Longbothem of the buck teeth. During our love-talk she said she fancied me because I wasn't pretty like Alec, or rich like Stuart, but ugly like the back of a bus. That was why her pet name for me was Number 14, the bus which stopped at her house.

"Hold on very tightly, please, Number 14!" she giggled, so I said she should fit a car bumper round her teeth. She howled so loudly that her father came out to the porch in search of the cat.

As a teenager I knew lots of silly little courting jokes to whisper in a girl's ear, like "Your teeth are like the stars, darling—they come out at night," and "Your eyes are like pools, sweetheart—football pools," and "Your lips are like petals—bicycle pedals," and "Your ears are like shells, honey—artillery shells". Alec supplied me with a new one: "Darling, your tooth is shining in the moonlight," and many more such gems, until it dawned on me why girls kept leaving me to go out with Alec. His success with girls was phenomenal because he had mastered the art of pleasing them by going all sincere and helpless the moment they met, almost as though he had been taken ill.

"Do you think your Gran danced with Bonny Prince Charlie, Aunt Dot?" I asked, not too sure of my time scale.

She looked at me over her Woolworth's reading glasses. "No, Peter, nor did she dance with William the Conqueror. Now try not to disturb me while I read the Deaths."

"Do you know how many people are dead in Cudford Cemetery, Aunt Dot?"

"No, my child."

"All of them. Ha, ha, ha, ha!"

Aunt Dot checked the Deaths every night in the *Echo,* using a candle to reinforce the electric light, as part of her self-imposed duty of keeping the family together, as she phrased it. Our family displayed a great reluctance to being kept together, despite Aunt Dot's efforts, and appeared more eager to break up on every side. I presumed she checked the Deaths so carefully to ensure no member of the family slipped through her net unnoticed, but she also kept tabs on all her contemporaries' families, too—the Nells, Flo's and Ada's, all dearly beloved and sadly missed, whom Aunt Dot had successfully outlived. She invariably read the verses aloud—'One of the best has gone to rest.'—often wiping her eye during a particularly poignant poem recording the final break-up of a marriage by the untimely departure of one of the partners, usually the husband, to the Hereafter to prepare accommodation for his spouse later on.

Aunt Dot was a devout believer in monogamy, that state of married bliss extending to the grave, wherein the husband had no eyes for another woman all his life, worshipping only his wife until she finally extinguished his passion by burying him in Cudford Cemetery.

It symbolized the idyllic, sexless union so dear to the Victorians, from which children, if any, suddenly appeared in group photographs, like waking up and finding a meteorite in your garden.

On the other hand, Aunt Dot allowed herself ardent admirers who followed her faithfully through the years, waiting in vain for their virgin goddess, at first virile young bucks, then tottery old gentlemen, until they too figured in Aunt Dot's favourite column in the *Echo*.

The facts did not quite fit the picture, because Aunt Dot's late husband had had eyes for several women down the years, and Aunt Dot's faithful swains had filled in the waiting period by marrying and re-marrying far beyond the norm of unrequited love. In fact, Aunt Dot's husband, Sydney, spent much of his married life in pubs, which he called refugee camps for husbands, and he was known to be particularly fond of the Bold Forester in Cudford, where women were not encouraged, not only as a customer but also on occasion as a lodger above the tap bar. Sydney made no secret of the fact that he liked war, especially those on the scale of World War I, which he regarded in the light of free foreign holidays for thirty million men unaccompanied by their wives. Rumour alleged that he had gone so far as to petition the Government to start another one shortly before his demise.

Uncle Sydney seldom spoke when not in the Bold Forester, having been born of an over-possessive mother who performed that chore for him whenever he opened his mouth, and this oral function was taken over by Aunt Dot upon marriage. She was able to put his thoughts into words on the basis of an almost telepathic communication between husband and wife, thus: "No, he's had quite enough for one night, thank you, and does not want another drink." Similarly, she was sufficiently clairvoyant to see into the future on his behalf, thus:

"No, Sydney won't be able to play darts tomorrow night because he wants to take me to the pictures."

Aunt Dot had adapted to the cinema with the ease she had adapted to the motor car and the aeroplane earlier in her life. She liked to see Queen Mary in particular on the screen, and when the Queen waved from her carriage Aunt Dot waved back enthusiastically, crying out: “I remember your Grandmother, Queen Victoria, your Majesty”.

Some years later her daughter, Aunt Mabel, refused to watch *Songs of Praise* on television if it was supper-time because she considered it irreverent for the congregation to have to sing and see her eating her supper in front of them. Likewise, when the Dean of St Paul’s delivered a sermon I was required to stand in front of the screen while Aunt Mabel sipped her gin. If a play displeased her she always forbade me to switch off or change channels lest the actors should lose their jobs on her account; so we had to endure everything in the name of full employment. During these plays she often warned actors who were in danger of attack from behind, and she was especially prone to exposing actresses who were taking advantage of unwary males or good women.

It would have been easy to mock Aunt Mabel on this score but I reminded myself that she came from an era when there were no cars, television, radio, aeroplanes, pneumatic-drills, motor-bikes or articulated trucks to break the heavenly silence that must have hung over the world since the beginning of time right up to Aunt Mabel’s coming-of-age. So I willingly changed chairs with her when Hughie Green persisted in winking at her from the screen, and even fetched bread-crumbs to scatter round the set during visits to Bird Island, and looked under the TV table to ensure that the Saint had not dropped his gun there, and searched beneath her bed before retiring, lest the missing body in the Whodunit had been hidden upstairs during the News.

Hanging on the wall was a fascinating sepia picture of Aunt Dot and Uncle Sydney posed on their wedding day like wax-works. Uncle Sydney stood to attention, except that both arms were positioned akimbo to resemble a two-handled vase, as if Aunt Dot was at liberty to put her own arm through either handle. She had chosen the left handle by hanging a gloved hand through it. Uncle Sydney had been married in military uniform, brass-buttoned and bemedalled, crowned by a pillbox hat and strap above a symmetrically perfect moustache shaped like a coat-hanger, the ensemble supported below on a pair of robust boots, indicative of his determination to march to the honeymoon resort.

Aunt Dot was one huge wedding dress, bustle, train, veil, hat, gloves, bouquet, horseshoe, ribbons, flowers, jewellery, beads, muff, feathers, prayer book, fan, leg-o'-mutton sleeves, frills, curls and several unidentifiable accessories essential to a Victorian bride. She must have had a bottom drawer like a haberdashery warehouse, and Uncle Sydney once told me how Aunt Dot's legs had been designed by nature on the dining-room table principle, solely to keep her body off the floor.

Beneath the wedding-cake hat so little of Aunt Dot's face was visible except nose and mouth that there was scant pictorial evidence to support the theory that Uncle Sydney had married Aunt Dot. It could have been anyone, or even a dummy supplied by the photographer. As a child, I gazed at the picture for hours, trying to solve the mystery of why Aunt Dot had been married in a palace of Imperial Rome. They were posed on the marble steps of some mighty edifice, flanked by statues of Mars and Julius Caesar, leading up to the Temple of Jupiter. Through the fluted columns of the portico I could see the Vestal Virgins performing a dance, while in the extreme background there was a tantalizing glimpse of the Roman Legions fighting the Sabines. Adding to the mystery was the faded caption on the border of the picture : 'Bert Langer & Son, Popular Studios, 27a High Street, Cudford. (Opposite Station.)'

"Were you married during a battle, Aunt Dot?" I inquired puzzledly.

"I certainly was, my child. There was the Boer War in South Africa and your uncle's family on the home front."

"Is that Uncle Sydney's family fighting in the picture?"

"In a manner of speaking, yes, Peter. Or it could be the reception."

"Why did you have a pagan wedding, Aunt Dot?"

"Because I married into a pagan family. Your uncle always thought he was a Centurion in the Imperial Guard instead of a Sergeant in the Hussars."

"Why did you wear your wedding cake on your head, Aunt Dot?"

"It was safer there than at the reception. If you look closely you will see a crate of beer hidden beneath my bridal train for the same reason."

"Why are the bridesmaids dancing in the temple with no clothes on, Aunt Dot?"

"I expect your uncle had pawned their dresses."

In actual fact, Aunt Dot was anything but pagan, being High Church to a degree. She attended St Mildred's for the purpose of worshipping Father Dee, a worthy cleric whose histrionic personality sometimes relegated God to a side chapel, and who was considered by my aunt to be the English Pope. Today Father Dee is dead and his beautiful church has been prostituted as a warehouse pending its demolition to make room for the modern short-cut to Heaven, a motorway—but his influence and good works live on despite progress and roadworks.

I found it extremely disconcerting to have Aunt Dot praying for me when I started teenage courtship in Cudford. After my first date with Hilda Longbothem she took me aside to her bedroom, where we knelt in prayer while Aunt Dot raised her eyes to the ceiling to ask that I might be given strength for my ordeal. At first I thought what a good idea this was under the circumstances, but I soon realized that the strength I needed was to overcome carnal desires and to despise weaknesses of the flesh, that I might go through life like a lay monk and not see Hilda Longbothem again. I learned to countermand her prayers by silently reversing all her requests, praying to see Hilda Longbothem again as soon as possible, and to be given strength to cope with all the other girls I had my eye on locally. Furthermore, I added a special prayer that

Aunt Dot might not find out about them, especially Bunty Tope, who had already offered me sixpence to take her into the back row of the Troxy Cinema.

Soon I was offering thanksgiving prayers in respect of Margaret McKay—my first introduction to the most feminine and desirable of the female species, the Scots lassies. Margaret McKay, with her demure ways, saucy tongue and delightful laughter, rapidly had me praying that my family should move house to Scotland, that I might reside at the source of supply of these irresistible charmers whose Robbie Burns' dialect was for me the language of love.

Learned, too, that life goes full circle, for soon I was praying for strength to overcome carnal desires and reject weaknesses of the flesh in case Margaret McKay wrecked my prospects of becoming a professional footballer by leaving me a burnt-out roué at the age of fifteen.

I remember my Uncle Sydney telling me that the ideal age for marriage was fifty-five, provided your bride was wealthy and in poor health. Uncle Sydney had a most peculiar facial expression difficult to describe in words. It was as though he kept opening a jam-pot and finding a wasp inside which flew out to sting him. Another eccentricity of his was to rise from the meal table for the purpose of emptying the tea-leaves on the carpet, then sweeping the carpet all over with a longhandled broom. This process resulted in a dust-free brown carpet.

Uncle Sydney also arranged daily rows with his wife to keep her happy. He explained to me how women liked rows, and how many marriages broke up for the lack of them. He said that in the past there was no radio, let alone television, so people had rows instead—whereas today people had to be content with watching rows on television, which wasn't the same, just as seeing cookery programmes was no substitute for eating food.

Uncle Sydney explained the three ways to have a row with women. The first was to disagree with what they said; the second was to agree with what they said; the third and easiest method was to say nothing. The most successful husbands said nothing, thus allowing the wife the whole show without the inconvenience of competition or interruption. When Uncle Sydney died, Aunt Dot declared she missed their rows more than any other facet of a long married life.

Another thing Aunt Dot liked was gossip, especially about fast women. A frequent caller was Madam Maude, who went to Paris a lot on unspecified business I could never fathom. As a child I loved to be in the room when she called because Aunt Dot made larger-than-life grimaces behind her back to my relations and mouthed silent words to them, like ‘all lies’ and ‘don’t mention Fred’.

When Madam Maude had departed, presumably to Paris, Aunt Dot invariably informed the company that our visitor was too fond of John Thomas, and that her obsession for this individual would prove her undoing. My inquiries as to who John Thomas was always seemed to throw the company into confusion and I was reminded it was past my bed-time.

“If Madam Maude loves John Thomas so much, why does she go to Paris with Uncle Fred?” I asked Aunt Dot puzzledly.

Uncle Sydney looked in his jam-pot, saw a wasp, then exclaimed that I had answered my own question.

“Don’t be disgusting, Sydney,” Aunt Dot admonished him. “As for you, Peter, you shouldn’t display such unnatural curiosity in what the grown-ups say.”

I went over and dumped my curls on her lap to forestall bedtime, then gurgled a bit to bring out her maternal instinct. “Peterkins only wants to know who John Thomas is, Auntie,” I whined. “Lots of the ladies talk about him and Madam Maude loves him, yet he never comes here to see us. Isn’t Uncle Fred jealous?”

“Don’t bother your head with such nonsense, child, and stop calling yourself Peterkins as though you were still a normal infant instead of a precocious little eavesdropper.”

"I've even looked him up in Kelly's Directory but I can't find him, so I expect he lives in Paris."

"Here's sixpence for some sweeties tomorrow, so go to bed now and try to dream about puff-puffs and Red Indians like other children of your age."

"How do ladies jump into men's trousers, Auntie?"

"Bed, child!"

"Would Uncle Fred teach me to play slap-and-tickle, Auntie?"

"Off to bed with you!"

"Why does Madam Maude always blush when Uncle Fred says that, Auntie?"

Another occasion I shall never forget was Aunt Dot's birthday party when she stood up to make her memorable speech about her great age and how one could live too long on this earth. I recall how the family nodded agreement and said "hear, hear", and my Uncle Ted whispered something about leaving them the money before they were all dead. Then Aunt Dot sat down and disappeared from this earth as I pulled her chair away from under her—a stupid and dangerous prank I still regret to this day. The company was so shocked that brandy had to be administered all round until some members of the family were actually drunk with remorse, and my father patted my head in such a way that I got a fat ear. But they all said I was only six, so I couldn't be held responsible and remarked what a cute, repulsive child I was. My Uncle Ted explained to me what a dreadful thing I had done to my aunt and gave me a shilling.

To compensate for my behaviour I piped up with my little jokes about Aunt Dot being so old that she needed three birthday cakes to hold all the candles, and that if she lived much longer Saint Peter would send down for a doctor's certificate. Everybody laughed and said what a precocious, revolting child I was, to be sure, so I chuckled engagingly and offered my curly head all round for fondling and sweetie money.

When Aunt Dot had taken sufficient brandy to recover from

the fall and the family had had enough of my new laugh, which I produced by covering the lower lip with my teeth and going fee-fee-fee-fee-fee for as long as they would stand for it, Uncle Ted inquired what I would be when I grew up.

"Judging by the way he's going on now he'll probably grow up to be an orphan," my father predicted.

"If he grows up," Uncle Sydney warned. "What would you like to be, Peterkins?"

"I should like to be rich," I replied without hesitation. "And I should like to be a money-lender, and I should like to be a lover man like John Thomas."

"It is my opinion," Aunt Dot said coldly, "that if he studies hard he could become a qualified idiot."

"Then you could leave me all your money, Auntie—fee, fee, fee, fee!" I ran round to Aunt Dot and thrust my head on her lap to remind her I was her ultimate heir. To keep the family on their hospitality toes, Aunt Dot let it be known that she had Money, and the family let it be known that they could do with it while still in possession of their faculties. Uncle Ted had gone so far as to give her a pamphlet on how to avoid death duties by an early dispersal of wealth, but I, with the ingenuousness of youth, once confronted her wearing my Dick Turpin mask and brandishing my Dick Turpin cap-pistol to deliver the familiar ultimatum of "Your money or your life!"

Such was the influence of the cinema during my early days that I shocked the family by producing a plan whereby we could obtain our inheritance without detection following Aunt Dot's nightly glass of stout and her resultant departure to the next world with the glass still in her hand. Rich aunts were ten-a-penny in the movies I saw every week at the Troxy, wherein their role was to get knocked off while the audience were settling in their seats and stowing their coats underneath, in order to get the plot going and provide the money for which the principal actors were to murder each other during the rest of the film. We knew from the movies that only bank tellers and Fort Jackson sentries had a shorter life expectancy than rich aunts, their acting careers prematurely terminated by bullets, arrows and arsenic in that order, almost before the house lights had been lowered.

My father was extremely angry when I explained my plan to him, declaring I must be severely punished by being sent to bed early. I tried to cry in case he noticed it was already past my bedtime, and dumped my curly head on his lap.

"Peterkins thought you would be pleased with him for planning something you often said you would do yourself, dad-dah," I whined, getting hold of his hand and putting it on my head.

"I think it is high time you and I had a private talk together, my boy," father said.

"If it's about the birds and the bees again, dad-dah, can we get on to genes and chromosomes, like we're doing at school?"

I attended the Convent of the Holy Angels, where they had to struggle on without the aid of modern educational theories, relying on good tuition and hard work to produce results. I was now eight years old and already studying such subjects as Biology, Algebra, French, Latin and Greek. Despite this old-fashioned approach to learning, we were all happy, normal children without psychological or neurotic complications, nor were we too exhausted to play football, cricket and tennis in our free time.

"No, Peter, I want to talk to you about your obsession with money. Now, your mother gave you a nice teddy-bear money-box some time ago. Have you been using it?"

"Yes, dah-dah. I save my sweetie money and my pocket-money and my presents."

"How can you save your presents?"

"I sell them to my friends, dad-dah."

"So how much is in your money-box to date?"

"Thirty-eight pounds, fourteen and fivepence ha'penny, dad-dah."

"Ye gods!"

Like most adults I spoke to, my father seemed shocked every time I opened my mouth, like at school where most of the boys were studying for the priesthood or missionary work. I was there on a much less positive basis, having derailed a tram with the aid of our kitchen poker, as I described in *Pook's Tender Years.* When Bishop Maloney visited the Convent of the Holy Angels to ask the boys about their careers, he smiled serenely at future priests and missionaries until he came to me. I replied, "Fleet Gunnery Officer, Monseigneur," which seemed to wipe the smile off his face, even though Reverend Mother Blake warned him I was a Protestant.

Bishop Maloney received a second surprise when he crossed over to the girls to see who wanted to be nuns, where he observed pretty little Daphne Coombe my ex-girl-friend, slightly marred today by a black eye she received in a dispute with me over this very vocation of nunhood. Bishop Maloney had a word with Mother Blake, whereupon she told me to open all the windows in the hall owing to the warm weather. While I was performing this chore I noticed that Bishop Maloney was blessing all the other children. I hurried back and knelt down in front of the Bishop with my eyes shut and hands clasped in order to be blessed, but now all the other children were kissing his ring.

Mother Blake came over and told me I could close the windows now because of the draught. I complied as quickly as possible, then joined the kissing queue, but Bishop Maloney was now blessing our rosaries. Being a Protestant I didn't possess a rosary so I pinched Daphne Coombe's and hurried back to the Bishop, only to find he had suddenly begun to bless Mother Blake. I knelt down beside her in blessee pose on her left, just as the Bishop turned to the right to commence a general prayer for all Roman Catholics in the room.

"Bishop Maloney forgot to bless me, Mother Blake," I complained.

"Oh, what a shame, child. Never mind, go and fetch the holy water and he'll do it then."

"Where is the holy water, Mother Blake?"

"In the Chapel of Rest, Peter."

"But that's nearly half a mile away."

"So you must hurry, child, or you'll miss him."

I set off across the Convent grounds for the Chapel of Rest as fast as my little legs would carry me, but when I returned breathless with the jug of holy water I saw all the children singing on the steps of the main building. Mother Blake called out, "Join in the singing, Peter," so I did with gusto.

After three verses I said to Daphne Coombe, "What are we singing for, little nun?"

"We're singing good-bye to Bishop Maloney," she informed me in treble song. "We're singing farewell to his Grace tra-la."

"Where is he then?"

"He's gone back to Ireland far over the sea; Oh, 'tis such a pity he cannot take me, tra-la."

"Sing up, everybody!" Mother Blake cried over our heads, so I stood there singing as loudly as I could, "We're singing good-bye to Bishop Maloney; We're singing farewell to his Grace, tra-la. He's gone back to Ireland far over the sea; Oh, 'tis such a pity he cannot take me, tra-la."

The high moral tone of the Convent of the Holy Angels was one which did not look with favour on pupils murdering rich aunts for their money, yet it demanded that one told the truth—even if you had murdered her. Thus I was slightly hurt that my father did not believe how much was in my money-box until he had counted it for himself. When he had satisfied himself I had told the truth I made sobbing noises and wiped my eyes with his tie. Then I said, "Dad-dah doubted Peterkins' word, didn't dad-dah?"

"Yes, I'm afraid I did, because I couldn't imagine any child of your age amassing so much money. I'm sorry, Peter. While we're at it, for heaven's sake stop snivelling and calling me dad-dah—my friends at the club wonder if you're mentally retarded or something."

"Shall I call you pah-pah, dad-dah?"

"Call me anything you like but don't drag it out as if you're in pain. Another thing, Peter, you're too old now to go around ramming adults with your head for sweets money."

"Supposing—just supposing—I could save fifty pounds in my money-box by next Christmas, would you double it like Alec's dad-dah does?" I did not add that the sum doubled by Alec's father was seven shillings.

My father laughed at the notion, so I gave him the big blue eyes and pouting lips. "All you need now is a bar of soap and you'd be Bubbles," he chuckled. "Yes, Peter, I'll take you on for fifty pounds provided you don't . . . er . . . well, provided your Aunt Dot isn't involved in any way. You mustn't have bad thoughts about your aunt even in fun, understand?"

"Don't go away, dad-dah, because I have a big surprise for you. I'll run upstairs and fetch it."

Momentarily my father experienced an uneasy feeling that I had gone to drag Aunt Dot's body down to the living-room for his inspection, but I soon reassured him by returning with my china piggy-bank. Opening it I proudly counted out fifteen pounds, three shillings and ninepence, plus odd farthings and foreign coins.

"I've managed to save up fifty-three pounds, eighteen and fourpence, dad-dah," I announced triumphantly, doing the sum in my head, then doubling it. "So now you've made your lovely promise I've got one-hundred-and-seven pounds, sixteen and eightpence—enough to buy a new Ford motor-car and I'm only eight. Aren't I a lucky little shod?"

When my father had recovered from the revelation of my early business acumen he took me to task over what I had called myself. He said, "Where on earth did you pick up that vile expression, Peter?"

"Oh, it's Uncle Sydney's pet name for me," I explained. "He often uses it when he's a wee bit drinky."

"Do you know what it means?"

"I think it's something to do with horses' hoofs, dad-dah."

"Good. We'll leave it at that. Now you come along with me to the Post Office and we'll open a savings account for you. That way you won't lose my money."

"And I'll earn a lot of interest, too, dad-dah."

"Do you know what interest is already, Peter?"

"Principal multiplied by Rate multiplied by Time divided by one hundred equals interest, dad-dah. We learn it at school."

"Remarkable! Could you work out how much interest your hundred pounds will earn?"

"Five pounds, dad-dah."

"No, Peter—two pounds, ten shillings."

"No, dad-dah, five pounds. Auntie Dot has promised to double it for me."

"Now I know why Uncle Sydney called you a lucky little shod. What made her do that?"

"Because I promised not to poison her stout, dad-dah."

As my father donned his hat he gave me a long searching look.

TWO

Aunt Dot often told me the family history in all its ramifications but the part I liked best was about my great-grandfather, the celebrated writer, Thos. Wm. Pook, Esq., Gent., late Blenheim Towers. I extracted the above entry from the parish register, wherein he had been entered in beautiful copperplate, marred only by the Victorians' strict economy with their ink.

For years I laboured under the illusion that his name really was Thos. Wm. Pook, Esq., and that he was the Gent who arrived late at some function at Blenheim Towers. This did not strike me as remarkable because all the other Gents in the parish register also arrived late at their various destinations; page after page of unpunctuality in what I termed the late book, like the one we kept at school.

The adjacent entry of another celebrated writer, one Geo. Jas. Payne, intrigued me, too. He was not a Gent. but a Paup., and was recorded in the book for having been late at Cudford Workhouse.

Aunt Dot constantly impressed on me what a great writer Thos. Pook had been, but it seemed that his works proved so popular throughout the world of letters that there was none extant for me to read. On the other hand the family papers showed that a great many admirers wrote to him, mostly begging letters demanding the payment of bills, settlement of loans and return of goods. Some of these admirers seemed to be souvenir-hunters, like Jem Judd (Stationer), of Cudford, who wished to collect Thos. Pook's paper, pens, nibs and ink, while others sought his clothes, boots—and even his rooms.

In order to maintain the literary tradition in our family Aunt Dot presented me with the family typewriter instead of donating it to Cudford Museum. It was an original Borton-Price machine, probably their prototype, with the typeface mounted on a wheel which spun round when you pressed a key and then banged the paper with considerable force to imprint the letter. It had what was known as a legal carriage, three feet long, for typing leases, wills and Acts of Parliament, or you could produce your own newspaper on it or emboss wallpaper. Owing to the vibration the machine set up and its factory-like noise in operation, I was allowed to type only when the house was empty, but even then the neighbours complained to my parents about it.

My initial success as a writer came at the age of nine, when Aunt Dot submitted a story entitled *Mary Quite Contrary* to a competition sponsored by a national firm of garden fertilizers. I had written many stories before but this was the first one I had managed to type out in full on the Borton-Price machine so perfectly that other people could read it, and so carefully that the machine had not torn up my work as I went along. I wrote the story in a day but it took me three weeks to type it fit for public gaze. The competition judges must have thought they were handling the Magna Carta rather than a story script, and probably this factor led to its winning first prize.

With the entry I sent a carefully worded covering letter: *Dear Sir, I am very interested in garden fertilizers and storywriting because my great-grandfather was the celebrated novelist. Thos. Wm. Pook, Esq., Gent., whose works are now unfortunately unreadable. I am very keen to win a year's free supply of garden fertilizer and a Remington junior Portable Typewriter, and as you read this manuscript you will understand why. My aunt says it is ruining my eyesight and keeping the neighbours awake. I am only nine years of age, but in case you do not believe me I enclose a photograph of myself when I was only eight, taken with my Uncle Sydney, who says I might well win this competition because I am a lucky little shod. Your sincere admirer, Peter Pook.*

MARY QUITE CONTRARY

In the northern part of Finland stood a little cottage and in it lived a farmer and his wife. The woman, like all contrary people, was stupid, and she always said no when she was expected to say yes, and always said yes when she was expected to say no.

As Christmas was near, the husband wanted to have the house full of visitors, so he went to his wife.

He said, "Wife, Christmas is near and we cannot have white bread because it is too expensive."

"What!" cried the woman, "no white bread! Anyone would think we were beggars."

"All right," said the man, "just a little white bread since your heart is set on it."

This continued till the man had everything he wanted: coffee, white bread, wine, visitors, fruit, nuts and coal.

Just before Christmas they were crossing a river spanned by a single plank bridge, and after the man had crossed to the other side he warned his wife to be careful when she crossed. But as she was so contrary she started jumping and dancing in the middle—and all of a sudden the plank gave way and she was carried off by the current.

The husband shouted, "Help, help!" until some haymakers heard and came to see what the matter was. The man told them, so they said, "Go downstream and find her," but the man said that she was so obstinate that she had floated upstream.

Then he went home and enjoyed the party .

The original story I wrote was twice the length of the above extract, only because I prefaced it with a geographical survey of Finland in order to set the scene. Where I obtained the idea or such insight into feminine psychology I cannot recall at this distance of time; suffice to say the story won me the coveted Remington typewriter which has withstood the battering of time and travel over the years so well that it has produced over a million words of

Pook books—including this one. The garden fertilizer I sold to my Uncle Ted, which was a mystery unto itself because he lived in a flat.

Inflamed by such early success I wrote for our school magazines continuously, but professional acceptance was much harder to achieve. In my late teens I had collected so many rejection slips that I decided the world was not yet ready for me. Then I wrote an academic article entitled *Is Time an Illusion?* which I sent to *Family Help.* This was an elementary discourse on the theory of relativity, for which *Family Help* was not yet ready either. However, when the Editor returned *Is Time an Illusion?* to me he enclosed a nice little note saying that he might be interested in an article from me on something like *How to Mend a Clock.*

Sinking my professional pride, I consulted a watchmaker friend of mine and managed to write *How to Mend a Clock,* which the Editor bought for two guineas. I quickly followed up such a literary triumph, based on my experience with Aunt Dot's family heirloom, by selling *How to Mend a Typewriter.* This led to *How to Mend a Tap, How to Mend a Fountain-pen and How to Mend a Fuse.*

I now saw myself as the Somerset Maugham of the repair world, so, in order to raise the literary merit of my work, I invented a Mr Bob Fixit, probably the most accident-prone man in fiction. Every Saturday Mr Fixit took a stroll down the road but he could not go fifty yards without meeting Mrs Brown wheeling her punctured bicycle, or Mr Smith struggling to light his pipe with a defective cigarette lighter, or little Johnny crying over his broken toy. If Mr Fixit entered a pub, all the lights went out as he opened the bar door; if he visited the cleaners, the iron went up in smoke; if he shopped at the butchers, the scales broke under the weight of his order. Although Mr Fixit brought great joy into his victims' lives by mending everything on the spot I could never rid myself of the feeling that his footsteps must have been dreaded by the tradesmen of the town.

When Mr Fixit's sister showed him a photograph of her daughter the frame felt to bits in his hands, and nobody in their right mind would entrust him with a piece of valuable china.

I tried desperately to break out of this rut, sending Mr Fixit to watch a football match, where, directly he took his seat in the south stand, the goalkeeper broke his leg. I entitled this article *How to Mend a Leg,* based on the St. John Ambulance manual, *First Aid to the Injured,* but the Editor rejected it on the grounds that it cut across his Medical Advice column, and warned me to get back to taps.

The irony of it was my inability to repair anything myself, being of an unmechanical mind that left our household littered with damaged articles, but it seemed that the readers of *Family Help* possessed insatiable appetites for repair work or enjoyed the thrill of reading about it in the style of a do-it-yourself Dickens.

When Mr Fixit attended a funeral—perhaps of a reader of mine who misinterpreted the instructions in *How to Mend an Electric Fire*—and the bell ceased tolling in the church tower, I sensed I had reached the end of my tether. The Editor pointed out that *How to Mend a Church Bell* had an extremely limited appeal in the home, so I gave Mr Fixit a dog named Sniff.

Now when Mr Fixit took his Saturday stroll Sniff dragged his master to all sorts of situations in the repair world not normally apparent to humans, such as elderly ladies lying on the floors of their lonely flats overcome by faulty gas-stoves, or trapped in lavatories through defective locks.

Now and again I slipped in a rogue article like *How to Mend a Broken Heart,* but the Editor, Jock Campbell, was adamant that I should not trespass on Nurse Dawn's territory in the magazine, a lady of infinite wisdom who covered Love, Babies, Lustful Lodgers, Warts, Fat, Mothers-in-Law, Unwanted Hairs and Women's Ailments.

Time came when for the life of me I could think of nothing more to mend that could conceivably be broken by man, beast or nature, so I begged Jock Campbell to let me do a travel series by way of a holiday from odd-job man. He agreed, provided the articles showed how people abroad mended things in their homes, igloos and tents.

For my new breakthrough in international repair work I introduced a character named Colonel Crane, who, for obvious reasons, never travelled without his faithful dog Scratch. I also gave Colonel Crane an opening tag-line for use each week as he found himself in a new part of the globe. It went like this: "Well, bless my soul, Scratch, what can that interesting object be up yonder? Surely not the Great Pyramid of King Cheops, who died nearly sixty centuries ago?/Surely not the Panama Canal, which first connected the Atlantic and Pacific Oceans back in 1914?/ Surely not the mighty Statue of Liberty which stands at the mouth of the Hudson River, New York?/Surely not the mighty Niagara Falls, 167 feet high, separating Canada from the U.S.A.?..."

Scratch played his part like this: "Well, bless my soul, Scratch, what can that interesting object be that you have dug up in mistake for a bone? Bless my soul, Scratch, it is a bone! Surely not the remains of a mummy from the Dynasty of King Tutankhamen?"

Whatever Colonel Crane saw or Scratch dug up or brought to his master in his jaws—like the boa-constrictor he sniffed out in Venezuela, or the shrunken head he mistook for a play ball in Borneo—the next line was invariably the same: "Bless my soul, Scratch, I must hurry up and tell the readers of *Family Help* all about our exciting discovery."

Dear old Jock Campbell wrote to me—not to the four corners of the earth but to Cudford, where I was travelling a great deal to the public library for more adventures—about this series of articles: 'Dear Peter, Bless my soul, thank you for your latest, in which your bloodhound managed to sniff out the Great Wall of China. The stories are quite interesting and unusually presented, but I cannot detect in them an awful lot of household hints as we agreed upon. See what you can do.'

I did not answer this letter. Instead, by way of a leg-pull, I sent in an article entitled *How to Mend Sydney Harbour Bridge,* full of instructions like 'Visit your local hardware store and purchase a box of one million seven-eighths rivets', and 'You will require a pair of steps two hundred feet high and an eighty-gallon pot of undercoat'.

The joke proved to be on me because Jock Campbell printed the article in the next issue of *Family Help.* As always, he took no chances with his readers, inserting a notice above the title saying: 'This will make you laugh'—just as above my former articles he had stated: 'This will help you', and over the serials he warned: 'This will make you cry.' Even above the Crossword he put: 'This will puzzle you', as though his readers needed guidance as to whether they should laugh or cry over any given feature, or would be confused over the ghost story unless told: 'This will frighten you.'

Once in jest I queried his announcement on the Cookery Page that 'This will make you hungry'. I pointed out that, in view of the recipe given, it was illogical. It should have read 'This will fill you up' or even 'This will make you sick'. Food which made you hungry was a rare bird.

Jock Campbell replied in a characteristic letter, headed, 'This will make you wiser': 'Dear Peter, The secret of good journalism is to find out what the customer wants, then tell him he wants it, then give it to him. But to be on the safe side you have to tell him that what you're giving him is what he wants—and because you've got a lot of it, you have to tell him he wants more. Finally, you have to explain what his reaction should be to a particular feature; this gives him a feeling of security—otherwise you would have readers crying over the Crossword or being frightened by the Dress Patterns.

'Several customers wrote in to confirm that *How to Mend Sydney Harbour Bridge* made them laugh, so let's have some more. What about *How to Mend the Gobi Desert?* Don't forget to write!'

As I struggled through the night trying to write on that most difficult of all subjects, *How to Mend the Gobi Desert,* it occurred to me that Jock Campbell didn't mind what you contributed to *Family Help* provided it was a series about mending things. I had noticed that even his current serial concerned the torrid romance of a jobbing plumber who fell in love with the maid of the house where he was stripping down the hot water system and decalcinating the boiler, explaining each step of the operation to his beloved in the dialogue as she played plumber's mate on her half-days. It was the only love story I ever saw with a pull-out diagram of a Jackson-Smith back boiler.

Soon I found myself in another rut, scraping the humour barrel dry trying to tell the cosseted readers of *Family Help* how to mend such large edifices as the Eiffel Tower and the Aswan Dam—but at least it had got me started on the funnies, despite those readers who wrote in for more detailed instructions or sectional drawings in order to complete the job.

Meanwhile, back at the ranch, as they say, my love life took a strange new twist. People were extremely impressed when they learned I was a young writer.

"I write, you know," I used to say at parties.

"Oh, how wonderful! I've always wanted to be a writer. I'd write a novel if only I could find the time. What is your pen name?"

"Peter Pook."

"I've never heard of you, but that's probably my fault. What sort of things do you write?"

"Humour."

"Oh, that! I thought you were a real writer. I expect you could do with some funny jokes then."

I learned early on never to tell people I wrote humour or mention *Family Help.* I found it expedient to say vaguely that I wrote biographies or about the political scene, which seemed to impress people. Sometimes I told them I wrote technical hand-books for displaced persons or historical trade fillers, religious thrillers and science-fiction operas—but never comedy.

I had been a tall thin youth up to the age of thirteen, when Aunt Dot began to feed me on near-raw steaks, eggs and cheese in large quantities. Aunt Dot believed the trouble with world was undernourishment, a theory which resulted in premature deaths of her dog and canary through over-eating.

At the same time my father enrolled me for a postal course of body building called Power-Surge. So successful was this course that at the age of sixteen I passed the final tests and gained my diploma as a Perfect Brute, Grade One (Junior), and the Principal of Power-Surge, Bruce Bold, recommended me to go on for Perfect Brute, Grade One (Senior), at two thirds the standard fees, tempting me with the prospect of being entered at the Earls Court Show as the Biggest Brute of the Year.

I was too shrewd to fall for the Earls Court bait, because, unless Bruce Bold entered me in the Ladies' Section, I stood no chance, being a comparative dwarf of only six-feet-three. Nevertheless, I enrolled for the Senior Course, which—as I have told elsewhere—led me, not to Earls Court, but to Cudford General Hospital's hernia ward.

I was fond of displaying my physique around Cudford Swimming Club, smelling strongly of coconut oil and vinegar, our formula for bronzed Adonises of the beach and thirsty flies. I was rather worried at the time on two counts. First, the weird experience in my bedroom recently, where, having completed the evening's Power-Surge exercises with two hundred press-ups, I was alarmed to discover all my muscles throbbing unbidden. I felt an overwhelming desire for fresh air, so I went down to our garden. Suddenly I heard myself rousing the neighbourhood with a kind of primeval mating call of unnatural power, whereupon I climbed the only tree in the garden with consummate ease and zipped a branch from the trunk as though it had been paper.

My second concern was whether I should see a doctor about the size of my pectoralis major, which was proving an embarrassment to me, especially in mixed company on the beach. Paul Wells got a cheap laugh from the crowd by suggesting I was changing sex and would have to wear a bra with my swim trunks.

Paul Wells was a shortie, being barely six feet tall, but massively broad and already wrestling professionally on the South Coast circuit. Swimming all the year round, his body was so weather-exposed that it was changing from brown to a kind of dirty grey.

"Don't worry about it, Paul," I consoled him, "nature's changing the colour of your skin to match your mind."

"OK, Peter, if that's the way you want it let's have a show-down."

To us a showdown was really a showing-off contest in front of the girls on the beach. I was secretly jealous of Paul's skill as an acrobat, having nothing to offer against it in that class. He sped lightly over the shingle, ran up the side of a beach hut and flipped neatly into a back somersault to land on his feet. Then he sprinted towards a high pile of deck-chairs, dived over them head first, somersaulting deliberately so that he hit the shingle with his bare shoulders on the far side. It was the supreme test of toughness, and to prove he wasn't hurt he walked up the beach on his hands.

Everybody clapped except me. I was trying to think of some feat that would equal Paul's without killing me in the process.

"Follow that, Muscle-bound!" Paul shouted triumphantly.

I saw Wanda Wells gazing at me expectantly. Of all the attractive girls in our crowd two stood out. First there was the dark perfection of Helen Hoyle, the classical beauty who was to become Miss Cudford the following year—then there was Wanda Wells, the tall blond with green eyes below brown eyebrows. I often looked upon Wanda and wondered how nature, plus a little artificial aid, could have produced such beauty outside of a rose garden. Her face wasn't perfect like Helen's, but this was because she had dimples and a cleft chin and a slightly retroussé nose—but what made everyone turn and stare was the colour scheme of golden hair, honey skin and green eyes.

I walked slowly over to her. "Hello, gorgeous," I said calmly.

I had to say it calmly in case my pectoralis major started throbbing uncontrollably in public. If this happened I was a dead duck, so I stood before her completely relaxed lest the nervous tension of the occasion should start my adductor longus off too. Over-development had made my legs particularly susceptible to involuntary throbbing when I stood on them, and I knew from experience that once my adductor longus started up, my gracilis and quadriceps extensor would follow suit, fluttering like leaves on a tree.

"Hello, Peter," Wanda replied. She was not remarkable for conversational floods but the sound of her low smooth voice sent my dorsals rippling across my back with excitement.

"Your brother put on a great showdown, Wanda."

"Oh, him—yes, I suppose so. I expect you can do better."

This praise from our local goddess thrilled me so much that my pectoralis major began to throb involuntarily. I clapped my left hand on it and swore to myself that I would abandon the body building course indefinitely now that I was going out with girls.

"I'll do my best, Wanda."

"Oh, doesn't Marcus remind you of a Greek god, Peter?"

"Not without his laurel wreath." It shattered me, the way girls changed the subject to Marcus without rhyme or reason. I looked across at the Greek god as he licked Helen Hoyle's ice-cream, and wondered what the girls saw in this slim young man whose sole claim to fame was his ability to run the quarter-mile in under 50 seconds. He possessed the unlined face of eighteen, so unlined that it seemed his features were painted on by a sign-writer.

"Marcus can run like the wind," Wanda sighed dreamily.

"You have to when you can't fight."

"Did you see him win the 440 yards in 49.8 last Saturday? It was 49.8, wasn't it, Marcus?"

This time check was solely to catch the attention of our Greek god, who simpered back, "I'm having a go at Helen's ice-cream, Wanda. Ha, ha, ha, ha!"

"By the looks of things he'll have a go at Helen next," I said sourly. Despite what Bruce Bold wrote in *Brute Strength* about girls preferring musclemen, our lot seemed to prefer normal fellows with pretty faces. Even Rodney Kane had his admirers, a young man you practically had to carry out of the water if he ever mustered up enough courage to go in. When Wanda talked to me her eyes were always looking over my shoulder, so that at first I thought she had a vision defect, but when I turned round there was invariably Marcus in the background—Marcus licking Helen's ice-cream; Marcus having sun lotion rubbed on his chest by Patricia; Marcus having his curls combed by Doreen; Marcus photographed by Rosemary; Marcus begging for mercy as Jean sat on him; Marcus registering bliss as Melanie fed chocolates into his mouth; Marcus feigning slumber as Peggy fanned him to keep the flies off his coconut oil and vinegar. Another thing I could never fathom was the way everybody regarded me as an expert photographer, so that when the group photos were taken I could never get in them because I was always given the camera. Peering into the viewfinder I knew what I would see—Marcus surrounded by girls, with the other fellows lined up behind and Paul upside-down in a one-arm balance.

"You have to be very strong to take good snaps," Wanda explained, handing me an eight-ounce Kodak every time I suggested we should be taken together. "But mind you don't break it."

"He'll only break it if he stands in front of it," Paul jeered.

Squinting into the viewfinder I was amazed to see a smiling Marcus supported on either side by Wanda and Helen, while Paul performed a front planche in the foreground. I clicked the familiar scene miserably.

"How about Marcus taking one for a change?" I demanded.

"Sure, Peter, of course I will, if you think I'm strong enough to work the button."

"Good heavens, man, they sell these to children. They're not fitted with a three-hundred-pound spring."

Having handed the camera to Marcus with a warning not to rupture himself with effort, I posed for the photograph—but I was surprised to find I was posing alone. In front of me was Marcus holding the camera, supported by Wanda and Helen on either side. To the left Paul was performing back-flips.

"We're helping Marcus," Wanda explained. "He doesn't know anything about cameras."

"But he's only got to push a tiny button, not invent the camera for mankind. He won't learn how to take photos if he's always in them. I'm fed up seeing him in every picture in my album."

"Perhaps it would be safer if you took it, Peter. After all, we can't afford to waste film."

"How the hell can I possibly take a picture of you and me together, Wanda?"

"Then Paul had better do it."

We lined up for the big picture while Paul focused the camera. I tried hard to look like a Greek god and happy simultaneously, until Paul waved his hand at me.

"Move in a bit, Peter—at the moment I can only see Marcus and the girls."

"Would you like me to put my head between Marcus's legs?" I inquired bitterly.

"No, sit down in front of the group, then I can get you in."

I strove to look like a seated Greek god trapped in a forest of legs, and waited for Paul to press the button. When the photo was developed there was no sign of me, only a head and shoulders group of Marcus and the girls.

Paul stopped turning cartwheels on the sand long enough to call out, "Don't talk to my sister all day, Peter. What about the showdown—do you quit?"

"Blow, squirt," I told him in the cinema language of the day. "Your act was just halfway for kiddies. I'll show you what grown-ups do."

I said this to stall for time because I wanted to ask Wanda something very personal. "Will you come with me to the club's Christmas Ball, Wanda?" I inquired in a whisper, hoping she wouldn't notice this was only July. But you had to get in early with Wanda, who was booked up like the Queen Mother.

Wanda smiled her wonderful smile, causing my trapezius to isolate and jam. "What a super idea, Peter, and how sweet of you to ask me," she purred. "Of course I'd love to come."

Success went to my stomach as my rectus abdominal seized up through nervous tension, causing me to lean forward like a hunchback with cramp. I pretended to brush sand from my toes rather than let Wanda see I was temporarily crippled, and disguised my pain noises as a debonair laugh.

"Your legs are twitching, Peter," Wanda observed. "Just like horses do to shake off flies."

"Yes, I'm slightly over-trained, Wanda. I intend to lay off gym work for a while." Actually, I intended to give it up for ever. I had already written to Bruce Bold about my condition, but as always his reply advised me to seek the answer in yet another Bruce Bold manual, price ten shillings, plus postage, entitled *How to Control Muscle Control,* thus sending you further down the bottomless pit of body building so skilfully dug by the master of *Brute Strength,* who even had exercises to develop the tiny muscles controlling one's eyelids. These latter exercises I had abandoned in case I became the victim of a facial tic.

"So that's a firm date to come to the Christmas Ball with me, Wanda?" I whispered so no male should hear.

"Well, Peter, there's just one tiny snag."

"Your ball gown has been struck by lightning?"

"No, it's just that Rodney has already asked me."

I gasped with astonishment. "But how could that be, Wanda?—the dance committee don't even arrange it till October, then they start selling tickets at the end of November. This is only July."

"Rodney is on the committee, Peter. But I refused him anyway."

"So you can come with me then?"

"Well you see I had already promised Marcus."

"Marcus! I suppose he asked you directly the doctor told your mother it was a girl."

"Now don't be jealous, Peter."

"Well, let me book you for the following Christmas."

"That's the one I've promised to Rodney to make up for this year. He's going to take Helen this year instead."

"How about the Christmas after that?—Or has Marcus dated you up to retirement?"

Wanda blushed, lowering her long lashes as though absorbed in my bulging calves. "Oh, silly, I expect I shall be married by then."

"Can I have a dance with you at your wedding?"

I was annoyed because this meant I should have to attend yet another Grand Christmas Ball in the tenacious arms of Hilda Longbothem of the buck teeth, the girl voted most likely to end up in a Ladies' Choice Waltz without a partner.

My chagrin was interrupted by Paul Wells, demanding satisfaction on the showdown. "Don't wait till dark, Peter," he needled me. "We want to see you play hopscotch in daylight."

I smiled sadly at Paul, then asked Wanda if she would keep the contest in the family by helping me. She stood up, lovely to see in her new white swimsuit, demure and embarrassed by the limelight. "Let your body go quite relaxed," I told her, placing the palm of my left hand firmly on the small of her back. "Now lean backwards with complete confidence. I won't let you fall."

So saying, I performed a deft overhead press to hold Wanda high above my head on a one-arm support—a ninety-eight pound heft, some fourteen pounds lighter than my training schedule. Then, to call Paul's bluff, I let my feet perform basic hopscotch jumps down the slope of the beach.

Wanda's screams shattered the still air unheeded, for I was deep in the world of showdown bravado, aglow with physical elation and eager to let the crowd see the climax of strength allied to skill. I was simply cavorting with barbell six on high, and the fact that barbell six was shrieking for the gods in their mercy to put her down worried me not.

On sprung legs I ran up the steps of the diving-stage to show my prowess to the holidaymakers staring from the promenade, staring as I spun on my toes, ballet fashion, to whirl Wanda round in the air and throw my head back in the abandon of the dance. But this posture brought Wanda into my line of vision, showing me not only flailing arms and legs but also that there was a lot of Wanda sticking out of the swimsuit which I had never seen before. Her body seemed to buckle and twist, whereupon the halter of her swimsuit fell loose and wrapped itself round my supporting arm. The sight caused me to panic, so that I lost balance long enough for Wanda to fall. Rather than let her hit the wooden deck of the diving-stage I thrust her outwards so she would plummet into the sea—which she did like a screaming comet from the heavens.

In that split second I instinctively tried to save her by gripping the halter of the swimsuit, but there was a tearing sound as Wanda was ripped out of her swimsuit like a banana from its skin and her naked body disappeared beneath the waters.

I stood on the diving-stage pale and trembling as I realized what had happened, like a sex-cinema projectionist leaving work. Paul was running along the diving-stage shouting, "My sister can't swim, you idiot!"

I waved the swimsuit stupidly. "I saved this," I gasped.

Paul pushed me into the sea on a double rescue bid, where the immersion jerked me back to my senses. Within seconds we had located Wanda and brought her to the surface, my mind rent with horror at the realization that my hands were supporting her naked body.

Wanda knew it too, for she shrieked, "Take your hands off me, you monster, take your hands off me!"

"Keep hold of her or she'll sink!" Paul shouted.

Modestly I shifted my grip so my right arm was around her waist—or what I thought was her waist until I learned from her screams that I had misjudged her anatomy, her waist being higher up. Once we were within our depth, Wanda refused to be rescued any further, covering her bosom with her arms and addressing me in terms I had never heard before from a goddess.

The nightmare ended when Helen and Doreen rushed into the water with a beach towel for Wanda, then assisted her up the shore to a haven of female refuge and consolation. Silently I untwisted the white swimsuit from my forearm and handed it to Paul. "I'll buy her a new one," I said wretchedly.

"While you're at it, buy yourself a new set of friends," Paul snapped. "You're about as welcome here as a wasp at a seance. Later on I shall probably do you over on account of my sister."

I smiled sadly at Paul. "Let it rest, sonny—you're too young to die," I advised him gently. "Just admit you lost the showdown without hiding behind your sister, and I promise not to be cross."

As I walked up the shingle on my own the crowd broke out with a spontaneous burst of indifference, showing their appreciation of my feat by giving me more beach space than a washed-up mine. Smiling bravely through my tears I mounted the diving-stage and loosened up with a pike and jack-knife from the high board before collecting my towel.

Surprisingly enough, there was a girl in a floral dress sitting on the towel whom I could not recognize. She smiled shyly at me and bade me sit beside her. "That was quite a show you put on—I enjoyed it," she said softly.

"It was nothing really—just my lucky day, plus complete coordination of mind and body utilizing strength for peak power efficiency. I write, too, you know—thriller poetry for the technical glossies and things."

The girl laughed unexpectedly. "I'm Scottish," she told me archly.

"When I heard your voice I didn't think you were Portuguese." I made this little jest solely to stall for time so my muscles could slide gently back into rest position without locking. I breathed deeply into my diaphragm to reduce pulse rate and thought about meadows and cloud.

"My name's Bonnie Bold—Peter," the girl volunteered in a tiny voice.

"My name's Peter Pook, the well-known author of *How to Lose Friends and Injure People.* You speak to me entirely at your own risk."

Bonnie squeezed my hand rather than shook it, smiling coyly into my eyes to let me know I had at least one friend left.

THREE

It was flattering, the way Bonnie hung upon my every word whether I said anything or not. Every time the Scots brogue hit me I rubbed myself down with the towel to re-park my muscles.

"It's my power training for Perfect Brute (Senior Division)," I explained, in case she thought I was having a localized fit, "but I'm giving it up now I'm eighteen so I can lead a normal life and take girls out."

"I'm thirty-four, Peter," Bonnie whispered.

"So you could be a grandmother. You certainly don't look it."

"Lots of folk say thirty-four is a woman's peak."

"Lots of folk say you can move your peak along with you as you get older. Bruce Bold, the editor of *Brute Strength,* reckons a man never reaches his peak—that's why you have to keep buying his books to climb higher. I'm pulling out before I drop dead on the slopes."

"Do you go out with the girls here at the club, Peter?"

"Sometimes. Mostly they think I'm a Greek god up to the neck, but above that I change into a Greek bus. They go for the pretty boys like Marcus."

"I think you're most attractive."

"So do I—but they say this broken nose spoils me; but for that I'd be ugly."

"I'm not beautiful like Wanda."

"You're not beautiful, Bonnie; you're not particularly pretty—you're irresistible. I may play hard to get but keep trying and talking Scots because you'll win in the end. Eventually you'll break down my resistance and then I'll be all yours. It may take minutes, or even hours, so never give up."

"Do you go far with these girls at the club, Peter?"

"Well, we went to London last year on a club outing."

"I meant do you go far in . . . well, love and things."

"Oh—not really, Bonnie. You see, wherever you take them

there's a church surrounded by two hundred guests right in front of you. Even if you kiss them you find yourself inside a jeweller's shop holding a ring gauge. I'd rather give a girl an eternity chest-expander or a pair of matching barbells. . . ."

I stopped abruptly because I could feel an engagement ring and a wedding ring on the hand I was holding, and momentarily I wondered if Bonnie was such a fast worker that she came equipped for instant matrimony, like awarding medals before a battle.

"I'm married, Peter," she said softly.

I towelled myself briskly to reduce muscle flutter, cursing Bruce Bold and all his works for making me wear my heart on my serratus magnus for all the world to see. We knew from the movies that bad guys who got involved with good guys' wives had a shorter life expectancy than gangsters' molls or stoolpigeons, whereas good guys involved with bad guys' wives received flesh wounds in their deltoids, injuring them for only one scene while they won an Oscar for pain acting.

As Aunt Dot had warned me about married women, and my father had warned me about unmarried women, and Uncle Sydney had warned me about all women, I was not short on trepidation. Uncle Sydney used to puzzle me as a child by insisting one spelt the word woman with a capital T. "T-r-o-u-b-l-e spells woman, Peterkins," he taught me authoritatively—a spelling I shocked the nuns with at the Convent of the Holy Angels until they convinced me of the more orthodox form.

Bonnie squeezed my hand with reassurance. "Who are you going out with now, Peter?" she inquired timidly.

"I usually end up with Hilda Longbothem of the teeth rampant. The crowd here call her Longstop, like in cricket. She'd make a buxom Greek goddess if she was like the ones in the British Museum minus their heads."

"You are unkind, Peter."

"Well, she's a swell dame really, but she calls me her number 14 bus and tells people she likes going out with me because I make her seem pretty. How would you feel when she introduces me to folk and says I've been in a car accident?"

"Is that because of your boxing, Peter?"

I scratched my triangularis sterni puzzledly. "How is it I've never seen you before, yet you know so much about me, Bonnie?"

"Perhaps . . . perhaps I've read about you, Peter," she said diffidently.

"Maybe you read about me in the *Cudford Echo* when I broke the junior record for the military press in weight-lifting. There was a full-length picture of me in bed at the Observation Ward of Cudford General Hospital."

"No, I didn't see that, Peter, because I live in London. Actually, I'm down here on holiday. Let me give you a clue, my name is Bonnie Bold."

"That's ridiculous; it should be Bonnie Bashful. The only Bold I know is Bruce Bold, the Grand Master of Muscle, without whose help and encouragement I shouldn't be in the mess I am now."

"I'm sorry, Peter, but I'm his daughter-in-law."

This news took me some time to digest. I blushed to think of the letters I had written him in the past about my personal problems as I struggled through adolescence, ranging from unsightly pimples to premarital sex. Because of my outstanding literary talent and the intriguing nature of my queries, these letters were usually printed in full on the medical page of *Brute Strength* under such banner headlines as 'The Wages of Sin is Pimples', and 'Put Sex Behind You'.

The medical page was conducted by Doctor Russell, a Physician of Muscle, who, when I wrote to him about Hilda Longbothem, alarmed me with the scare headline above my letter: 'Cut It Out, Peter!' At first I was flattered to see my name in print but when I realized my personal problems were being publicized all over the world—despite Dr Russell's declaration every week that our letters enjoyed the strictest professional confidence—and other readers abroad began to send me improper remedies and suggestive letters,

I adopted the pen name of Puzzled Peter. What puzzled me most was that the answers to my questions were to be found only in Dr Russell's books, price ten shillings, plus postage, starting with *Let Power-Surge Outlaw Sex* and *The Celibate Way to Success.* These volumes were so persuasively written that I was gradually turning into a kind of muscular monk.

I shall never forget how upset Hilda Longbothem was when, unbeknown to me, she received Bruce Bold's follow-up brochure by post, with a covering letter which began: 'My Dear Friend and Sister, I just can't wait to get working on your neglected body, so that the next time some fellow makes a pass at you, just you pick him up and dump him down on the sidewalk where he belongs. . . . Simply write *Yes* on the enclosed prepaid card and we'll rush you Unit Two of Spectacular Womanhood for Red-Blooded She-Males—Unit One is in your hands right now, free; free because this vital moment of your life is no time to worry about cash. Let us worry about that while you enjoy Spectacular Womanhood. . . .'

I tried in vain to convince Hilda that Bruce Bold's tracking literature went out to everybody whose names were even hinted at in correspondence, like when I told him how much I owed to Aunt Dot's steak diet and by return of post Aunt Dot received Unit One of Bruce Bold's Explosive Longevity For Veterans.

"But it's ridiculous, Bonnie," I protested. "You're so desirable that I just can't imagine your being connected with Bruce Bold in any way. If members have anything to do with women he fines us and makes us do thirty days' double Power-Surge. That's why I'm so over-trained at the moment. I still owe him five guineas from last spring."

"Would you like to kiss me now, Peter?" Bonnie asked in the beguiling singsong accent of the North.

"I reject weakness of the flesh because it begets weakness of the muscle. . . . I'm sorry, dear, I automatically quoted the fend-off formula from Unit Six, Look What Happened to Samson."

"I promise not to cut your hair or report you, Peter."

"I'd sure like to kiss you, Bonnie, but not till I've put my track-suit on. I'm a bit like a racehorse these days. It's nice sitting here, letting the crowd see how popular I am with you. Tell me some more about myself."

"You write the funnies, Peter," she smiled apologetically.

"Now how could you possibly know that?"

"I'll give you a tiny clue. My maiden name is Bonnie Campbell."

"You'll tell me next that you're related to Jock Campbell, the Editor of *Family Help.*"

"I'm afraid I am, Peter. I'm his daughter."

Quite calmly, my face a mask of inscrutability, I sat there gasping and dumbfounded by this revelation. Only the flickering of my levator menti betrayed that I was stunned. Some one kept repeating, "It's a small world," and I discovered it was me. She would know about Mr Fixit, Colonel Crane and their ever-probing hounds, Sniff and Scratch. I was fascinated by this girl who had appeared from nowhere, yet possessed my most intimate secrets.

"I write, too, Peter," Bonnie whispered, resting her head lightly on my shoulder as if the very thought of it exhausted her. "Every week in *Family Help.*"

"What do you mend—clothes? I'm not allowed to touch clothes because of a 'A Stitch in Time'."

"No, Peter, my mother runs that feature."

"I hope you didn't write that love story about the dental mechanic who fell for the girl with ill-fitting teeth."

"I mend broken hearts and things, Peter. I'm Nurse Dawn."

"Nurse Dawn!" I cried. My mind rushed about in turmoil, struggling to recall the last letter I had written to her. It had concerned my crush on Wanda Wells, asking if there was anything I could do to make myself more attractive to her and win her love. Nurse Dawn sent me a letter of sympathy, together with a lucky pixie to wear round my neck. After three weeks of fruitless endeavour I tried to present the lucky pixie to Marcus, hoping to kill his chances stone dead with it.

When I wrote again to Nurse Dawn reporting my failure she sent me a leaflet entitled *Personal Freshness,* sponsored by a leading soap manufacturer, and a booklet called *Dance Your Way Into Her Heart.* For three months I practiced the steps with Alec, until the time came when we could dance reasonably well, but only together. This course affected Alec all his life because years later when I met him abroad I noticed he was still dancing backwards with his wife.

Then suddenly I shook with embarrassment when I remembered the letter about Secret Exercise 63 for developing the fascia of the neck. There was a rope-end hanging over the window-sill of my bedroom, the end of which I was required to clench firmly between my teeth, then endeavour to walk backwards across the room. This simple feat was made difficult by reason of the far end of the rope being secured to our garden roller, but by dint of practice I was able, not only to pull the roller along the garden path, but also five feet up the wall of the house. Bruce Bold emphasized the necessity of performing this exercise in one's bedroom in order that complete rest was available immediately following the exertion.

During the second week of this I lay exhausted on the bed, clad only in my leopardskin drawers, sweating as I massaged my neck in an effort to prise my head off my chest and back on to the pillow. Then I slept. At first I had a nightmare in which I was being hanged by the neck for murdering Marcus, but soon I began to dream about Wanda. In the dream I managed to haul Wanda up the side of the house and into the bedroom by my teeth.

"My word, what strong teeth you have, Peter," she exclaimed admiringly.

"Oh, I wouldn't say that, Wanda. Anyone with tremendous power and intensified training could do the same. Why, three of our senior members can actually haul a London bus by the same method."

"How fascinating, Peter!"

"I'm not up to that standard yet, but I intend practicing on a Daimler saloon for when we get married."

"Marvellous, Peter! You'll be better than a horse. Just think how that will look in *The Tatler*—you pulling your bride from the church to the reception for my five hundred friends and relations."

"Then I'll pick you up in my teeth and carry you over the threshold of our cave . . . I mean our new home."

"How thrilling, Peter! You make me sound just like a bone. Poor Marcus couldn't do that. He's still in hospital since you shook hands with him at our engagement party for my five hundred friends and relations."

"Have you got him from under your skin yet, Wanda?"

"Completely, Peter. Can't imagine what I ever saw in him. I can't stand men with weak teeth."

Then a terrible thing happened. I woke up the entire household by falling out of bed with Wanda, whose scream brought my father running into the room under the impression there had been a break-in. Throwing open the door he discovered me searching under the bed for Wanda.

"Have you got him, Peter?" my father demanded.

"No, she's disappeared completely."

"A woman burglar, eh? Don't waste time, we'll search the house and garden immediately. My oath!—there's the rope she used to climb in. Quickly, Peter, she must be still on the premises."

It was a weird set-up, my father checking every cupboard for a burglar, while I did the same to locate Wanda. Even when he phoned the police I dared not tell him it was Wanda we were looking for, rather than an intruder.

The nightmare had been so realistic that only after some days did doubts enter my head of its validity. On the third day I met Wanda in the street but she displayed no sign of passion. Instead, she said, "Have you seen Marcus, Peter?"

"No, Wanda, I haven't," I replied, in a tone implying that if I had it would not flood my soul with ecstasy. "What's new with you?"

"Oh, nothing special. Marcus took me to the Troxy to see *Helen of Troy.*"

"How was she?—ha, ha, ha, ha!" I laughed to let her see I had cracked a joke and that unrequited love had not detracted from my irrepressible nature, on the laugh-clown-laugh theory.

"I must dash, Peter. If you see Marcus tell him I'm looking for him, please."

"I'll send out a search party to drag the canal."

"Oh, don't be horrid, Peter! Bye."

Although the dream worried me a lot I dared not write to Bruce Bold or Doctor Russell, A Physician of Muscle, because they would fine me again and put me on double Power-Surge to purge my mind of women. This was the notorious Cathartic Calisthenics, which not only purged your mind of women but left you too enfeebled even to go out and look for one. Consequently I wrote a long letter to Nurse Dawn, telling her all the facts of the case and seeking her advice.

Her reply was sympathetic and even longer than mine. She had passed my letter on to Gipsy Rosa for an astrological analysis of the dream, while she herself undertook to solve my problems by consulting a third party called Fred. Apparently this character Fred—whom she misspelt as Freud—was an expert in my line of country, and, although we had never met, seemed to know all about me. I was surprised to learn that my dream proved I was obeying man's second strongest instinct by wishing to propagate the species in order to ensure the survival of the human race. Furthermore, by means of my physical culture activities I was carrying out Darwin's doctrine of the survival of the fittest or natural selection. Fred also stated that the dream expressed my readiness to take my place in the Descent of Man, and that the striking symbolism of my teeth in the courtship ritual was compatible with the Origin of Species.

This scientific analysis of my problem was accompanied by a

printed form containing 120 intimate questions about myself, to be answered by ticking or crossing little blocks, whereby I might solve my problems by remitting one guinea and placing myself in the experienced hands of the *Family Help* Marriage Bureau. In addition, the envelope contained a copy of Frampton's Engagement and Wedding Rings catalogue, Steinberg's Easy Plan Furniture brochure, a personal letter from the Managing Director of Cudford Building Society, and a free voucher for Gug-Gug Baby Foods.

During the ensuing weeks I received several unsolicited letters concerning such matters as Birth Control for All, Visit Our Toy Fair, Wedding Photographs that Delight, Borrow Without Security, £1,000 For Your Wife If You Die Suddenly, and Confidential Divorce Inquiries Undertaken.

It was while I was trying to puzzle out why a national insurance company should offer to pay £1,000 for my wife if I died suddenly, unless they were in the white slave traffic on the side, that the letter arrived from Gipsy Rosa. It told me I was Taurus the Bull, and that as Venus would soon be in the ascendancy I was extremely vulnerable to affairs of the heart. There was a fair woman in my horoscope but this was only a passing phase, for true love would come later. Gipsy Rosa saw a dark man who was unfavourable to me but I was not to worry about him because his influence would soon fade. I possessed considerable creative ability which I must not waste, for success would surely come, either as a writer or a father, or perhaps both. My lucky colour was red, I liked money, and a sense of humour was my saving grace.

As I read on I marvelled more and more at Gipsy Rosa's supernatural sagacity, but it was the final paragraph which both intrigued and thrilled me. 'Your stars and planets are especially propitious for the month of July this year, when a dark lady will enter your life from afar to change it considerably and bring you great happiness.'

The prediction came back to me with startling impact as I gazed at Bonnie sitting beside me, with her head on my shoulder and her arm around my waist, like Shakespeare's Dark Lady of the incomparable Sonnets. And merely listening to her voice told me that one couldn't come from further afar than Scotland. It was incredible.

Bonnie opened her handbag and offered me a De Rezke Minor from a cigarette case, but I recoiled from such temptation with as much panache as I could muster. "Do you mind if I smoke, Peter?" she asked apprehensively.

"Certainly not, Bonnie—you're on holiday and a woman of the world. I'm not allowed to smoke, drink or . . . or anything while in training. Even dancing is taboo."

"But I sent you *Dance Your Way Into Her Heart,* remember?"

"Ah, I only got as far as my friend Alec, because we couldn't follow the steps unless we danced together. I certainly didn't intend taking him to the club's Grand Christmas Ball as my partner. As it was we got thrown out of Cudford Palais by the manager when we tried to practise together to a live band. Now he tells me he daren't ask a girl because he can only dance backwards with his right arm out and his left hand on her shoulder. He's been to the Palais since, but the girls won't dance with him and he's terrified in case some man asks him for a waltz. He figures the booklet should have been called *Dance Your Way Into Court.*"

"I am sorry, Peter. I loved receiving your letters."

"I never dreamt I'd be sitting here with Nurse Dawn, though Gipsy Rosa sent me a fantastic horoscope predicting all this. I was in trouble and suddenly you're here beside me, just as if you'd come through the post like your letters."

"Perhaps I can help you even more this way, Peter. The personal touch, you might say," she replied, brushing my orbicularis lightly with her lips. This was only one muscle short of my own lips and the effect on me was galvanic, especially on my left leg. I held it down with both hands, at the same time massaging the thigh to prevent the leg jumping about on the beach. When Hilda Longbothem kissed me good night at my front door it was like kissing a small ivory fence, and just as unemotive. She used to whisper, "Do you love me, Peter? Why don't you kiss me passionately?" and I used to reply, "Because I don't want to get hurt, Hilda." She believed I meant my feelings would be hurt, not that my lips might get ripped off, so I always played along with it rather than appear unkind. Yet Bonnie had only to caress me to produce a nervous breakdown without the traditional months of worry beforehand.

"If you came to the holiday flatlet we've rented perhaps we could thrash out your problem together, Peter," Bonnie suggested hesitatingly.

"Thrash out which one, Bonnie—my old one or the one you've just given me? And how can I come to your flatlet if your husband is there?"

Bonnie sighed. "Oh, my husband wouldn't take a holiday, Peter. All he lives for is his work, so I hardly ever see him. Russell hopes to take over *Brute Strength* when his father retires. At present he writes as Doctor Russell, A Physician of Muscle. Our love burns like the Olympic torch—about once every four years."

Once again I sat there stunned by this new revelation Bonnie told me so casually. I should sooner have believed the Pope was engaged than that Dr Russell was married. In his articles he always referred to sex as the Devil's Drill or Coffin Calisthenics, declaring that a true athlete used his bed only when too exhausted to stand up. He hinted it was high time the biologists evolved a more sophisticated method of procreation, quick and simple like having your ears pierced. If you want a matchstick, he said, you don't have to fell an oak tree to make one. If one of our members got married Dr Russell wrote of him as 'our late brother who fell mortally wounded by an arrow through his aortic ventrical in the battle of the sexes. With the going down of the sun we shall remember him; yea, who shall forget his clean-and-jerk at 300 pounds?'

"But I never dreamt that Dr Russell had a wife, Bonnie," I

exclaimed bewilderedly.

"I sometimes wonder myself, Peter. When I put the children to bed at night and they want to say good-night to daddy I have to let them phone through to his office in London and record a message. But we're all together at Hogmanay because he insists that is a family occasion when we must all be united in the true Scots' tradition. So every year I take the kids into town and we have a family reunion party at his office. He dresses up as Father Christmas and gives them presents, like grip-improvers and Unit One of Infant Expansion. Folks get quite a shock when they first see my youngest coming home with me in his pram. When we reach our house he climbs out and carries the pram up the steps."

"So who's sharing the flat with you here in Cudford, Bonnie?"

"My sister."

"Is she married too?"

"Yes, her husband is a surveyor."

"Locally?"

"Borneo. He went out three years ago to survey the country for mapping, but last year we received a report from Brunei that he had not come back to base, so they presumed he had got lost up-country. Here's a picture of him just before he sailed."

Bonnie produced a photo of him, clad in topee, bush-jacket, shorts and jungle boots, holding a theodolite and fly-whisk, taken on Platform 12 of Waterloo Station, but I was staring at the girl by his side carrying two suitcases and an earthenware water-cooler. Although she was not wearing the bandanna and brass ear-rings she displayed every week in the oval picture on page 7 of *Family Help,* nor gazing into a crystal ball against a background of the Zodiac, the features were unmistakable.

"Who is his bearer?" I asked sharply.

"Oh, that's my sister, Margaret."

"Don't people mistake her for Gipsy Rosa?"

"She is Gipsy Rosa."

"It's a small world, Bonnie." I said this automatically because it seemed to be my new motto. As if to emphasize this global shrinkage Bonnie snuggled closer to me so I had to speak directly into her left ear.

"As Gipsy Rosa possesses extra-sensory powers, Bonnie, could she not help find her husband?"

"She's tried ever so hard, Peter. She warned him before he left England that he'd get lost. I know it seems silly but even on Waterloo Station he was lost. The boat train left from London Bridge. Now she can't see him in the crystal ball, just a blank space surrounded by jungle."

"What about his stars?"

"Margaret didn't dare let him know what the stars foretold. They said he'd go on a long journey across the ocean and disappear into a strange land. Because of this she gave him a St Christopher medallion to wear round his neck but he lost it in Southampton Docks while he was searching for his luggage. That's how he missed the ship."

"Surely the last person to get lost is a map surveyor?"

"The headman of the village said Harold had mislaid his Gunter's chain and went off into the foot-hills to look for it. He was never seen again."

"But surely he didn't go alone, Bonnie?"

"He had no choice, Peter, because his party of bearers had gone up-river in search of him the previous day and couldn't find their way back to base."

"Is Margaret very upset by Harold's disappearance?"

"She's upset, naturally—but not surprised. She misses him terribly and I think it's only fair to warn you that such a long separation has made her . . . well, frustrated and passionate."

"Like the famous painting, 'When did you last see your husband?' "

Bonnie laid her smooth cheek on mine. "Unfortunately, we lassies are brought up to be reserved and modest in Scotland—almost frightened of men, you might say."

"You certainly change when you cross the border then."

"So, Peter, you mustn't be annoyed if she behaves a little unfemininely at times."

"I'll simply laugh it off and give her twenty-four hours to hand me back my clothes."

"You shouldn't tease, Peter. After all, you've experienced the torment of love and she may be able to help you with your problem."

"I can hardly ask her about you behind your back, Bonnie."

This reply so embarrassed Bonnie that she fell across me to hide her confusion, burying her head in my face. "You're a wicked, wicked man," she sighed. "No girl is safe with you around. Oh, you're a terrible man!"

"If I continue to behave so badly I shall soon be an ex- member of this club, Bonnie."

"My mother warned me about men like you, Peter."

"She told you how to find one, too."

"Oh, it's a good thing I shall be there when you meet my sister."

"Two of us should be able to keep her at bay."

Gently I brushed Bonnie's silken hair from my eyes in order to survey the club membership. Paul was practising his fantastic racing dive by sprinting down the beach to hit the water with his chest where it was barely six inches deep. Wanda was playing a Bing record on the HMV portable which reposed on Marcus's stomach. Helen and Rodney were indulging in the wildly erotic pastime of eating the same apple simultaneously; Helen with some delicacy but Rodney displaying those ping-pong eyeballs and cavernous mouth of a potential cannibal in love.

The sun was a warm orange floating on the western horizon of a sea which dozed lazily, as though it too was in holiday mood. Life was pretty good, I thought to myself, as Bonnie shyly took my hand and led me up the beach.

FOUR

Aunt Dot's birthday party was always a great occasion in our family but never had the clan gathered in such numbers as the one which celebrated her hundredth anniversary. Surmounting the cake was a telegram from a delighted and slightly astonished King George, while surrounding it were the gifts from less delighted but more astonished relatives.

Uncle Ted in particular resembled an athlete who set out confident of victory, but now fearing he might be outrun—or even lapped. He had gained much support in the family for a proposal to gratify Aunt Dot's ambition by sending her up in an aeroplane, but when the idea reached her ears she declared that if God had intended man to fly he would have equipped him with wings, and that she had no intention of leaving this earth either by charter flight or by hearse. Furthermore, when the time came for her to visit her grandchildren in New Zealand she would go by ship, not by air, whereupon Uncle Ted expressed the opinion that it would be a long way to travel just to place flowers on their graves.

Fortified by her unconquerable spirit—which she obtained from a Johnny Walker bottle—Aunt Dot commenced her annual birthday speech with the remark we knew so well. "When you reach my age, dear family. . . ."

"Not a chance," Uncle Ted observed to his glass.

"When you reach my age you will realize that you can live too long."

"Hear, hear," the family groaned in chorus.

"She means us, not her," Uncle Ted corrected them.

"You see, dear family, I have outlived all my friends. . . ."

"And most of her relations," Uncle Ted confirmed.

"So what have I got to live for. . . ?"

"I've been asking that for years," Uncle Ted remarked.

"I shall tell you. The only things that keep me alive are your love, affection and devoted care."

"There must be a traitor in the family," Uncle Ted suggested.

"Now as you all know, I have a certain something tucked away in your Uncle Sydney's strong-box. . . ."

"It must be the secret of eternal life," Uncle Ted said, refilling his glass.

"And the day will come when it will be handed over to you almost in its entirety."

"It goes to the State when the deceased is without heirs," Uncle Ted reminded her.

"I say almost in its entirety because I still have to visit my grandchildren in New Zealand."

"So we shall owe your executors ten pounds apiece," Uncle Ted estimated. "Why not give us the money now and sail to New Zealand as the world's oldest stowaway?"

"Ah, my dear Teddy, how anxious you are for your share of the prize. You really must learn to have patience."

"That's what you told me years ago when you were scarcely out of your eighties. Since then I've learned to have so much patience that my friends call me Job."

I sat there simpering at Aunt Dot to let her see I was her favourite heir, and chuckling at Uncle Ted to let him see I was not short of time like him, and to conceal my speculation of being his heir as well. Aunt Dot had once hinted that one day this house would be mine to cherish as the family seat, so, as I looked around the room, I wondered what her reaction would be could she but see the first petrol pump going in just where she now sat, as the new filling station took shape on the site.

We were not a sentimental family. Uncle Sydney's dress sword was Aunt Dot's most treasured possession, yet when Snuff Bros., the local antique dealers, had appealed to the nation for dress swords for urgent shipment to America, where there was a desperate shortage of them, she sacrificed Uncle Sydney's for ten pounds, telling Mr Snuff senior, "Those poor Americans, how they must have suffered!" After Mr Snuff had explained the plight of the

Americans to her she sent over further aid in the shape of Uncle Sydney's medals and spurs. Subsequently, a great deal of Uncle Sydney's possessions crossed the ocean, including his shaving-mug, moustache-cup and brass shell cases.

Uncle Ted remarked at the time that he hoped the family would be consulted before Aunt Dot had Uncle Sydney exhumed for export, which raised the legal question of posthumous emigration.

Aunt Dot had long decreed that we must not talk shop at her birthday parties, by which she meant we were not to argue about her money or how much we would receive when she finally sank.

"There will be enough for everybody," she assured us, "and of course I want my brass oil-lamp to go to Teddy."

"I can hardly wait," Uncle Ted groaned. He was extremely worried about the legacy of the oil-lamp, having a premonition that it might be all he would get, or that Aunt Dot was providing it for him against hard times when he could no longer afford electricity.

Today Aunt Dot announced, "Please don't quarrel on my hundredth birthday. There will be enough for everybody, and of course I want Teddy to have my Bible."

Uncle Ted looked up, taken by surprise. "Where's my oil-lamp then?"

"Oh, that has gone over the ocean for those poor Americans. They're so desperately short of oil-lamps, Mr Snuff assures me. The dear man gave me three pounds for it."

"But you said it was your most treasured possession because its light fell on Uncle Sydney when he passed away."

"No, Teddy, my Bible is because I read it to him as he went."

I caught Aunt Dot's eye and chuckled engagingly to let her see I wasn't jealous of Uncle Ted's new legacy, so long as I got the house for a filling station. I felt safe, figuring that Snuff Bros. could hardly ship that.

"I haven't forgotten you in my will, Peter," she smiled back. "I expect she's left you her hymn book," Uncle Ted said. "No, that goes to Flo. I want Peter to have his Uncle Sydney's army bugle."

"Whereabouts in New York will he be able to buy it?" Uncle Ted inquired.

"Oh, Auntie Dot, how wonderful!" I exclaimed, registering extreme bliss and squeezing her hand. "Just what I've always wanted. Fancy I shall be able to stand in the garden and blow it at sunset." I pointed through the window to where the greasing bays would be located in the new Bugle Garage, though I felt a trifle disturbed at the possibility of my ending up with a bugle and no garden to blow it in, unless Aunt Dot meant that the bugle went with the house.

Aunt Flo wasn't too thrilled about the hymn book bequest either. No one disputed Aunt Flo's psychic powers, and this ability to see into the future had endowed her with an extremely long face which had lost the art of smiling. She had carefully checked on Aunt Dot many times with cards and tea-leaves, always with the same result—a death to the house, followed by an unpleasant surprise concerning a dear one. Uncle Ted insisted on interpreting this omen as Aunt Dot coming to live with them until they too passed on, but Aunt Flo maintained he would no longer think this when the will was read and the solicitor presented him with a Bible and an envelope containing his account for settlement.

Uncle Len supported this theory, likening the will to a kind of State Lottery where the tickets were extremely expensive and the prize-money non-existent. In support of this view he quoted the disturbing rumour which had swept through our family last winter that Aunt Dot had applied to Cudford Council to participate in their Free Coal for the Aged scheme. However, Uncle Ted insisted this was merely a subterfuge on Aunt Dot's part to appear destitute, and typical of the Pooks not to pass up anything going free. He cited Uncle Len's economy measures on the buses, where he travelled half-price as an Old Age Pensioner, while his son Philip travelled on his knee as a non-fare-paying infant.

At eighteen I was really too young to worry overmuch about legacies, confident that eventually the family treasure would funnel down to me if I played my cards right. I sat there half listening to the Pook saga I knew so well, thinking about the exciting new world Bonnie had introduced me to the previous evening. It was the first time I had visited a girl's flat alone, quite different to taking Hilda Longbothem home.

When Hilda took me home at night it was like going into hospital, the way everybody waited on you as though love had left you paralyzed. Mrs Longbothem gave you a large cup of scalding coffee, accompanied by three slices of cake Hilda had baked herself, which Alec called duck-sinker. Mr Longbothem spoke above the radio noise about his problems in the grocery trade, not by way of conversation but as a monologue delivered by a compulsive talker. Simultaneously, Grandma showed you photographs of the old days, taken slowly from a box containing four hundred prints, each of which revived a memory in Grandma's running commentary on her life. Then suddenly you found yourself part of a play being acted by Hilda's younger sisters around your armchair, which was really a throne and you a king having his supper and addressing his subjects with his mouth full. At the same time you were a boxing referee for a fight between Hilda's two brothers, who, because you were immobile, kindly fought round your chair.

Mrs Longbothem brought in trifle for your lap, while Hilda, to prove her domesticity, sang and played at you from a nearby piano, usually *Home Sweet Home*—a song which made me long for mine. It all made you wonder whatever the Longbothems did until I arrived to become the focal point for a kind of indoor fete.

But above all I dreaded Mr Longbothem's coloured slides. To enjoy these I was required to peer upwards through a small kind of telescope aimed at the electric light bulb, while Mr Longbothem fed in an inexhaustible supply of tiny pictures of ant men, ant women, tombs, mountains, waterfalls, ant soldiers on the march, ants being married, ants playing football, beaches covered with ants, dancing ants, ships loaded with ants, picnicking ants, college ants en masse, singing ants and individual ants leaning against ruined castles. Mr Longbothem knew all the ants by name, and when I viewed any given slide of massed ants it was imperative I learned which ant was he and the names of all surrounding ants, their life histories and where they lived now, if not dead.

Although I constantly changed eyes as my sight failed and my retinas became white lamps surrounded by sparks when my lids closed, Mr Longbothem opened more boxes of slides from the old tea-trolley which transported them; boxes of holiday ants, relation ants, wartime ants, school ants, sporting ants, business ants, infant ants, club ants and even flying ants.

"Now, Peter, see if you can spot me here at our last reunion," Mr Longbothem commanded, inserting into the telescope three hundred regimental ants stacked in rows on a picture no bigger than a postage stamp.

"That must be you in the back row, one-hundred-and-eighth from the left," I said hopelessly. I felt brainwashed, tired and dizzy. To make matters worse, Hilda had abandoned the piano for her knitting needles, on which was taking shape my new pullover for the winter, which had to be smoothed out over my torso for fit every ten rows. The garment was growing in four colours—red, green and amber body with orange sleeves—as though I worked on a motorway and must be visible for one mile in each direction. Moreover, Hilda was incorporating four stitches in it; rib, cable, moss and stocking stitch; and by some knitting miracle I cannot explain, the word PETER was appearing on the chest section in blue wool. Tonight I was horrified to observe that what I had taken to be a pattern design on the back section was now sufficiently advanced to reveal the word PETER right across the shoulders. I told her it was heavenly and tried to remember from school whether wool burned.

At the conclusion of the slides I rose too quickly from the armchair in my eagerness to go home, instead of waiting till the vertigo passed and normal vision returned. Whether I opened my eyes or not I could see nothing except a white glare surrounded by sparks, but at regular intervals a blueprint diagram of the electric light bulb's filament appeared in both my eyeballs with disturbing clarity, followed immediately by a short burst of forked lightning without thunder.

I tried to thank Mr. Longbothem for such an interesting evening but I couldn't see where he was for sparks. Then suddenly I fell heavily to the carpet, my right arm striking the tea-trolley of slides as I went down at his feet.

I was immediately surrounded by women, children and dogs as Mr Longbothem helped me to stand up again. I apologized, pretending my foot had caught in the carpet, then let Hilda lead me out of the room by the hand to say good-night in the porch.

"Are you all right now, Peter love?" she asked me worriedly.

"Just dandy, Hilda," I told her, holding her closely for support. Although the porch was dark, it appeared to me to be floodlit, yet I couldn't see anything except an impression of the lamp filament surrounded by pink spaghetti in motion.

"I think you looked at Daddy's slides too long, Peter. You went through five boxes tonight."

"I'm all right, Hilda, honestly. It's just that I can't see. Could you switch off the porch light for a while?"

"It is off, Peter, so you can kiss me quite safely."

"But I feel utterly sexless."

"Oh, dear! Never mind, think about your nice new pullover and you'll soon be better. I know how careless you are with clothes so I worked your name on it. Now you won't be able to lose it."

"Nobody will be able to lose me either."

"I thought all those nice bright colours would cheer you up this winter."

"People will think I'm on fire, Hilda."

"Nonsense, Peter. I want you to wear it when you take me out."

"Take you out where? Unless we stroll hand in hand along the main line to London. The drivers will think I'm a fog signal."

"Oh Peter, you're impossible. I've a good mind not to let you kiss me goodnight, just to punish you."

"I'll be off then."

"Come here, you wretch! You men are all the same. All you want a girl for is to take advantage of her at the first opportunity. You'll soon discover I'm not that kind of girl."

"Please put me down then, Hilda. I promise not to take advantage of you."

"Ah, that's what they all say—then what happens?"

"You realize they're speaking the truth."

Hilda held me tightly in case I took advantage of her. "Oh, you men, with your smooth tongues—don't you ever think of anything but sex?"

"Of course, Hilda—I often think of you."

"There you go again, you naughty thing, you can't get your mind off it. Heaven knows what my parents would think if they knew what kind of a fellow you are, Peter. They certainly wouldn't let me stay out here on the porch with you."

"They'd probably march you inside handcuffed and lock you in your bedroom."

"Don't keep harping on about my bedroom, you wicked man. You'll just have to wait till I'm a bride."

"My rule is never touch a married woman. . . . "

"Not somebody else's bride, idiot! You know very well what I mean. Now I'm going to let you give me just one kith and no more."

I started with alarm to hear Hilda say kith because this lisp came on only when she was excited to flash-point, inflamed by the pressure of my chin on the top of her head so she couldn't look up. Hilda used red lipstick lavishly, so I wore old ties to take the worst of it, though there was little I could do about the mascara and powder. After last year's Grand Christmas Ball my tuxedo looked like I had been making pastry with too much jam filling. Hilda had worn a low-cut gown, so that even when I took her arm my sleeve turned white, and the fluff from her lamé stole prompted Paul to inquire if it was snowing outside. To prevent my chin resting on her head Hilda had worn a spiky tiara that was quite dangerous when we danced together, like silver barbed-wire. No man could have possibly been unfaithful to his wife by going out with Hilda on the sly because even if you wore overalls to take the rouge, powder, mascara and talc there was no escape from her science-fiction perfume, outrageously labelled *Harem Girl's Secret,* which clung to my wardrobe for weeks as if there had been an accident in a scent factory.

"Kith me quickly, Peter, before Mummy thinks you're seducing me," Hilda persisted. "You know how she worries about me."

"She knows you're safe with me, Hilda. Your Dad said you'd be safe on a battleship at sea."

"They don't know you like I do, Peter. One little word of encouragement from me and you'd have all my clothes off, even though we're not officially engaged yet. Now you can kith me before I change my mind and send you packing."

It was difficult to see how Hilda intended to send me packing when she had me pinned against the front door. I tried to placate her by planting a passionate kiss on her forehead, breathing heavily to indicate powerful emotional stress as I did so, at the same time concealing from her the fact that the ornamental cupid she wore in her hair had unexpectedly gone up my left nostril in the process. Hilda exhibited more jewellery to the square foot than any girl I knew, from earrings and bangles to bunches of cherries and lucky charms. At dances we spent much time searching for her parts as they dropped off, and at the last Grand Christmas Ball, during the Gay Gordons, her triple-row pearls splattered the floor like a sudden hailstorm.

"You are cold tonight, Peter," Hilda groaned after I had kissed her forehead good-night. "Why is it you never seem to kith me properly?"

"Because I don't want to get hurt, Hilda." It was out before I could stop it, and I could have bitten off my tongue with shame. Why didn't I have the courage to say I didn't want to get injured and have done with it?

"I promise never to hurt your feelings, Peter—so if you're too shy to kith me, I'll kith you instead. Just take your chin off my head so I can reach you. . . ."

As I was in the act of bracing myself for the kiss, another female voice called out, "Are you quite all right out there?"

"Yes thank you, Mrs Longbothem," I replied.

"Not you—me!" Hilda snapped crossly. "Just coming, Mummy."

"You really should let Hilda come in for bed, Peter. It's past midnight."

I let Hilda come in for bed in the most unexpected fashion. Mrs Longbothem opened the front door, causing me to fall backwards into the hall with Hilda on top of me, like a well rehearsed scene from a permissive movie.

Mrs Longbothem screamed, then pulled her daughter off me while Mr Longbothem helped me to my feet. "I expect you need a drink after that, Peter," he said.

"Drink!" cried Mrs Longbothem. "You stand there and offer this . . . this wretch a drink! Hasn't he abused our hospitality enough before he takes advantage of our daughter on her own doorstep?"

"Perhaps he. . . ."

"Silence, Harold, you only upset me. Hilda, go straight to bed—I'm shocked to find you allowing Peter to act like a married man before you're even engaged. Whatever will the neighbours think?"

"Peter loves me," Hilda said defiantly. "He wasn't doing anything wrong because he's too shy. I believe he was trying to pluck up courage to propose to me when we fell into the hall."

"Oh, the poor boy! You young lovers are so secretive. Harold, give Peter a drink, then he can propose properly in the comfort of the drawing-room. Fancy, how like a man to make the most important decision of his life out on a cold porch. I remember so well how Harold couldn't face my parents, but insisted on proposing to me by telephone."

It was unnerving, the way Hilda used to ask me round for coffee to this house where all doors led to the altar. On one occasion she had let me in dressed as a bridesmaid in readiness for her cousin's nuptials on the morrow; on another, she happened to be trying out her mother's wedding dress; on another, Mr Longbothem fed into the telescope a whole box of wedding slides depicting a kind of history of marriage within the Longbothem clan, wherein a tiny tot of a bridesmaid in one slide appeared as a bride in the next, a matron-of-honour in the next, and a tottery old lady in the next.

At one time I found myself spending many Saturday afternoons in churches with Hilda, an unwilling witness to unions of people I had never met before and never saw again. At these ceremonies I stood beside a new Hilda, unfamiliar in large coloured hats like lamp-shades and wearing glasses for better surveillance of fashion, singing *Eternal Bliss Upon Thee Fall* in a voice lacking enthusiasm for the blessing invoked. At the subsequent receptions I stood among sundry lamp-shades sipping that special kind of sherry you only get at weddings and health spas. In this way I myself began gradually to appear in Mr Longbothem's slides, at first on the outskirts, then imperceptibly moving towards the central position.

Thus I found it strange that there were no parents at Bonnie's place. It was the first time I had visited a girl's flat under such conditions and I felt sure she must have some parents lurking in the next room, waiting to pounce on me.

Bonnie had warned me about her sister Margaret, but her tone of voice hinted that she would protect me from her.

When we arrived at the flat Bonnie expressed surprise that Margaret wasn't in yet. "Just as well, Peter," she remarked. "It will give me an opportunity to talk to you about your problem alone. Once she comes I'll have no chance. Now sit down on the settee and make yourself comfortable."

"I like the flat, Bonnie—it's great."

"You'll like it even better later on. Drink this to help you unwind. It's ginger ale."

"Strong for ginger ale, Bonnie."

"Yes, there's a dash of Scotch in it for luck. Don't let Margaret get you tight though—she's fond of her wee dram these days."

I drank the ginger ale and felt I should be already tight when Margaret arrived. Bonnie put a record on the HMV, filling the flat with soft mood music from the Black Watch Pipe Band on the march. "I do hope you like bagpipes, Peter," she said, handing me another glass of ginger ale.

"What have we got for supper—porridge?" I jested inanely.

"I thought the skirl of the bagpipes would relax you, Peter."

"But that's the battle call of the Highlanders they're playing, Bonnie. I don't know the name but I heard it in a war film when the Scottish regiments were going over the top to attack. The Germans called them the ladies from hell because of their kilts."

Bonnie laughed softly. "Shall I put on my tartan skirt, Peter?"

"Shall I call myself Fritz?"

"Now no more joking, Peter," she replied, putting her arms round me, "because we must thrash out your problem before Margaret arrives back. I must warn you quite bluntly that she is looking for a man, if you know what I mean."

"Will she bring him back here?"

"You're here already. Now let us concentrate on your problem."

"Which one, Bonnie?"

"Why, Wanda, of course."

"Oh, that one. I'd almost forgotten about it. I used to have a crush on Wanda, but she prefers Marcus to me. In fact, she prefers anyone to me. She thinks I'm ugly."

"I don't, Peter. I think you're handsome."

"Well, you saw Wanda this afternoon—I expect you think she's ugly."

"No, Wanda is very pretty, much prettier than me, but with a man it doesn't matter whether he's handsome or ugly."

"That's what all the girls tell me. Then they go out with Marcus and Alec. Take Rosemary for instance. She said she hated Alec's type because he's too good-looking for a man, so I said come out with me tonight and stop complaining. She said she'd love to but she had a date with Alec."

"But you've got Hilda."

"Once I got mumps—but they went. At the club she's been voted Spinster of the Year. Paul reckons our members should be covered by Lloyd's against fire, tempest and Hilda."

Bonnie rested her lips on my right ear, as though I suffered a hearing defect. "Perhaps your trouble is you're so mature, Peter."

"I always was precocious as a child, Bonnie. I remember trying to join the British Legion when I was eleven, thinking it was the local branch of the Foreign Legion."

"What I meant was that you might be happier with an older woman."

"Someone like my Aunt Dot?"

"Someone about my age, Peter. Someone who wouldn't worry about your looks all the time."

"You mean a pen-pal overseas?"

"No, darling, someone close to you who understands your problems because she too has problems."

"Any woman who isn't married by then has the kind of problem I don't want to share, Bonnie. There are limits, you know. I've already hinted to Hilda that I hope to be a monk."

"But this girl might be married, Peter, like me. Her husband neglects her, but she is a woman and wants to be treated like a woman."

"Give her your seat in a pub and buy her a port-and-lemon?"

"Little courtesies help, of course. But there is a deeper side to it. What did you say in one of your letters about your body?"

"Bruce Bold suggested I left my body to the nation. From which I gathered they would only bury my head and face."

"He meant that you have a beautiful body, which you must not throw away, Peter."

"Wouldn't that be rather difficult?"

"He meant that you must not waste it. You should give it to the woman you love."

"I tried that with Wanda but she wouldn't take the face that goes with it."

"That is because she is so young. Girls of her age are still in love with love—they think only of a comely face. When she is older she will begin to appreciate more important qualities in a man."

"Like how rich his dad is?"

"Like his personality and manly physique. Then you will know the joys of real love, Peter."

"It'll be too late then, Bonnie. I shall probably be married to Hilda."

"Surely tonight would not be too late, Peter?"

"Tonight!" I panicked internally at the thought of becoming the plaything of this femme fatale, who lured me with her bagpipes and whisky. Bonnie seemed to sense my distress because she gently wiped the sweat off my brow with a handkerchief that filled my nostrils with the scent of heather, then she laid my head on her bosom and began to croon an ancient Scottish lullaby in which a body repeatedly met another body coming through the rye, followed by a line I could not understand, all about gin a body kiss a body, need a body cry?

I tried to join in with *Auld Lang Syne* to distract her, but she bade me hush because she was going partly into the Gaelic, sweetly singing lovers' threats, of which I could understand but snatches like, Ae fond kiss and then we sever! and O, gie me the mon that has acres o' charms; Fair fa' your honest sonsie face, Great chieftain o' the puddin'-race!

"Cood that be a wee bit Rabbie Burns, ye ken?" I inquired in my new accent.

Bonnie laughed. "Aye, Peter. It's *To a Haggis.*"

"That's not particularly flattering, is it? I know I'm no oil-painting but surely I'm not that bad. I thought you were singing a love song to me."

"You're ma wee haggis, Peter."

"How romantic! I suppose if you hailed from Spain I'd be your wee onion." I felt extremely depressed about my image with girls, what with the back of a bus and now a haggis, not to mention Wanda's oblique reference to me as a Greek door-knocker. When Doreen returned from a visit to Paris she announced she had seen my bust at the Louvre, which flattered me immensely until she added that in wet weather water spurted from my mouth and ears on the end of a rain spout.

"That's really a compliment," Bonnie told me. "It means that you're delicious and I could eat you for supper. You see, a haggis is a sheep's whatnots, all minced up and boiled in oatmeal."

"It's hardly what you'd call the language of love, Bonnie. I don't suppose there's many love songs about haggises like there are roses. I always seem to miss out on the romantic side of life. Last St Valentine's Day Hilda sent me a Mickey Mouse card containing a pair of ear-flatteners."

Bonnie kissed me on the ear. "Oh, Peter, you worry too much about your looks. I think you're rugged, like a man should be, not a pretty boy like Marcus."

"But he gets all the girls."

"He hasn't got me though. Now, if you're so self-conscious I'll switch the light off."

"Surely I'm not so ugly that you want to put the light out!"

"Oh, dear, I mean self-conscious about making love."

It was remarkable how, at that very instant, the standard lamp went off as though it was on a time-switch, but I divined from a slight jerk of Bonnie's body that she had activated it with her toe.

"I couldn't solve your problem by post, Peter, so I'll do it by personal interview," she whispered, but I was soon to learn Lesson One in the love manual, that one problem can only be solved by the creation of two more.

FIVE

There was so much noise going on outside that it gradually permeated my brain until it woke me up. I felt pretty sheepish, lying there in the guest bedroom, befuddled with whisky and bloated with the haggis supper.

Bonnie had kindly offered to put me up for the night in the guest bedroom owing to my inability to leave the premises unless I went on all-fours, and had in fact assisted me from the lounge to the bed by using her tea-trolley to support my upper torso. So unaccustomed was I to alcohol that I did not so much feel drunk as gravely ill and sinking into a coma. Several times I requested Bonnie to return to the lounge for the purpose of fetching my body and reconnecting it to my head, but she assured me I had brought it with me, and, by tilting my face forward, showed me where it lay lifeless.

Suddenly the door opened, the light came on and a girl stood by my bed. She was taller than Bonnie—about eight feet six from where I lay—but directly she opened her mouth in the familiar brogue of the wild Highlands I sensed it was Margaret.

"Who air yew then?" she demanded, almost as though she was singing the opening line of a ballad.

"I'm Peter Pook, ye ken, lass," I sang back, "and lang may your lum reek the noo'."

"Oh, I see. What have you done to your face—had a wee tumble from a horse?"

"No, as a matter of fact I'm smiling at you."

"Does it pain you, mon?"

"This is my natural expression. I'm what Bonnie calls ruggedly handsome—not pretty-pretty." Things have come to a sad state, I thought to myself, when you have to tell people when you're smiling. My morale sank to a new low.

"Don't cry, Peter—you mustn't take it to heart so. They say Oliver Cromwell had warts as well."

"I'm not crying. It's just that I've stopped smiling."

"Oh, I see. I'll put the light out, then we can get to bed."

"I'm already in bed."

"Move over then."

"But this is the guest bedroom, Margaret."

"I know it is, but this is a flatlet, not the Dorchester Hotel. There's only one bedroom, and this is it."

"But Bonnie said I could sleep here."

"So you can, Peter—there's room enough. You've heard of mixed bathing—well, this is the same, only indoors. We call it mixed sleeping."

I lay there sweating, as Margaret got in beside me, and the scent of heather swept across my face as if we were camping on a Scottish moor.

"Talk to me, Peter. I love to talk in bed."

"Well, as a kid I was a curly-headed charmer, but what with boxing and rugby I've gone off a bit."

I felt Margaret's hand slide across my defenceless chest in the darkness. "Why are you trembling, Peter?" she whispered.

"I'm over-trained just now and suffering from muscle-flutter."

"But you're not frightened of me, are you, Peter?"

"Yes, I am. I'm frightened of Bonnie, too, after the evening I've been through."

"If you were in Scotland they'd build a kirk round you, then you could die in peace."

"What does a remark like that mean, Margaret?"

"It's an old Scottish saying. Ask Bonnie."

"I certainly will when I see her. By the way, where is she now if this is the only bedroom?"

"She's the other side of you. She likes to turn in early."

At first I thought Margaret was trying to scare me with a macabre joke, but when I put out an exploratory hand in the dark I was horrified to feel a body there—a female body. A voice said, "Oo! I'm warning you, Peter, I'm giving you exactly eight hours to take your hand off me."

There was no mistaking Bonnie's voice. I jerked my hand back and lay there trembling as my situation dawned on me. The stimulus of fear set all my major muscle systems throbbing, their combined action jerking me so violently that the bed began to rock end to end with the steady rhythm of a steam camshaft.

"How old are you, Peter?" Margaret inquired.

"I'm only eighteen."

"Do you want to be nineteen?"

"Of course I do."

"Then stop shaking the damned bed to pieces."

Bonnie said formally, "Peter, I want you to meet Margaret; she's my big sister."

"You can say that again," I gasped. Even the movies had no precedent for being in bed with two women—married ones at that. Recently I had seen a picture called *Leap Year Bride,* in which the groom died on his wedding night and I wondered if such a story was possible in real life.

"Peter has a big problem we're trying to solve," Bonnie confided in her sister as though I wasn't there.

"Yes, I've seen it, Bonnie. Have you thought of plastic surgery?"

"Oh, don't be rude about his face, Margaret; he's most self-conscious about it. His problem is women."

"So I should think, judging by tonight."

"No, he can't get the girl of his choice—a beautiful girl called Wanda."

"I don't doubt it—there isn't room for her."

"This unrequited love has given him a kind of inferiority complex—he thinks women don't want anything to do with him."

"I must say he shows it in an odd sort of way, with one each side of him. Perhaps he's a Muslim and thinks anything less than four wives is loneliness."

"Anyway, I thought with your help we could cure him by shock treatment. . . ."

"I haven't got that problem any longer, Bonnie—I swear it," I protested vehemently.

"See how bravely he tries to hide it, Margaret? Isn't that just like a man? Lie still, ma wee haggis, and we'll soon have you better. We'll prove to you that there's at least two lassies who want you."

"Please let me take your word for it, Bonnie. You're both married—I'm not."

"Then imagine this is your wedding night, Peter, and you're alone at last with your brides."

"We're in a hotel on our honeymoons?"

"Exactly."

"And I'm being arrested for bigamy?"

"Of course not."

"Two jealous husbands try to take my brides away from me? A bullet penetrates my protective confetti and enters my heart?" I kept talking to take their minds off the shock treatment. Having already learned that I couldn't cope with Bonnie, I was prepared to talk till dawn to keep her big sister at bay.

"Let me explain, Peter. For many centuries life has been extremely dangerous on the Isle of Skagh, where Margaret and I hail from, off the coast of Scotland, because many of the menfolk were drowned."

"If they knew you two I expect they ran to the cliffs and leapt into the sea, Bonnie."

"No, they were fishermen, and because so many of them were lost there was always a shortage of males."

"So you want me to take up fishing?"

"Now, if the population of Skagh was to be maintained there was no place for a shy man, obviously."

"He was sent out fishing without a boat?"

"No, Peter, he had to undergo the ancient Skagh custom of Fash wi' a Bawbee. After that ordeal he was no longer shy of women."

“Because they had knocked his brains out?”

“Oh, no, Peter, the lassies of Skagh are renowned for their gentleness and femininity, but they know their duty—that the population of the island must be maintained, so they keep up the tradition of Fash wee Bawbee if there is a reluctant male in their midst.”

“They make him fish with a baby?”

“What happens is he is given a bottle of whisky to drink, while the lassies of the island dance round him. Then each girl in turn makes advances to him, and if he agrees she gives him a bawbee.”

“You mean he becomes pregnant?”

“Oh Peter, a bawbee is a halfpenny.”

“So he can give up fishing and retire on the proceeds.”

“On the other hand, if he refuses he has to give her a bawbee. This seldom happens, but if it does she cries out ‘Skagh wa’ hoo’! Skagh wa’ hoo’!’ at such an affront to her sex. Whereupon the man is required to pay a forfeit.”

“He is publicly hanged from a bed-post?”

“No, he is stripped of his clothes, then made to carry the lass on his shoulders Skagh wa’ hoo—once round the island.”

“How far is it round the island, Bonnie?”

“Just short of eight miles, some up, some down.”

“Does he have to run all the way?”

“No, he usually staggers most of the distance, but he must finish within three hours. Then comes the final ceremony.”

“They attend his funeral?”

“The affronted lass stands over him and repeats three times, ‘Fash wi’ a Bawbee the noo’, mon?’ Whereupon the man must take back his bawbee and say, ‘Aye, lass, Ah weel’. If he is unable to speak yet, a friend must say it for him.”

“After that the lassies of the island put him to bed,” Margaret confirmed happily, “and make him choose his bride before cock-crow. Then directly the sun breaks over Ben Doondoch he is pulled bodily from the bed and carried to the kirk, where the Pastor stands over him and reads the banns three times. At each reading the man must answer, 'Aye, Ah weel', and each time his bride-to-be bangs his head on the flagstones to impress his pledge on his memory. Only then is he allowed to dress and go off in his fishing boat, in the knowledge that never again will he be shy of women."

I lay there sweating, making a mental note never to visit the Isle of Skagh, even as a tourist. Was this the reason, I asked myself, why countries as far afield as New Zealand and Tasmania were choked with Scotsmen, always singing and bagpiping about Ma Wee Heeland Hame, yet never returning—fugitives from those beguiling lassies of Skagh? I wondered if all those Scotsmen one met in Canada, South Africa and Australia were, in reality, ex-fishermen who had sailed away from the Isle of Skagh with their nets, and kept sailing—until they could safely domicile themselves abroad as engineers, accountants and doctors.

I lay on my back as stiff and still as possible, scarcely breathing, in the hope that the girls would assume I had fallen asleep and do likewise. The air was drenched with heather, as if I was lying in a bush of it, and I recall an irrational fear that I might attract bees about me. After some ten minutes I judged by Margaret's breathing that she had gone to sleep, and soon I figured that Bonnie had followed suit. So I relaxed slightly and prepared for the long vigil through the night.

When the hand lightly touched my stomach I was so taken by surprise that I choked back a scream of terror into a squeak. I lay still, waiting for the next move but nothing happened. Yet I sensed that something cold was there on my stomach. I listened to the regular breathing of my hostesses, then gradually brought up my left hand, inch by inch, to investigate the object. My fingers discovered a small, round disc fitted neatly over my navel like a tiny manhole cover. My sense of touch told me it was a coin of some sort, about the size of a half-penny.

Then I heard Bonnie whisper, "Fash wi' a bawbee, Peter?"

I racked my brains, trying to remember the counter-password.

"Aye, lass, Ah weel," leapt into my mind, so that only by clapping a hand over my mouth was I able to suppress it. The only other phrase I could recall was Skagh wa' hoo' but this I dismissed lest it entailed my carrying Bonnie round Cudford on my back.

My thoughts were interrupted by a dreadful occurrence. Margaret turned over in her sleep, throwing her left arm across my chest, at the same time mistaking my face for the pillow. She was now breathing into my ear, while I breathed through a curtain of silken hair. Her skin was soft beyond telling, so that I lay there as one in a trance, bemused by a strange feeling that there had been accident in Heaven and an angel had crash-landed on top of me. My mental retina was also receiving a series of pictures I identified as Hogarth's *Rake's Progress* in colour, wherein I figured as a kilted debauchee.

I started with shock as a voice whispered in my other ear, "I think Margaret's having a nightmare."

"She's not the only one," I gasped.

"Oh, she's a true daughter of Ben Doondoch if ever there was."

"Is that her father, Bonnie?"

"It's the great mountain of Skagh. That's why she's such a wild one—she was born half-way up its north face."

"Was her mother a mountain guide then?"

"'Tis an old tradition of the island that the higher a child is born the bonnier it will be."

"I guess you were born on the summit."

"Her trouble is that she misses her wee Gordon so much, Peter."

"But you said her husband's name was Harold. The one who is lost in Borneo."

"Ah, wee Gordon was her first husband. He put out from Skagh Harbour and was never seen again."

"The first man to row the Atlantic single-handed?"

Just then Margaret stirred slightly, gripping my neck in the crook of her arm. "I'm so glad you're back at last, wee Gordon", she sighed into my ear.

"I'm not wee Gordon, I'm big Peter."

"Sh! She's talking in her sleep. Tell her you're wee Gordon back from the sea, then she'll slumber peacefully."

"I'm wee Gordon back from the sea," I confirmed.

"Where have you been, wee Gordon?"

"Well, in view of what I said previously, I've been to the sea, Margaret. That's how I'm back from it."

"Why have you been so long, wee Gordon?"

"I lost an oar and went round in circles." It was remarkable, how these girls, even in sleep, always presented you with a kind of verbal questionnaire to fill in.

"But meanwhile I married again, wee Gordon."

"I'm not surprised. The next day probably."

"And now ma wee Harold's gone awa'."

"It was the only way he could get some sleep."

"D'ye ken where ma wee Harold's gone ta?"

"He sailed o'er the sea to bed."

"It says in my stars I'm to wed a Sassenach before Hogmanay."

"I should stick to your own countrymen and marry Hogmanay first. Keep Sassenach in reserve for the end of the fishing season."

"They say he's a fair bit younger than me."

"Once you're married he'll soon be a fair bit older than anyone."

"Bonnie says he'll have to change his name to McPook when he weds a lassie from Skagh."

Momentarily I wondered what Hilda Longbothem would think when next we met and she saw my hair had turned white in three hours. I felt scared and inexperienced beyond measure—worse now Margaret had named me as her next victim. Moreover, I couldn't stir, so effectively had the two girls pinned me down.

"Do you still feel lonely and neglected, Peter?" Bonnie whispered into my left ear.

"Not now I'm frightened and suffocated, dear."

"See how *Family Help* came to your aid? Remember our motto?"

"'Kill or Cure'?"

" 'If you are lonely and unwanted, consult our experts'."

" 'Merely complete free advice coupon and look in your bed'."

"Do you like my sister, Peter?"

"I think she's a beautiful creature of the wild islands."

"Don't forget you have to choose a bride before cockcrow."

"But this is Cudford, not Skagh, Bonnie. I'm too young for marriage yet."

"Oh, Peter, you can't take a lassie to bed and not do right by her. On the Isle of Skagh there is a dreadful old custom for any man who dared do such a thing. . . ."

"Please don't tell me, Bonnie—I've had all I can stand for one night."

Suddenly Margaret increased her grip round my neck as she whispered in my right car, "Fash wi' a bawbee the noo', mon?" and I was astonished to hear myself replying, "Aye, lass, Ah weel."

Thus began the most memorable night of my life, packed with tradition and custom, during which I was installed as an honorary Skagh fisherman and given the freedom of the island in a manner I had never before connected with such ceremonies.

I did my best to look inconspicuous at the club's Grand Christmas Ball, held as usual in the King's Hotel, Cudford, but when I tell you that the Press photographers were continually firing their flash-bulbs wherever I walked, it was a difficult task. I made a record number of visits to the Gents, mainly to escape the cameras and adjust my dress. The commissionaire on the main door had already tried to bar my entry, on the grounds that this was not a fancy-dress occasion but strictly formal, until I explained that I had the honour of wearing the traditional wedding regalia of a Skagh islander.

I was secretly rather proud of the kilt and jacket in scarlet and gold, though I felt a bit frilly round the neck and cuffs. The kilt set my legs off very well, and tucked in one of the stockings was the symbolic dirk for cutting up bait. My sole objection was to the glengarry, because not only was it hard to balance on the side of one's head—which I solved by wearing it dead centre—but also there hung down from the front the traditional black streamer of a betrothed mon, as Margaret put it.

This streamer was a constant reminder to all, and especially to oneself, that I was engaged. Because it terminated at chin level I found it impossible to eat or drink without it dangling in the refreshment like a fishing-line. Margaret said it was bad luck to remove the glengarry, and a flagrant breach of custom to tie it back. As a consequence the streamer was invariably wet and sticky to the touch, as so many of my friends discovered when they frivolously pulled it, crying, "Hold very tightly, please," or "Kindly flush after use."

I had temporarily lost the use of my left hand owing to the massive gold betrothal ring thereon, which felt as if I was clutching a golf ball. Inscribed on the band was the legend, in Gaelic, informing female readers that I could not consider their advances to me without first observing the ancient Skagh custom of cutting my throat.

I was very much in love with the beautiful Margo—as Margaret was called in Skagh—so much so that I had to force myself not to think of my betrothal night because it made me break out into a cold sweat and tremble all over. Even tonight when I danced with her my knees often buckled visibly below the kilt and she had to support me. Alec declared that dancing with Margo was like going to bed to music, because she melted into one's arms and placed her moist, parted lips against one's cheeks in an extremely sensuous fashion, making a tango seem like an illicit weekend.

Margo's ball gown was the sensation of the evening. It is difficult for a man to describe it, except to say that it was simple, black, and apparently unfinished, as though they had run out of material half-way up, relying on her long dark hair to cover her back and her fiery eyes to take our minds off her bust. She wore no jewellery to hide her magnificent shoulders, and Paul told me confidentially in the Gents that he dared not dance with her again without a chaperon being present.

Margo kept telling me I was her lord and master, so I kept asking myself how was it I had a black eye. My left eye was almost completely closed after she had kissed me good-night the previous evening, following her protestations that the Skagh lassies were so gentle, feminine and submissive. I had learned to be most wary of Margo when she did a Madonna and slid into my arms as helpless womanhood, soft and virginal—with the result that I had to visit the doctor to have a dressing put on my ear lobe. At first he was going to give me an injection for rabies until I confessed that I had been bitten by my fiancée.

I felt embarrassed in the extreme as he examined my black eye, apparently under the impression I was engaged to an alsatian or something, and he asked me if I had got my broken nose in the same way. I explained how it was the result of boxing, whereupon he laughed and said I was a glutton for dangerous sports.

I was very annoyed with myself, the way my knees kept buckling when I danced with Margo, as though I had had too much drink. I noticed Marcus dancing with Wanda, yet simpering all the time at Margo over Wanda's shoulder. Surely, I thought, he's not going to steal Margo from me? I couldn't think this for long because I had to concentrate on my knees, endeavouring to keep them straight to prevent buckling at the joints, despite the inconvenience of dancing stiff-legged.

"Who is that grinning mon with the staring eyes?" Margo demanded.

"All the men are staring at you, Margo. Which one do you mean?"

"That wee Jock yonder."

I winced as Margo threw out her arm and pointed right in Marcus's face. "Oh, he's Marcus," I replied miserably.

"Och—he's a face like a cod!"

"A Greek god?" Margo's broad accent often made understanding difficult.

"A North Sea cod, mon. Praise the laird for your ain wee bonny face, Peter. Gie us a kiss to tak' the taste awa'."

As often happened when Margo kissed me, she had to support my body-weight while I regained the use of my legs. I felt extremely flattered by her remark, yet at the same time I wondered at her judgment. "Do you really think I'm so good-looking, Margo?" I fished, savouring such unaccustomed compliments.

Margo flashed her eyes and teeth. "Och, mon! On the Isle of Skagh ye'll be the handsomest devil ever kissed by a lassie."

The Isle of Skagh jumped up in my estimation, especially as Margo was determined to spend our honeymoon there. "You must woo me in the shadow of Ben Doondoch if our first bairn is to be a boy"—though I wondered about the looks of the male population if I was considered handsome.

At that moment Hilda Longbothem danced by in the unenthusiastic arms of her father, the silver barbed-wire halo on her head shaking with indignation at the sight of me in my traditional wedding attire. Catching my eye, Hilda glanced pointedly at Margo, then threw her own eyes up to the ceiling in disapproval. Instinctively I looked at Margo's bust, once again experiencing the sensation that I was about to fall headlong from the summit of Ben Doondoch into the gorge below. It was odd how, at that precise moment, Margo kissed me once more, at the same time extending my left arm for me so that the great betrothal ring almost touched Hilda's nose. Then the music ceased.

We were so close to the Longbothems that I had no option but to introduce them as we left the floor. Margo ignored Hilda, having eyes only for Mr Longbothem, standing demurely by him like a girl caught in her bath with barely time to get a towel up.

Hilda was extremely cross with me, impatiently brushing my streamer from her face. "What is this ridiculous get-up, Peter, that you have to come to the Grand Christmas Ball looking like an advert for porridge? And if you must wear that stupid glengarry, why is it on back-to-front?"

"This is the correct way, Hilda. The streamer is to show that I'm betrothed, in case people don't see my big ring here."

"For a moment I thought you had got your finger stuck in a brass cartridge-case. How could you humiliate me so, backing out of our ball date at such short notice that my father has to escort me?"

"But I told you last August, Hilda. That was four months ago, when I became spoken for, as we say north of the border."

"Then you have the gall to turn up here in front of all our friends with that half-naked female, who, one presumes, is wearing the traditional wedding nightdress in public."

"Your dad seems to like her well enough, Hilda."

"My father is merely being polite to a guest."

"Is that why he keeps kissing her hand?"

"Oh, to think that I once let you kith me, you horrible man! What does it say on that hideous ring of yours?"

"It's an ancient Gaelic pledge that . . . er . . . under certain circumstances it would be necessary for me to kill someone."

"Kill who?"

"Myself actually."

"For doing what?"

"Well, for being unfaithful to Margo."

Hilda let out a little scream. "Would you really do that, Peter?"

"I'd have to. That's what this small dirk in my stocking is for. Margo carries a similar one in her handbag."

"So she would kill herself rather than be unfaithful to you?"

"No, Hilda, she'd kill me if I funked it."

"Supposing I took you away from this Margo?"

"I'd have to come to you by hearse. Then we could get buried in Cudford Cathedral."

Hilda shuddered. "Oh, Peter, you're so morbid! Let's have a dance together for old time's sake to cheer you up."

"I can't, Hilda, because I've been spoken for."

"But she's been dancing with other men."

"She says engaged couples may dance only with each other or with other men. I suppose that's all right on the Isle of Skagh but down here it means that I have to sit out."

"I'll ask her myself."

Margo flashed a glance at Hilda and promptly agreed to our dancing together while she danced with Mr Longbothem. The band struck up a waltz and we set sail across the floor. I noticed that Mr Longbothem was sweating in Margo's arms as though she was dragging him clear of a car crash, and it was pathetic to watch his knees buckling as he tried to be convivial to his partner.

Hilda saw it too. "Really, Peter, it's awful to see Daddy making a fool of himself over that woman of yours. Thank heaven Mummy isn't here to witness it."

"She does that to all the men."

"Well, I think it's disgusting. Honestly, the more I know of men the more I'm sure that I shall never marry."

"Don't give up hope, Hilda. The song says that somewhere, somewhen, there's someone waiting for all of us."

"Oh, shut up! That sounds more like a hymn than a song."

"I'm sorry, Hilda, but my streamer has got caught in your barbed . . . your tiara whatnot." It had, too, and jerked the tiara clean off her head. While I was untangling the streamer I heard a commotion on the far side of the dance floor.

"Quickly, Peter, I think it's Daddy," Hilda screamed. "I believe he's collapsed."

Hurrying over to the scene, I saw many hands helping Mr Longbothem to his feet. He was wiping his bald head and protesting that he had slipped during a turn. Margo was retrieving his spectacles from her bra and replacing them on his nose. "They fell in my bodice as he went down," she explained worriedly, "otherwise they might have been smashed."

"Oh, Daddy, are you all right?"

"Yes, thank you, dear. If Peter will just assist me to the bar for a Scotch . . . no, better make it a brandy . . . I'll be fine in a jiffy. The exertion and stuffy atmosphere made me a trifle dizzy. I had that nasty sensation of falling headlong from a mountain into the gorge below. Don't mention it to your mother, Hilda, there's a good girl; it would only worry her."

"You're darn right it would worry her," Hilda snapped, glaring at Margo. "Next time you cavort with a woman like that you ought to be roped to a guide or you'll end up where your specs went."

This barb so hurt Margo that her high cheek bones registered infinite regret, and she was obliged to cling to Paul for protection, those long black lashes lowered in contrition. She said nothing, letting her heaving bosom send out distress signals, so that Paul kissed her brow reassuringly—and seemed taken by surprise when he was promptly kissed back on the lips.

I assisted Mr Longbothem to the bar for a brandy, where he confessed to me that he had not had such an experience since he was blown up by a land-mine in the last war. I listened patiently to the first three years of the war, but shouts of "Bridegroom! Bridegroom!" from the dance floor forced me to leave him halfway through the 1917 offensive on the Western Front, some weeks before the land-mine was due to go off.

Returning to my party, I found Dave Parnell, the *Cudford Echo* reporter, pulling Paul off Margo so he could photograph her for tomorrow's edition. Paul was trembling and red-faced, crying "All right, send for the police then, but I was only trying to console her."

Marcus was shouting, "Nobody's going to send for the police, Paul—just let go of her for the photographers. Can't you see you're squeezing the Mayor?"

Paul wasn't the only one squeezing the Mayor of Cudford, because Margo already had one arm round him in an effort to pull clear of Paul. Directly she was free, her other arm encircled his

Worship as she kissed him gratefully for her deliverance. Dave Parnell, never slow to grasp a human interest item, flashed the kiss with his camera. I could see that wild look in the Mayor's eye as a bit of the Skagh magic rubbed off onto his mayoral chain, but he quickly recovered his aldermanic dignity with a smile, although I sensed he was secretly testing his legs for stability.

"Ah, here's the lucky bridegroom at last!" Dave Parnell announced.

"How many of them are there then?" somebody exclaimed from the rear of the crowd.

Dave lined up Margo and me for the photograph with our arms round each other's waists in connubial pose, but when I touched her hand it was large and hairy, and I discovered it belonged to the Mayor. I learned that he was in the centre of the group, with his left arm round Margo, who had changed shape and seemed to be in some danger of bursting out of her dress.

When Dave's pictorial requirements had been satisfied, the Mayor of Cudford gave me such a quick handshake that I scarcely had time to get my hand up; then he slowed down, to give Margo such a long kiss that Dave intervened with, "Can you spare a few minutes for some details of the courtship for my write-up?"

Margo smiled shyly, then put her hand inside my jacket to extract the copy of *Family Help* she insisted I carry at all times. "We owe everything to *Family Help* magazine, if your Worship the Mayor will accept this copy as a memento of this wonderful night of rejoicing."

The Mayor bowed low as he took the magazine for the civic archives, marvelling at the power of such a journal to produce Margo.

"Please tell us how *Family Help* comes into such a love saga," Dave probed.

Margo blushed prettily, holding her hair back with both hands. "I'm just a simple Scots girl, far too shy for interviews, Dave, so let Peter tell you his own story."

"My name is Peter Po. . . ."

"Before he begins I merely want to add that I love him dearly, and will try to make him a good wife."

"My name is. . . ."

"Also, I must thank *Family Help* for bringing us together."

"My name . . . ."

"Just by filling in a little coupon. Tell them why you filled in the little coupon from *Family Help,* Peter."

"My . . . ."

"Peter felt lonely and neglected by the opposite sex, so he filled in the little coupon from *Family Help.* You see, *Family Help* has a motto which you can probably guess."

" 'No reader shall open his mouth'?" I suggested.

" 'If you are lonely and unwanted, consult our experts'."

"So, Peter, tell us how you consulted the experts," Dave inquired of me.

"I merely turned over in bed. . . ."

"We already knew Peter's case history, so we came down to Cudford personally to help solve his problem. After our very first interview he was no longer shy of the opposite sex."

"I was engaged, too."

"So now you don't feel lonely and neglected any more, Peter?"

"On the contrary, I can't get any peace, Dave. Margo has brought a host of new friends into my life, day and night. If we go to a party, all the other guests come home with us. The insurance man called last Tuesday and he hasn't left yet. In fact, Dave, I'll lay ten to one that you'll be able to continue this interview tomorrow morning when I bring your tea in and wake you up."

"Where on earth shall I be sleeping then?"

"Next to the Mayor of Cudford, I guess."

Dave laughed delightedly at the prospect. "This is a fantastic change in your situation, Peter, and real hot copy. Now tell me about the colourful apparel you're sporting tonight."

I stood to attention proudly and adjusted my kilt for hem-line.

It was what would be termed today a mini-kilt, extremely short to show off a good leg—so short in fact that I had to wear the sporran on my stomach.

"This is the traditional betrothal dress of a Skagh islander, which I am permitted, even compelled, to wear because my engagement to Margo makes me a naturalized inmate of the island. Have your camera at the ready, Dave, for I am about to show you something you have never seen before."

"Your traditional wedding drawers under the kilt?"

"No, Dave, a Highland Fling."

"But I've often seen that."

"Not without moving the feet." I was secretly peeved at the way Margo stole the limelight, so I had been practising my own version of the Highland Fling in the privacy of the bathroom. Raising my arms high above the head and going up on my toes in conventional Fling pose, I let the muscles of my legs have full play in advanced muscle control without moving the feet. My iliac, sartorious, adductor longus, gracilis and quadriceps extensor muscles took on the steady rhythm of the dance, bobbing and throbbing in double time, till the crowd began to clap out the beat with their hands except Hilda, who ran distraught to join her father at the bar.

"Revolting, isn't it?" Margo said to the Mayor delightedly.

"Utterly vile, my dear. One dreads to contemplate what the rest of him is like."

"He can even oscillate his orbicularis palpebrarum."

"Your married life should be far from dull, my dear. I trust you will practise birth control."

"This enables him to isolate his eyeballs."

"A fitting tribute for your womanly charms, my dear. I myself have been doing it for the past hour. Ah, I hear the orchestra striking up the last waltz, so, my dear, will you give an old man the pleasure of this dance?"

Margo smiled archly. "I'd rather dance with you instead, your Worship."

"Ha, ha! Perhaps your fiancee will take my wife as a fitting climax to the festivities?"

"Why is she kneeling down, sir?" I inquired, seeing the lady for the first time.

"Not kneeling, Mr Pook, merely on the short side. Petite, shall we say?"

I wondered if petite meant short and fat, but I smiled bravely as I tried to get some kind of hand-hold on the Mayoress, finally compromising with a head-lock which gave people the impression that I was dancing without a partner. We stumbled round the floor while I endeavoured to solve the problem of her feet, so many of which emerged from under her long gown that I thought she moved on the caterpillar-track system of a tank. No matter where I trod she had sets of feet there before I could plant one shoe, and if I retreated I found spare feet behind me and to either side.

"I'm afraid I'm not used to these modem dances," she apologized far below me.

"It is the waltz, madam," I replied, puzzled. Perhaps in the old days you needed four pairs of feet for the quadrille.

"You're so tall that I keep tripping you up."

"My fault entirely, madam—having only two feet I quickly run out of supports. Perhaps you would be kind enough to confine the majority of your feet to the centre, while I use the sides."

By spreading my legs coat-hanger fashion I managed to create a freeway where my partner could dance on her own in the central reservation, a posture which made me feel rather like a dock-side crane hoisting a bale of cotton.

The Lady Mayoress raised her face for speech, now we had mastered the art of standing upright and following the other couples in the anti-clockwise circuit of the floor—the kind, homely face that always makes me think of tea, cakes, ironing and desertion. "I expect you'll want to be taking up dancing now you're engaged," she smiled, gliding backwards on an endless-belt of small shoes. "Every groom is duty-bound to dance with his bride, you know."

"If I ever dance with my bride it'll have to be round a great big maypole to fit all her partners in," I replied coldly, just as Wanda sailed past aboard Marcus.

"Lucky you!" Wanda called out, smiling her wonderful smile.

"Social climber!" Marcus laughed.

I smiled back with my teeth, as Margo approached supporting a tottery Lord Mayor in an arm-and-bust lock. "Och, darling, yew're na more and na less than a wee de'il of a flirtie!" she sang to me, blowing kisses at twenty paces.

All the men in our vicinity began to blow kisses back to her. Then the band struck up the National Anthem and we stood to attention for the finale, to sing *God Save the King.* It may have been Margo's broad dialect or my overwrought imagination, but as I listened to her voice singing above the rest of us I could have sworn she added the words *for me* to the opening line of the Anthem.

SIX

Of all people it was Aunt Dot who introduced me to the motor trade for the purpose of making a living, because, being old-fashioned, she could not bear the thought of Margo keeping me when we were married, nor the thought of Margo starving if we depended on my outstanding literary talent.

I just could not get in the money, even though I had gone to the fountainhead by working in one of the Big Five banks, where they kept temptation out of my way by paying me £5 —not per week or per day but per month. At this time my name was fast becoming a household word in literary circles, and as I was now grossing two guineas a week by my pen I was forced to the conclusion that the household word was *Broke.*

With feminine perspicacity, Aunt Dot pointed out that if I sold one car a week at a profit of £10, it would be the equivalent of two months' slavery in the bank or one month's journalistic genius on a typewriter. This sounded all very fine, but, characteristically, she told me how to do it.

My premises or motor showrooms were to be the forecourt of Aunt Dot's house, almost in the centre of Cudford. Rental, one peppercorn, to be paid annually in advance. The next step was to obtain stock, and to this end Aunt Dot and I compiled the following advertisement for insertion in the Used Cars section of the *Cudford Echo,* at twopence a word:

Elderly gentlewoman in reduced circumstances urgently requires cheap reliable car to visit husband who is unable to move. No dealers.—Write Box 729.

At first I was appalled by what Aunt Dot had dictated to me. "Uncle Sydney is dead," I protested.

"So the advert says, Peter. You will be able to drive me up to the cemetery to visit his grave and check that he is still unable to move."

"But why mention him at all, Aunt Dot?"

"Because some kind person may be touched on the heartstrings and let us have his car cheap."

"Even if that happens, how will we pay for it?"

"Uncle Sydney will finance us, Peter."

"Vivisection?"

"No, I am in the process of selling his silver sports trophies to those poor Americans."

"But they were his most treasured possessions. He said they were never to be taken out of your china cabinet."

"Exactly. And to show how I respect his wishes I am selling the china cabinet with them."

The advertisement produced several replies, two of which were suitable. The first was a black 1936 Standard Nine De-Luxe, with wire wheels, sunshine roof and green upholstery, owned by a bank manager, in immac. condit., as they say in the trade. I recall only two points from the conversation Aunt Dot had with the owner. The first was in reply to the bank manager's inquiry as to her husband's health, when she replied firmly, "I am informed on the highest medical authority that he will never move again." The second was the manner in which she fixed the price of the vehicle—"You tell me it cost you £147 10s new, therefore I am sure you will accept half that sum as a fair second-hand price—£63 15s."

It was not until the deal had been concluded and the bank manager departed that I detected Aunt Dot's faulty mathematics. When I taxed her with it she said, "To whose advantage is it, Peter?"

"Why, ours of course, Aunt Dot."

"Oh, dear! Still a bank manager, of all people, should have spotted the error so we'd best say no more about it. It would only embarrass him."

The second deal I did myself, sweating with nervous tension as I gambled with high stakes for an Austin Seven two-door runabout which had lost its hood during a recent gale, with the result that the upholstery had turned rain grey, with a leaf motif. After two hours of hard bargaining and demo runs, the owner said to me in a confidential tone, "I'll bend down to tie up my shoelace, and while I'm not looking, you jump in the car and steal it."

We bargained for a further hour, when the man looked all round to ensure there were no eavesdroppers about, then whispered in my ear, "I'll tell you what we'll do, Peter. You write your birthday in my diary, and when it comes I'll give you the car as a present."

We adjourned the negotiations until the following day so both parties could consider their positions. On the morrow the man said to me, "I'll accept your offer, Peter, provided it's cash and in notes of small denomination so I can get out of the country to South America."

So I clinched my very first deal—perhaps hard to believe in this affluent age—whereby I obtained an Austin Seven hoodless coupé for £2 15s, in immac. condit., provided you weren't going far and the weather was fine. The seller became a close friend of mine in the future—Mr George Craig—and when, some eight years later, I was stationed in the Far East he kindly stored a Vauxhall I then owned free of charge. In 1946 he cabled me: 'Vauxhall deteriorating in storage. Recommend immediate sale. Current price £100. George.' Pleased with the price I cabled back: 'Sell Vauxhall £100 less your expenses. Peter.' George wired me £90, with which I was delighted until I returned to England and learned of the post-war famine prices then being paid for cars. I spotted the Vauxhall in Cudford High Street and by chatting to its new owner I learned to my horror that he had paid George £300 for it. Furthermore, he was willing to sell it back to me for £350. That was the only time I ever wept in a public thoroughfare.

Keeping the Austin Seven for my personal runabout, I washed and polished the Standard Nine like a baby, cleaning the green upholstery with hot Persil and blacking the tyres with Zebra grate polish. I also discovered that Vim sink powder would remove blemishes on the cellulose bodywork, and that Brasso brought the bumpers up like mirrors—until people inquired if the car was a new one.

To sell my treasure, Aunt Dot compiled another advertisement for the *Cudford Echo* which quite shocked me at the time:

'Elderly gentlewoman in reduced circumstances, emigrating New Zealand, must dispose of almost new Standard Nine De-Luxe Saloon, showroom condit. Sacrifice for early sale. £110 o.n.o. No dealers.—Box 797.'

"What does o.n.o. mean, Aunt Dot?" I asked.

"£110 or near offer," she explained. "Like £109 10s. This time don't put the advert in the Cars For Sale column; this type of advert will do better in the Personal Column."

"Like a charity appeal?"

"We need to touch people's consciences, Peter."

"How about yours, Aunt Dot? I suppose they wouldn't accept it under Church Notices?"

"No, Peter, the Personal Column will do nicely. Ask the Editor if he will insert it after the suicide one that's in every night."

Aunt Dot finally sold the Standard Nine for £105, showing a profit of £42—a small fortune in those days, equivalent to my working eight months in a bank, or hiring a maid for eighty-four weeks, or supporting eighty-four Old Age Pensioners for one week. It was our first baby and our joy was indescribable. Although far bigger deals were to come, never again was the thrill so ecstatic—not even in 1950, when I purchased a Ford Anglia, list price £340, for £200 in Johannesburg, South Africa; drove it to Durban, shipped it on the *Pretoria Castle* for £45 freight charge, bound for car-hungry Britain, and sold it on the dockside at Southampton to a dealer for £750. That was the crazy set-up in 1950, when a car manufactured in Britain could travel halfway round the world back to Britain—and still net me a profit of £500. It really was an extraordinary period, when Britain was exporting automobiles all over the world at the expense of the home market, yet at the same time entrepreneurs like myself were shipping them back to England as fast as we could for the fast buck.

A passenger on the *Pretoria Castle* trip was that dynamic car giant, Lord Nuffield, of Morris Motors fame. His physical fitness astonished everybody, as he defeated the ship's officers and passengers at the testing game of deck-tennis— not deck quoits, mark you, but deck-tennis! After he had soundly beaten me I remarked jokingly, "I'm shipping cars back to Britain, sir."

He smiled delightedly. "Pleased to meet you, young man. I'm the chap who keeps sending them out!"

At that time Lord Nuffield was in his seventy-third year.

Drunk with success, Aunt Dot and I next sold a Hillman Ten, an Austin Huntsman, a Clyno, an Essex, a Lagonda coupé and a Chrysler Airflow, the first streamlined car we ever saw. But when Aunt Dot purchased the flashy Hudson Terraplane it was so long that I could not fit it on the forecourt at all and was forced to park it round the rear of the house on the lawn. I told Aunt Dot we would never be able to dispose of it, at least not in a modest area like Cudford, but she was adamant, and her method is probably unique in the annals of salesmanship. This is the ad she instructed me to insert in the Personal column of the *Cudford Echo:*

'Elderly gentlewoman in reduced circumstances must sacrifice Hudson Terraplane, immac. condit., taxed and insured year, seat eight, low mil., owing to failing health. View appointment only, Sunday a.m. after church. Christian buyer preferred. No dealers or near offers. Would consider smaller car part-exchange. Easy terms available.'

I protested to Aunt Dot about the ad but she refused to alter a word of it, explaining esoterically that "We must meet craft with craft, Peter—if you sup with the Devil you need a long spoon. Always remember that folks can never stand their own medicine. I haven't failed you yet, now have I?"

I felt extremely embarrassed as the counter clerk at the *Echo* offices read the ad and counted the words. "Under what heading would you like it printed, sir—*In Memoriam?"* he inquired, twisting his nose as if the ad smelled. "Though you could do it cheaper in *Thanks For Sympathy*—it's only three-ha'pence a word."

"Personal column as usual, Percy, please. Immediately beneath the suicide one."

If I was embarrassed by inserting the ad, I was shocked when the first applicant arrived on the following Sunday morning and Aunt Dot bade me conduct him to her bedroom. His name was Mr Gilbert Budden, a master builder according to his card, whom I had to seat in a chair by my aunt's bedside. She hardly seemed ready for business, lying there on her back with her eyes closed and her mouth open, still wearing her nightcap.

"Is she ill?" Mr Budden whispered to me worriedly. "It's the anxiety of the car," I replied off the cuff. "She can't afford to lose money but she can't wait."

"Wait for what?"

"Wait to sell it."

"Why not?"

"Because she desperately needs the cash. She thinks about nothing else."

"Will she consider an offer?"

"Only if it's the same as her asking price."

"Could we try?"

"The doctor says any sudden shock might give her a stroke."

Even as I said it I blushed at the lies tumbling from my lips, but Aunt Dot refused to help me out by speaking herself. Involuntarily I glanced at her lifeless face and a strange premonition flashed across my mind that she had passed away in her sleep at last. I seemed to be conducting a business transaction beside a death-bed and a terrible sense of guilt fell upon me. I wondered what Mr Budden's reaction would be if I inserted a mirror in her mouth during the negotiations to see if I should stop the deal and refer Mr Budden to the executors of her will, if he still wanted the Hudson Terraplane.

"Shall I come back later, or tomorrow?" Mr Budden suggested, seeing my concern.

"That may be too late, Mr Budden. Whisper your offer to me

so I can break it to my aunt gently without shock."

Mr Budden learned forward from the chair and whispered, "I merely wanted to knock off, say, the odd fiver, if that's not asking too much. I don't like to beat the old lady down, but £495 seems quite fair to me."

"I accept."

The sound of Aunt Dot's voice was so unexpected that I jumped in my seat, and Mr Budden looked at me startled, as if half suspecting I was a ventriloquist. Then we both stared at Aunt Dot, who still displayed no signs of life.

"I thought someone said 'I accept'," Mr Budden observed to me.

"Yes, it was my aunt agreeing to your offer of £495."

"Remarkable! So it's a deal then?"

"The Hudson Terraplane is yours, Mr Budden. I can assure you that there is no danger of my aunt backing out. She must sell, even at a loss, because she badly needs the money."

Mr Budden smiled for the first time, a somewhat apologetic smile. "Would she mind if I pay you in cash, Mr Pook—that is, in notes instead of a cheque."

"I am informed on reliable authority that notes are generally regarded as money, Mr Budden—still legal tender, ha, ha!"

"Normally I pay by cheque, you understand, but in a business like mine it is handy to be able to do the odd cash transaction—it, well, it helps simplify my income tax."

"Snap, as they say, because an occasional cash deal assists my own books in that direction, ha, ha!" I didn't add that practically all our business was cash, which went straight into Uncle Sydney's old deed box in the attic, hidden under a hollow toy fort of my childhood. The last time a customer had paid by cheque I went into the Bold Forester for a pint and asked the landlord to cash it for me. He wanted to know how much it was for, five or ten, so I said £200 and he replied that I could buy his tenancy for that amount.

As the months went by, so Aunt Dot's advertisements in the Personal column grew worse and our business expanded. She began to advertise in *The Gentlewoman,* a delightful magazine for old ladies far removed from the jungle of the motor trade, wherein ladies' companions, governesses, nannies and parlour maids were in great demand. It also specialized in invalid chairs, commodes, leg-rests and comfortable homes for the elderly, but now a new type of advertisement began to appear in its columns appealing to retired gentlefolk of both sexes for their cars which they could no longer drive, that Aunt Dot might be able to visit her husband, who had lost the use of his legs permanently; or that she might see once again the countryside she loved before losing the use of her own legs; or that she might provide transport for parties of elderly gentlefolk who could not otherwise visit the seaside, with or without legs.

So successful were these adverts which tapped a new source of supply, that Lady Adele Layton-Neil actually presented us with her Bean four-door saloon free, and Aunt Dot had to stay in bed all day on the appointed date, waiting for Lady Adele to arrive for the official hand-over of the vehicle at her bedside.

I was appalled by my aunt's methods but she dismissed my fears by quoting what she insisted was the Pook family motto: "Only the good die young—Long live the Pooks!"

She had no qualms about accepting Lady Adele's Bean Supreme. "It should fetch £165, Peter, buffed up nice and advertised right."

"I don't mean that, Aunt Dot. Supposing somebody turns nasty and takes us to court?"

"They won't do that, not to a dear old lady like me. I'm in my dotage and don't know what I'm doing. When you reach my age you're not responsible for your actions. I'm just a silly old faggot awaiting the Grim Reaper. In law I'd be as guilty as a new-born babe. Imagine the judge telling me, 'Mrs Pook, society must be protected from old ladies like yourself. Five years hard labour.'

Then the warders would have to carry me off to Dartmoor in chains."

"It's not you I'm worried about, Aunt Dot. It's me."

"How old are you now, Peter? My memory is going fast."

"Nineteen."

"So you're a minor. You've got two more years until they can charge you as a responsible adult. You're in your first childhood and I'm in my second childhood. Neither of us is responsible in law for our actions. In fact, we're the ideal business partnership."

"But I'm not paying any income tax either."

"That's because you're not earning enough income to tax. You stick to £125 per annum and they can't touch you."

At that period the rate of income tax was 4s 6d in the pound, but the first £125 was tax-free. The next £135 was taxed at only ls 6d in the pound, but Aunt Dot refused to let me enter that bracket because she held that income tax was immoral and had herself never paid any on religious grounds, which I found difficult to follow, even when it was fourpence back in the nineteenth century. I often heard her say that the blackest year in Britain's history was 1799, when income tax had been introduced as a temporary measure, and the second blackest year was 1842, when it had been made permanent. I well remember as a child Aunt Dot taking me upon her knee and telling me, not Little Red Riding Hood and similar folk tales, but about how the Pooks had led the uprisings of 1799 and 1842 against the new taxes, even though they weren't paying any. Another thing she told me was how her grandfather, Jos Pook, had been imprisoned in 1797 for opposing income tax, but when I pointed out that it hadn't then even been introduced, she explained that it was under discussion in Parliament at the time. I thought it strange that he should be thus involved, because only the previous year he had been committed to prison for debt.

I didn't say any more about my earning £125 a year until I made over £125 in one week. This particular week really had me worried because the elderly gentlewoman in reduced circumstances was forced to sacrifice a Volkswagen V3, a chain-drive one and a half litre Trojan, a Crossley and another 918 c.c. Morris Eight. It was the most sacrificial week we had experienced so far, and Uncle Sydney's deed box was so full of notes that I must sit on the lid to close it. Under such pressure the notes looked as if they had been ironed. I had been at my wit's end to conceal the cars among Aunt Dot's apple trees at the rear of the house, because the nature of her advertisements made it imperative that only one car should be on display out front at any one time, lest the premises took on the air of a motor rally. It was also vital to have the correct car on show at the right time, for obvious reasons.

Another of my worries was the risk of fire in the house, not for Aunt Dot's sake but for the safety of Uncle Sydney's deed box up in the attic. From the tax angle, I decided it was time I entered the taxable class by entering the £126—£260 bracket at 1s 6d in the pound, but Aunt Dot would have none of it, repeating the Pook saga of taxation riots as from 1797 and declaring that any more such seditious talk on my part would render her liable to a stroke, whereby I should find my partner dead at my feet clutching a car log book in her lifeless claw.

In desperation I decided to consult my friend George Craig on the subject. He had a reputation as a tax expert because, although he ran several business enterprises, he seldom paid income tax except when the Tax Inspector called on him personally, begging him to contribute a little something towards running the nation. On these occasions George always made a point of finding a little bit on account from his wife's house-keeping, a painful affair that sent the Inspector away feeling thoroughly ashamed of his profession.

"I work on the diamond-mining principle, Peter," George once told me. "Digging for diamonds is so difficult that most people don't try it, or give up half-way. It's the same with tax men, they're only human. First, make sure your accounts are four years behind, then let them see you're broke. Meanwhile, have a small fire on the premises so nothing is traceable, show them your wife and six kids and offer to go to jail."

"How on earth do you manage to have a fire, George?" I asked.

"My last fire was back in April, during a thunderstorm. My office records were struck by lightning."

I arranged to meet George one evening at opening time in the Bold Forester, but he was late appearing. There was only one other customer in the bar, so I bought him a jug and we started chatting. It was not long before we discovered that not only did we both know George but we were both waiting for him. The man's name was Jack Pollard, a likable, humorous character I took to at once, even more so when I learned he was interested in cars.

Through the pub window he showed me his car, one of the old Argylls of treasured memory, and I began to tell him about the Chrysler Airflow I had sold.

"It was the first streamlined car I ever set eyes on," I enthused. "No sharp angles or upright windscreen—no sidelights, no head-lamps!"

"Both lights embedded in the mudguards—fantastic!

"No battery on the running-board, no spare wheel on the back!"

"No luggage-grid sticking out either! Eight cylinders!"

"Sit six adults in comfort—purrs like a cat at eighty!"

"My dream is a 2-litre Frazer Nash B.M.W., Peter, with six cylinders under the bonnet and independent front suspension . . . here, let me fill your jug, and have a whisky chaser to go with it."

We settled down to the luxury of pub car talk, the cares of the world—George included—forgotten in an atmosphere of Olds-mobiles, Packards, Mercs, Napiers, Alvises, Bugattis, Delages, Talbots and Hispano-Suizas. Jack seemed to know so much about cars and their histories that I inquired if he was in the trade himself.

"Afraid not, Peter—only wish I was. Certainly suit me better than my stuffy old office job. Still, people like you and George keep me in touch—and I can always dream. You fellows make a bomb while I drudge along for peanuts. That's life, I guess."

"Have another Scotch to help you forget, Jack—ha, ha, ha!"

"Happy driving—cheers!"

"I know just how you feel because I worked in an office myself, five quid a month and lucky to get it. Now I often make that in a day."

"You wouldn't be looking for a partner, eh?"

"Not a chance at the moment, Jack. It's the queerest set-up you ever heard—wait for it—I'm in business with my own great-aunt! She's a female Henry Ford for cars, and she runs the show like a church bazaar. Mark my words, before she's through with me she'll have me flogging bangers dressed up as a bishop."

Jack laughed at the fancy. "She sounds a real character, Peter. Some women have a natural flair for making money."

"She makes it so fast that I have to hide it in the attic. That's what I want to see George about. He's the top tax fiddler around here, so I hoped he'd give me a few tips."

"George has brought it to fine art—almost beautiful in its perfection."

"I mean, you can get away with the odd deal, but not the way we're heading. I want to know how I can fiddle on a respectable basis, like showing enough sales to pay 1s 6d in the pound without being done for 4s 6d."

"If George can't tell you, no one can, Peter. He should have been a chartered accountant for Shylock."

"You sound as if you've known him a fair time, Jack."

"George—many years. We're old friends, believe me. He's taught me more about tax evasion and tax avoidance than any man I've ever met. He should have a degree it in."

"Sounds like you cook the books a bit yourself, Jack."

"Ah, wouldn't I just!—but there's not much chance when you're pinned down on a monthly salary cheque. They don't let you claim for anything these days."

"Hallo, there's our George at last. I'll set up the drinks again."

By now the bar was half full and George didn't seem to see us at the far end. At least he seemed to spot us, then changed his mind and would have departed had I not called out over the customers' heads.

"We're over here, George," I shouted. "There's a jug coming up for you."

George made his way across to the bar with a very long face, I thought. He grunted, "Hallo, Peter. Hallo, Jack," then buried his face in the beer.

"Seems Jack is a mutual friend, George," I observed.

George made a strange face at me, enlarging his eyes, then looking pointedly at Jack. "I didn't realize you knew Jack."

"I didn't till this evening. We got chatting and found we were both waiting for the same man."

"Do you know who he is, Peter?"

"Only that he's the best car talker in Cudford."

"Well, I'd better introduce you without delay. This is Mr Jack Pollard, Chief Tax Inspector of Cudford District."

"Chief Tax Inspector!"

"Pleased to meet you, Peter." Mr Pollard was smiling, holding out his hand for the formal shake.

"Chief Tax Inspector!"

"But he has a jug like normal human beings. As Shylock says, 'If you treat us, do we not quaff?' "

"Chief Tax Inspector! But he said he was your old pal, waiting to meet you!"

"True—but the point is, Peter, that I wasn't coming to meet *him.* He knows I use the Bold Forester, so this is where he lies in wait for me when I'm . . . well . . . when I'm slightly in arrears with my Schedules A to Z. He figures a man isn't broke if he goes into a pub—but in my case you've just bought me a drink which I'm not in a position to return. I merely popped in to tell you that, and to ask if we could meet somewhere less expensive—like in a bus shelter."

Mr Pollard laughed jovially. "I know you better than that,

George—you always carry a little bit of Mrs Craig's housekeeping money on you, just to keep the wolf from the door. I'll buy you a Scotch to help ease the pain. As Shylock says, 'If you treat us, do we not pay up?' What about you, Peter?"

"I'll pay up!" I said it as one in a daze. It seemed inconceivable that I had blabbed my sordid financial chicanery to the Chief Tax Inspector himself. It was like a murderer boasting of his crime to Sherlock Holmes.

"Ha, ha!—I meant what is your pleasure, sir?"

"Scotch—double."

While Mr Pollard ordered the round I made urgent distress faces at George. "I've told him everything!" I hissed.

George's face registered panic. "About me?" he hissed back.

"No, me!"

George's face registered second-degree concern. "You must be crazy, man. I know you wanted advice but I didn't think you'd go to the fountain-head for it. If you must confess, a priest would be the lesser evil."

"I didn't realize who he was. He said he was a mate of yours, so naturally I thought he was bent, too."

"If you go to London you might bump into the Chancellor of the Exchequer—you could tell him as well. Can't you say you were only joking?"

"Joking for a solid hour, and offered to chop out his Argyll?"

"Tell him Aunt Dot is blackmailing you and you told him to expose her. Look out, he's got the drinks."

"Here's to happy motoring," Mr Pollard exclaimed, raising his glass jocundly. "Like Mr Wemmick in *Great Expectations,* I live two lives, gentlemen—one in the office and one in the felicity of an inn. What I hear outside the office is no concern of mine, ha, ha, ha, ha!"

"Then why do you always choose the felicity of an inn to dun me?" George asked sourly.

"Because, George, you never come to my office and you are

never at home. Furthermore, I have it from your own lips that you are unable to read or write, thus dispensing with the inconvenience of letters. Where else shall we meet, old friend, but in the convivial atmosphere of a tavern?"

"We could meet in jail. I've offered to go inside but you said it would break your heart."

"Such a primitive course merely creates a great deal of paper work for us, with no cash on the end of it, George. Our mercenary masters are interested only in money, not revenge."

While George handed over £4 from the housekeeping money and Mr Pollard duly wrote out a receipt, I excused myself and slunk from the Bold Forester to face Aunt Dot.

SEVEN

Aunt Dot was in bed, reading the *Auto Mart* ads without glasses by the aid of a candle. She held the candle so close to the print that there was grease further down the page and scorch marks higher up the page and a distinct smell of fire hazard in the air.

Hearing me, she called out, "Have you brought a customer for the Jowett, Peter?"

"No, Aunt Dot, I'm alone."

"Pity. We'll have to advertise it in the Diocesan magazine if we don't get a bite soon. It would be ideal for the clergy; so impressive, yet unostentatious. Heavens, my child, you're trembling like a part-exchange banger! Don't tell me you've lost a sale."

"Worse, Aunt Dot."

"You've taken a dud cheque on the Jowett?"

"Don't try to guess, please. I've been indiscreet about our business affairs."

"You've been opening your mouth to that George Craig again, I'll be bound. If I've warned you once, I have a dozen times about that man. He should wear a mask under a three cornered hat when he does business. I never trusted him from the start."

Aunt Dot made a habit of not trusting a soul but I ignored it. "I merely went into the Bold Forester."

"You're your Uncle Sydney all over again. Two gins and he'd give you the keys of his barracks' armoury. During the Great War they used him to confuse the German Intelligence system. They gave him false information and it was in Berlin before the pubs shut."

"But you always said what a quiet man he was, Aunt Dot."

"He was quiet if he was sober and hadn't met a spy. He was the only man in the British Army to tell the enemy where his regiment was stationed before they interrogated him, and he won his medal for being the soldier the Germans refused to hold prisoner because of the security risk. They sent him back across the lines before he could hear about their Spring offensive."

"But I always understood Uncle Sydney won his medal for bravery under fire."

"So he did, but it was the Allied guns firing as he returned. The only reason he wasn't shot was the fact that he was drunk and kept falling down the shell holes. Eventually he fell into a trench in the French sector, under the impression that they were digging the road up outside the Bold Forester."

I prayed that after a lifetime of Uncle Sydney, Aunt Dot would not find my confession so hard to bear, but, whatever her reaction, I simply had to get it off my chest.

"I told all our business to a friend of George's," I said wretchedly.

"Good grief, Peter—a friend of his is the last person to confide in! I'm only surprised that he's got a friend."

"But it was his tax friend. He works in the local tax office."

"Tax office! Why didn't you go straight to the police and tell them too? Why keep our affairs a secret? You're supposed to be a writer, so there would be material for an article there and more people could know about us. That would look good in *Family Help—How to Swindle the Inland Revenue,* as told to our reporter by Peter Pook from his cell window. Who was this man anyway?"

"A Mr Pollard."

"Jack Pollard! He's the Chief Inspector of Taxes for this district."

Aunt Dot gave a little scream and demanded the brandy bottle from her bedside table. She took a swig, then glared at me. "If I wasn't already lying in bed I'd faint. To think I'd live to see the day when a Pook would so dishonour the family name! I'd trust that Jack Pollard about as far as I could throw George Craig."

"I didn't know who he was at the time, Aunt Dot."

"If you had known I expect you'd have shot your mouth off just the same. You're as bad as your Uncle Sydney the night they threw him out of the Bold Forester, so he has to go round the corner to Cudford Police Station, where he demanded a double gin before closing time. Get that George Craig on the phone and find out if Pollard can be fixed. Do it right away."

Directly I broached the subject to George over the phone he panicked badly. "Take my tip, Peter, don't get in any deeper. Bribing a tax man is dangerous stuff, especially the head vampire. I once offered Jack Pollard a fiver on the side and his body arched like a bow. I thought he was going to have a fit standing upright. Lay off it, boy, it's too hot."

"Never mind that, George. Just tell me where I can get hold of him off duty."

"I'll tell you on one condition, Peter. Don't mention any name or involve me in any way. Tell him you and I have had a bitter quarrel and don't see each other any more. He's in the Bold Forester most Friday nights, drinking Scotch to try and get back the feel of a normal human being for the weekend. If he brings up my name, look angry and say you never want to see me again."

"Thanks, George. Wish me luck."

The following Friday I caught Mr Pollard in the Bold Forester about 6.30. Smiling pleasantly, he invited me over and accepted a drink, so I car-chatted him as though nothing was amiss until 7.30. By this time I considered him sufficiently mellowed for the main play, and I steered the conversation round to the 2-litre Frazer Nash B.M.W.—mentioning casually how I had bought one yesterday through the columns of the *Auto Mart.*

Mr Pollard's eyes brightened enthusiastically as I described the car in detail and accidentally let the instruction manual fall from my pocket to his feet. I was glad to observe him pick it up with boyish delight, scanning the data lovingly. "My dream car," he purred, more to himself than to me.

"Funny thing you mentioned that, Mr Pollard—I thought the same thing when she arrived this week. That's Mr Pollard's dream car, I said to Aunt Dot, just the very thing to take his mind off all those horrible taxation problems he has to handle."

Mr Pollard smiled broadly. "Nice thought, Peter, but that'll be the day when I can afford a Frazer Nash. On my salary I'll just have to soldier on with the old Argyll until she collapses under me."

I set up the Scotch again. "It so happens we're having our annual sale, Mr Pollard. Some sharp bargains going, if you know what I mean. We slash everything, not just a banger clearance. In such a cut-throat trade we have to be a jump ahead of rival bandits—ha, ha, ha, ha! Even the Frazer Nash carries a big knock-off during sale week; it's an all-stock vend—everything must be outed."

"Sounds interesting. Dare one inquire—just for fun—as to the sale price of the Frazer Nash? Break it to me gently, Peter."

"One guinea, Mr Pollard."

"One guinea!"

"One guinea, but you could use H.P. over, say, two years, interest free of course. No hidden extras at Pook's."

Mr Pollard's body arched like a bow, his moustache seemed to bristle and he looked down his nose. "Mr Pook, correct me if I am mistaken, but do I smell bribery in the air? Do my faculties detect an odour of corruption about us? If so, it is my duty to quit this ancient hostelry forthwith and take such action as is required by law."

I panicked internally, remembering George's warning, but there was no turning back at this stage. "All you smell is a bargain, Mr Pollard. There is no law against keen trading, especially if it's in your wife's name. I merely give you an early tip-off about our sale week. If you don't choose to snap it up, a less worthy customer will."

"Like Mr Craig?"

"Ah, I'm afraid George and I are not on speaking terms just now. We've quarrelled over business ethics, Mr Pollard."

"One can hardly quarrel over what one does not possess, Mr Pook."

"But I should like you to possess the Frazer Nash, sir. As

Shylock says, if you tempt us in the market-place, do we not purchase?"

"It is my painful duty to ensure that you appreciate your position under the Corrupt Practices Act of 1883, Mr Pook, which includes making a gift with the corrupt object of inducing the recipient to show favour to the donor."

"Good grief!"

"Also the Corrupt Practices Act of 1900, covering the giving, bestowal or awarding of secret commissions to induce business or advantage for the donor or his agent, and the allied Acts protecting His Majesty's Inland Revenue Officers engaged on their lawful occasions, *lex scripta et lex non scripts,* and *in totidem verbis."*

"But it was only a sale bargain. . . ."

"Therefore I hereby affirm that I accept the Frazer Nash."

"You accept it. . . ?"

"You sail mighty close to the wind, Mr Pook, but the law has always found difficulty in drawing the line between a gift and a bargain. Such a bargain in my wife's name would not be construed as a gift in the technical sense. On the other hand you must expect no favour from me, let that be quite clearly understood."

"I wouldn't dream of it, sir. . . ."

"Merely bear in mind that what I hear outside the office is no concern of mine—ha, ha!"

"Ha, ha!" So taut were my nerves that I echoed Mr Pollard's laugh in an unfamiliar treble.

"Furthermore, I shall take advantage of your H.P. terms to spread payment of the guinea over two years—ha, ha!"

"Of course, sir."

"And I take it as read that the vehicle is taxed—did I say taxed?—for the ensuing year?—ha, ha!"

"All part of our service, sir."

"And that you will give me a generous price for the vintage Argyll?—ha, ha!"

"Our normal policy, sir." No wonder George had called him

the head vampire and was suffering from financial anaemia.

"And that the Frazer Nash carries a twelve-month warranty, so I may enjoy trouble-free motoring while you enjoy trouble-free trading?—ha, ha!"

"You shall have my written undertaking, sir." Surely he wouldn't expect another Frazer Nash every year!" Should you break down through lack of petrol, we supply that, too, sir."

"Excellent, Peter. I see you run a highly efficient and worthy business enterprise that I may patronize with every confidence. There remains the question of engine oil."

"We top you up regularly, sir, and change completely as required. This applies also to the battery, radiator and rear axle. We check your tyres likewise, and it is our constant concern that your headlights be correctly aligned. Should the bodywork become dirty we wash and polish it. We run a free puncture service and also advise on route maps. Unfortunately we are as yet unable to supply a uniformed chauffeur with each car we sell, but we are working on it."

"I see we understand one another, Peter—ha, ha, ha, ha! If I may drop a hint, it has long been my ambition to become a member of the Royal Automobile Club."

"That goes without saying, sir. With your permission, your name automatically goes forward for election to the Jockey Club, too." Now I understood why Mr Pollard had been so insulted when George offered him a fiver on the side.

"So, Peter, be good enough to set up the Scotch, that we may drink a toast to happy motoring and prosperous trading. With bargains such as you are able to offer to a grateful public, I am sure they will flock to your door—including some of my own staff at the Inland Revenue. For, as Shylock says, "if you please us, do we not recommend?""

So I had given my first bribe, fixing none other than the Chief Inspector of Taxes, Cudford District, before my twentieth birthday. As I responded to the toast I wondered whether my astuteness would save my bacon or go a fair way to putting me out of business and into the bankruptcy court.

It was at this period that I read in *Family Help* an article entitled, 'We're Dyeing to Help You!' written by Dolores Gloria, one of her endless series designed to assist the plainer female reader to get her man. Miss Gloria London Beauty Consultant who resided in Wigan, left no part of the human form untouched in her quest for allure, so that if any girl followed all the advice she must end up a different person, like a distant cousin.

Although the articles were for women—and one gathered that only plain women read *Family Help*—I studied them for odd tips I could exploit to make myself more worthy of Margo. Miss Gloria emphasized that a woman's crowning glory was her hair, which not only supplied a lovely frame for her face but also acted as a beacon to attract attention to her in the first place. No woman, she declared, need worry about her lack of looks provided her face was framed, and partially hidden, by a breath-taking coiffure—although only last week in an article entitled 'Seven Years' Bad Luck!' she insisted that we had but to glance in our mirror to observe how our face was the dominant feature of aesthetic attraction.

Much taken with the latest article, I had to agree that our natural hair is dull, lifeless, and highly unexciting, like wearing old thatch to keep the rain off one's scalp. Why not copy the film stars, Miss Gloria asked, by exploiting the dyer's art and turning our old rope into exciting auburn tresses, sparkling with high-lights and throbbing with gorgeous colours?

I was particularly interested in her magic formula for obtaining radiant hair, as she called it. In those days there were not the sophisticated rinses I use today to discourage Boy Scouts from helping me across the road to the Bold Forester. The chief ingredients were Egyptian henna and yeast, the whole process reminding me of home brewing. Having bought the materials from the chemist, I followed Miss Gloria's instructions with meticulous care, ending up with a liquid of considerable viscosity closely resembling cold mulligatawny soup with a head on it.

As I stirred the liquid into a paste it seemed inconceivable that its destination should be one's hair, rather than a kitchen wall. Miss Gloria recommended the protection of rubber gloves during the application, but as I possessed none I stood in front of the mirror and applied the paste with a dessert spoon. Having deposited the contents of the bowl on my head until a pile had been formed, I carefully smoothed it down evenly with my father's putty-knife. Fortunately, the paste did not run. In fact, it seemed to be drying to the shape of my head like a potter's bowl. When finished I noticed I had ginger hands, so I washed them under the tap and found I now had bright ginger hands.

My next problem was the hour's wait while the dye took. It was imperative that I should not be called out during this period, so I had warned my family I was taking a bath, locking myself in and spending the time re-checking the instructions and scouring my hands. I could already see the high-lights and tints promised in the article, but these were on my hands, where I appeared to be wearing ginger gloves. However, Miss Gloria had begged us not to worry about the waiting period while the dye developed, although nothing was mentioned about worrying later.

After one hour I inspected myself in the mirror and was slightly perturbed to discover I was wearing a kind of ginger hat. The next step was to shampoo the hair thoroughly, but when I tapped the hat and found it was solid I wondered how to use the shampoo. I tried lifting the inverted bowl from my head but it seemed firmly fixed to my scalp. I finally solved the problem by repeatedly hitting my head with the handle of a lavatory brush, whereupon fragments of the bowl came away and dropped to the floor.

What I saw underneath brought me out in a hot sweat, for not only was my hair bright ginger in colour but it stood out straight in bunches. Trying not to panic, I shampooed it vigorously until the wash-basin itself seemed to be turning ginger. No matter how often I rinsed my hair the water turned ginger—in fact, what with the towels, the basin and the floor, the entire bathroom was changing colour. I held my head under the bath tap in an effort to flush away this vile colour, till the bath itself took on a ginger hue.

Miss Gloria had warned us not to be alarmed at this stage because the richer tones would develop later, so I dried the hair and combed it as best I could—but directly I removed my hand the hair regrouped into bunches. Staring into the mirror, I just could not believe my eyes. My hair was so brilliant that it seemed to be on fire, and it was surrounded by a faint halo like the corona round the sun. Whichever way I turned my head this nimbus was visible, as though I was a ginger-headed saint on a church window.

In desperation I raked out my old cricket cap from a cupboard, pulled it on and stuffed all surplus hair underneath it. My scalp felt hot and prickly, as if it resented the tea-cosy function of the cap, but I was determined to wear it at all costs rather than let the family see me in such a condition. In my mind was a plan to seek my barber and have him shave my head or dye my hair jet black, but when I reached the shop it was shut for the Wednesday afternoon early-closing.

Standing there in the doorway I wondered if my fears were groundless, merely induced by the novelty of the situation. Perhaps Margo might like it and find me more attractive. Growing more confident, I surveyed my reflection in the pier-glass lining the side of the shop window and gradually removed my cap. In the bright daylight I was horrified by what I saw. The dye had developed dramatically at the crown into a rich burgundy, though the fringes were still distinctly ginger. So bright was the effect that a halo was clearly visible in the pier-glass.

Sick at heart, I hastily replaced the cap, like blanking off a car fog-light, and glanced at my watch. It was nearly six o'clock, when I had promised to meet Margo on the London train, so I hurried round to Cudford Station.

The train was already stopping at the platform as I arrived, and I spotted Margo from afar stepping down from her compartment.

Directly she had checked my engagement ring and kissed me, she said, "Why the cricket cap, Peter?"

"I have a little surprise for you, Margo," I replied diffidently. "One that I don't want anybody else to see."

"You've caught ringworm?"

"No, dear. You know I'm not the handsomest man in the world, well, I've tried to improve things by . . . er . . . well, sort of livening up my dull, mousy hair. I thought you might like it and find me more attractive.

Before I could finish, Margo snatched off the cap and gave a little scream as my locks reformed on release. To my surprise she threw her arms round me and kissed me.

"You did that for me, darling? Gosh, how you must love me!"

"You really think it's an improvement then?"

"It's gorgeous, Peter. I adore it. What I love even more is to think what a sacrifice you are prepared to make for me."

"How do you mean, dear?"

"Oh, don't tease me. I have to leave you so often down here in Cudford while I'm working in London, so you dyed your hair to make sure no other woman will try to take you away from me."

"But the idea was to. . . ."

"Don't you dare put that cap on—I want the whole world to see how you treasure our love. Honestly, I think I'm going to cry in front of all these people."

Just as I was about to cry with her, a smiling porter passed by, calling out, "Would you mind leaving the station, sir?— we can't get the goods train through unless. The driver thinks the signal's against him."

"Ignore their stupid jokes, Peter," Margo snapped, "they don't know what true love is. My grandmother used to tell me that in the old days on Skagh a betrothed man had to shave his head until the marriage was solemnized, to warn off designing lassies. I never dreamt a man would do anything like that for me in this day and age."

"It wasn't. . . ."

"Whenever I see a rainbow in the sky I shall think of my Peter coming towards me—from now on it will be our secret sign, like the Olympic torch. Oh, darling, how you will stand out in the colour photographs of our wedding!"

It was quite embarrassing, the way Margo swamped me with affection on Platform 3, running her hand through my flaming bush of hair as though it excited her like the proverbial red rag to a bull. They say love is blind, and apparently colour-blind to boot, because she had not yet noticed my ginger hands—which I now kept in my pockets lest they should drive her to a frenzy of passion in public. I decided to break my hands to her gently, a finger at a time, preferably at twilight, at the same time assuring her I had not dyed anything else in the cause of true love.

Margo stayed down in Cudford till Sunday, but long before that my hair had consolidated its colour at a deep red, like an angry sunrise. "Red in the morning, shepherd's warning," Margo persisted in telling me, on the donkey's tail theory of weather forecasting, "but red at night, maiden's delight."

During this period I refused to accompany Margo to the cinema, for obvious reasons, so we visited our friends in order that Margo might show them how far a man will go to be faithful unto his beloved—an explanation I found most embarrassing in mixed company, especially when Hilda Longbothem asked me if I had walked under a painter's ladder.

It was on the Monday following Margo's departure for London that the O.H.M.S. letter arrived from Mr Pollard, in which he informed me that he was my obedient servant, and that he wanted to see his master at his office on the Tuesday. Assuming that he was experiencing some technical fault on the Frazer Nash, like running out of petrol or wanting it resprayed a different colour, I presented myself at Mr Pollard's outer office. I now lived in a pork-pie hat I purchased at Dunn's, removing it only when actually in bed, having grown weary of people's jibes and accusations that I was deliberately frightening young children and the elderly.

I stood outside a glass door marked 'Mr J. Pollard, His Majesty's Inspector of Taxes, Cudford District. Knock and Wait.' I knocked and waited as instructed, until a female member of the Inland Revenue opened the door to invite me inside.

"Mr Pollard will see you now, Mr Pook," she said, like a dentist's receptionist who knows all your teeth have to be extracted.

A short, stout gentleman with one ear-to-ear eyebrow rose from behind a desk and indicated a chair for my occupation. "Please, be seated, Mr Pook," he said sadly. "Perhaps you would like me to take your hat for you."

"Oh, so sorry—I forgot." I removed my hat, then waited to let him view me and recover his wits. I had long discovered it paid to say nothing, but to sit quietly while people reacted to the shock in their own way. I had also learned not to look at my victims whilst they were in the throes of embarrassment, or, even worse, trying to stifle their astonishment. The sole concession to their feelings I made was to wear gloves, to spare them the embarrassment of lowering their eyes and seeing my ginger hands blazing on my lap.

Being a tax official he recovered much quicker than normal folk, breaking the silence after only three minutes.

"Hm . . . er . . . are you keeping well, Mr Pook?"

"Yes, thanks. I'm in the pink—ha, ha, ha, ha!" This weak little joke was merely to put him at his ease by letting him see I could laugh at myself. Only last Friday, when my bank manager had sat before me stunned, I broke the ice for him by saying, "I hope my account isn't in the red, too—ha, ha, ha, ha!"

"Now, I have asked you to visit me in order that we might have a chat about your tax, Mr Pook."

"But I understood from the letter that I was to see Mr Pollard. He knows all about my affairs."

"Quite so, Mr Pook—I am Mr Pollard."

"I mean Mr Pollard, the Chief Inspector of Taxes. Knock and Wait—ha, ha!"

"Yes, I am he."

“Ah, but not Mr Jack Pollard. His brother perhaps?”

“I am indeed Mr Jack Pollard, Chief Inspector of Taxes, Cudford District.”

“With great respect, you’re not the Jack Pollard I met in the Bold Forester.”

“With great respect, I could not be—I am teetotal. My identifying credentials hang on the wall before you.”

“Surely there must be another tax officer named Pollard who works in this office?”

“I assure you there is no such person.”

“Does anyone here drive a Frazer Nash car?”

“That I can most certainly deny, Mr Pook.”

“It is most strange.”

“It is indeed most strange, Mr Pook.”

Mr Pollard glared at me intently, as if thinking that the strangest thing of all was my burgundy hair, coupled with my unwillingness to admit his identity. I thought that if he were to observe my ginger hands at this moment he would opine that sitting before him was a well-dressed lunatic. I wondered if the nature of his profession accustomed him to interviewing people whose tax worries had deranged them, so that they came in his office dressed as Mr Micawber or Napoleon. I even reflected that perhaps Mr Pollard was the statutory name for Chief Inspectors of Taxes, and that when such an officer retired or was put away his successor automatically assumed the title of Mr Pollard to ensure the continuity of the line.

“This may strike you as an odd question, but have you been Mr Pollard long?”

“For about half a century, young man. Before that I was Master Pollard. Before that I was Baby Pollard.”

“So your father’s name must have been Pollard?”

“Our conversation smacks of the painting, ‘When did you last see your father?’ Pollard is my family name, not my rank in the Civil Service or our Latin motto.”

"Does any female member of your family own a Frazer Nash?"

Mr Pollard leaned forward on his desk. "Let us be quite frank with each other, Mr Pook. You come to my office wearing, shall we say, a bizarre hair colouring, the like of which I have never had the misfortune to see before in my life, and waste my time disputing my identity—when you have obviously met someone else of the same name with whom you are confusing me. If I were wearing maroon hair you might have some grounds for suspicion, but I am not. It is you who is dyed up like a scarlet runner in a jam pot, but I do not insist you are not Mr Pook. Now, pray accept me for what I am and let us discuss the apparent irregularities and inconsistences in your tax returns."

"But there is something extremely sinister going on."

"Exactly. That is why I summoned you to this office, to inquire about your business transactions."

"But I explained all that to Mr Pollard."

"So now be so kind as to explain it to Mr Pollard the Second—such as why you appear to be operating a successful car sales enterprise, yet pay no tax?"

"Oh, because I'm only an employee on a low wage and very little commission."

"I see. So who is your employer?"

"My great-aunt, Auntie Dot."

"Then why does she pay no tax?"

"She is over age, sir."

"Do you mean she is over sixty?"

"She's over a hundred, sir. Hundred-and-one, I think. She doesn't believe in new-fangled ideas like income tax. She says the Window Tax and the Corn Laws were bad enough, without taxing income."

"The Corn Laws!"

"Yes, sir. She says her husband, Uncle Sydney, was nursed by Florence Nightingale in the Crimean War."

"Florence Nightingale!"

"Yes, sir, following the Charge of the Light Brigade. He fell off his horse directly the charge commenced."

"Was he shot?"

"He was drunk, sir. The horse went from under him, leaving him at base as a foot soldier. He was the only man in the Hussars without a horse. He had to be entered on the muster roll as a walking cavalryman. They made him march carrying a saddle in case something turned up along the route to Turkey."

"Did he eventually obtain a mount?"

"Yes, sir. He became the first Hussar to parade on a camel."

"Most extraordinary! Did Florence Nightingale really nurse him?"

"Aunt Dot has always said she did."

"Was he badly wounded?"

"He tried to ride the camel like a horse, sir. When they lifted him off, his legs wouldn't close. He was carried to the tented hospital and had to be laid out on two beds, like a coat-hanger."

I could see Mr Pollard was flabbergasted, as everybody was who listened to the endless tales Aunt Dot spun about her late husband, even though it was difficult to believe that a man who fought in the Crimean War could also have served in the Great War. When people queried this point Aunt Dot explained that in those days the enlisting age was much lower than today, Uncle Sydney having joined up as a Cadet Hussar on his fifth birthday.

"We're an eccentric family, sir," I told Mr Pollard as he struggled to grasp our eccentric tax problems, "but there is one boon I must beg of you. Owing to my aunt's advanced age she may go at any moment in the event of stress or shock, especially financial shock, so please exercise great discretion in this matter."

"Would it be possible for me to interview the lady?"

"Only at her bedside, if you promise not to excite her by speaking into her ear-trumpet. This runs the risk of waking her, when she will probably think you are Uncle Sydney returned from the Boer War."

“Should I bring the parish priest with me to be on the safe side?” Mr Pollard asked coldly.

“That should not be necessary, sir, provided you do not mention money or accounts into her ear-trumpet.”

“Pray tell me how one can possibly discuss tax matters without a passing word about money and accounts, young man? Or is the interview to confine itself solely with the Boer War and the Corn Laws?”

“Oh, under no circumstances must you refer to the Corn Laws, Mr Pollard. Even income tax would be less dangerous than that.”

Mr Pollard closed my file sharply. “Mr Pook, I can give you seven days in which to arrange for me to interview your great aunt about her motor business. Is that clearly understood?”

“Thank you, sir. I will consult with her physician to see if it can be arranged without jeopardizing her life expectancy. Meanwhile, I shall endeavour to clear up the matter of your namesake, who is in a position to explain the situation to you fully. Goodbye, sir.”

“Good day to you, sir—and here is your hat.”

“Thank you, sir. I call it my candle-snuffer.”

I left the building in a hurry, directing my steps around to the Flying Bull, where it was a safe bet I would find my dear ex-friend, George Craig.

EIGHT

It was barely eleven when I entered the Flying Bull but George, who always took an extended lunch-hour, was already there, chatting to several members of the motor trade about the current slump in business. He greeted me cordially and invited me to join him in a jar of anti-freeze, as he insisted on calling the Flying Bull's best bitter.

"You remember introducing me to Jack Pollard one evening in the Bold Forester?" I began, directly we had toasted our dying craft.

"No, I don't, Peter, but keep talking because it's nice to see you after so long."

"But it was only last week!"

"How come, when I don't use the Bold Forester since last Christmas—the landlord barred me for debt. Ask him yourself."

"Look, George, I'm not a customer with a smoking banger on his hands outside—I'm a fellow bandit, a fully paid-up pirate like yourself. You can talk freely, just as you would if you had friends. You know, like in the old days when there was honour among thieves. Tell me the truth, like you'd have to if you were shopping your mother to the police for the reward."

"Hard words, Peter. Jack Pollard is the local tax hatchet-man. That's all I know, and I'm supposed to be smart."

"I want to know who the Jack Pollard was you introduced me to and I gave him a Frazer Nash as new, one owner, gen. low mil., disc wheels, 6 cyl., sac. for immed. sale."

George mobile face registered showroom incredulity. "Don't tell me you gave a Frazer Nash to a complete stranger, boy?"

"You vouched for him; you said he was the resident profit leech; you squeezed up £4 on account."

"You really think a Chief Inspector of Taxes would hang around a boozer to collect four quid off the likes of me, Peter? You must be crazy! No wonder you dyed your hair vermilion. Besides, why present the enemy with a Frazer Nash?"

"To take his mind off my sales pitch, of course."

"Have you informed the police?"

"Ye gods, no!"

"Meet me in here Friday night and I'll introduce you to a man who can help you. Tell him the whole story from start to finish, then offer him a substantial bribe to get your Frazer Nash back."

"Is he another Jack Pollard?"

"No, he's Chief Constable Proudfoot of the Cudfordshire Police. Let me give you some free advice, Peter. I don't know anything about your little trouble but my guess is you've been taught a valuable business lesson to prevent you getting done."

"But I've already been done."

"Ah, but you got done in the trade, and that don't count. We all get conned in the trade in the normal course of business, but from what you tell me I figure your friend went out of his way to show you how to avoid dishonest practices by the public. As you must realize by now, one of the dealer's worst snags is that you can't trust the customers any more. There was a time when the customers were as straight as the trade, when retailers like you and me could make an honest living without treating every client like he was Old King Cole's top fiddler just come out of porridge. Why, today I often rip out the distributor flex before I lets a customer try the driving seat inside the showroom."

"Is it really as bad as that, George?"

"Bad? The other day two Islington hoods come in for a demo run in a V-8 Lincoln, so before we start I packs three of us in the back seat so we wouldn't be outnumbered, and put barely half-a-gallon in the tank so we don't end up as Lot 27 in a London car auction!"

"That's awful, George."

"Watch the judies, too. Last summer a talkin' doll come in for a demo run in an immac. tight-up Cit, so I thought nice tart, key-worthy, little sister image, let her go solo. Comes back later, tears and smiles, fallen in love with Cit but engine not powerful enough.

Engine not powerful enough—no wonder! When I re-parked the Cit for the night it hadn't got enough compression to mount a six-inch kerb ramp. That power-unit was so weak that it stalled if you engaged the clutch in neutral. Just to rev up we had to slacken the fan-belt and push it."

"What on earth could a girl do to an engine, George?"

"I'll tell you what she done, Peter—she pinched the damned thing. Her mates round the corner switched engines and left me with a clapped out knocker what didn't have enough strength to open and shut your distributor points, let alone pull a Cit. Imagine it, an as-new Cit powered by hot scrap-iron and gunfire. I wept, Peter, and do you know why I wept?"

"You'd got one of your own engines back?"

"No, boy; my tears fell on to the cracked block and battery fungus because it dawned on me how you can't trust the public no more, not even skirts. To think that years ago my dear old mother wanted me to enter the Church. No, Mum, I says, I'd rather be a motor dealer, which comes next to vicaring in the way of dedication, because I've experienced a call inside me to enter the transport world. Where did you receive this call, George? she says. At the Earls Court Motor Show, I says, in a phone box when I rang Eddie Somers for a job on his site. Do you think you'll be happy in the motor trade George? she asks me. Probably not, Mum, I says, but happiness isn't everything in life. I try to think of the more important things, like money and luxury."

"Gosh, George, I didn't realize what a philosopher you are," I told him admiringly. "In future I shall vet every client who comes in, like he wanted to join the Freemasons."

"Exactly, Peter. You catch on quick. I'm in disgrace with UCDA for being conned outside the trade, so I wanted to put you wise before you get done, too."

"Who's UCDA, George?"

"Used Car Dealers' Association, formed in 1930 to protect our interests and foster prosperity among its members. Give me a fiver now and I'll sponsor you—though that don't mean I can get you in unless you can put up a surety of fifty pounds to prove you're a bona fide used car dealer and not just a member of the public trying to con UCDA. But remember this, once they accept you into the brotherhood you're fully safeguarded and insured against fraud—in short, the ranks of the motor traders close round you so you can't get done from the outside."

"It sounds marvellous, George, but what worries me is getting done from the inside."

George dismissed the notion with a swig of anti-freeze. "Once they know you're a brother, a knight of the forecourt, a comrade in auction, a lord of the ring, they'll protect you till it hurts—even from each other. Why, the very slogan of UCDA—'Part-Exchange is No Robbery'—tells you whose side they're on. Just think what it means, Peter; instead of being a vulnerable lone wolf, you'll know that if ever you get done there's a fellow dealer like me standing right by your side."

"Impressive, George, most impressive. I should like to join very much, and feel that the trade was right behind me."

"Bumper-to-bumper, knock for knock, as we say in court."

"Whom do I make the cheque out to, George?"

"Just put my name there, Peter, because I'm the local branch secretary with powers to enrol you as a full member now you've put up the surety, and guarantee you complete coverage."

It seems strange now to think that I made out a cheque to George for fifty-five pounds, but I was barely twenty and George was a slick talker.

"Here's your Robin Hood badge you're entitled to wear now," George said, pocketing the cheque and ordering a celebration round of anti-freeze. He handed me a tiny lapel button of Robin Hood in traditional bow-and-arrow pose, except that the radiator of a car had parked itself between his legs. "Look closely and you'll see his bow is really a car bumper and the arrow is a dip-stick," George explained.

“Isn’t that rather blatant, a Robin Hood emblem, George?”

“It’s like when the Kaiser jeered at the British Expeditionary Force in the Great War, so we called ourselves the Old Contemptibles, Peter. Thus when dealers used to meet each other they’d say, ‘Hallo, you robbin’ hood,’ and the name stuck. So if a customer asks for your credentials you can reply with pride, ‘I’m a Robin Hood, and here’s my badge to prove it.’ ”

I popped the button in my lapel with a feeling of deep professional satisfaction that I now belonged to a vast brotherhood. “Funny thing is, George, that I can’t honestly say I’ve noticed the badge before.”

“That’s because you were an outsider and weren’t looking for it. From today keep your eyes skinned at sale yards, auctions and showrooms and you’ll find Robin Hoods all round you. They may even give you the high sign, like Masons do, thus.” Clenching his fists about a foot from his chest, George jiggled them up and down alternately some half-a-dozen times. “The high sign derives from the steering-wheel of a second-hand car with a lot of play on it, symbolizing your efforts to go straight despite a worn rack-and-pinion and wobbly hub bearings.”

“Absolutely fascinating, George. Is there some counter-sign I’m supposed to give?”

“Having seen the dealer declare himself to you, Peter, you acknowledge with this.” George again clenched a fist by his knee, jerked it upwards, then regarded his fist with surprise. “The acknowledgement sign derives from the car whose brakes have failed, so you resort to the hand-brake, which comes away in your hand like taking an umbrella from a rack.”

“That’s clever, George. It’s as exciting as being a Mason, yet much cheaper. Are there any more secret signals?”

George looked both ways to ensure we were unobserved. “Most important of all is the Universal Distress Signal, performed like this.” George’s right hand made urgent circular motions of cranking a car. “When you see another Robin Hood doing that you know he's in dead trouble, so you keep putting both your hands out thus, indicating that you will give him a push provided there's enough juice left in the battery to fire the ignition. Should you see a Robin Hood bobbing up and down in a kind of pump action he is telling you he's flat broke."

"How do you answer him, George?"

"I turn smartly about, then step out three hundred paces until I'm out of sight. I'll help anybody, except with money, but a skint Robin Hood isn't worthy to be in our trade. It's a contradiction of terms."

"Thanks a million, George; I've learned a lot this morning and I feel you've really established me in the profession

"Think nothing of it, Brother Pook—I've helped you, you've helped me, and that's how it should be."

From that day forward I searched diligently for the Robin Hood emblem, anxious to try out these esoteric signs of our craft on fellow members, yet I was unable to spot one anywhere. Thinking that perhaps our brethren were too modest to wear the button I gave the high sign to several dealers, who responded with signs George had made no mention of, though the symbolism obviously derived from a V-8 engine. I asked one dealer outright if he was a Robin Hood and he became quite aggressive, threatening to ram a can of heavy-duty oil up my nose if I didn't perform an impossible feat of sexuality on the spot.

Far from finding the motor trade solidly behind me I learned that they were solidly against me the moment I mentioned our professional organization or displayed our secret recognition signals—so much so that I discarded the lapel button and kept both my hands in my pockets. When I tackled George on the subject he explained how ours was a highly exclusive fellowship, warning me that I would encounter much professional jealousy from operators who either couldn't afford the entrance fee or whose business integrity was suspect.

"But I've never so much as clapped eyes on another member except yourself, George," I protested.

"You won't neither around the little men of Cudford, Peter. But wait till you trade up London among the big boys in the flash motor marts—then you'll see what kind of company you're in. Take no notice of these local backyard dwarfs who reckon they've had a bonza week if they peddle a sidecar."

"But I've got to work here in Cudford, not up the smoke, George. You said we stood bumper-to-bumper across the nation."

"Listen, Peter, if a ship is insured with Lloyd's of London the captain don't expect to find Lloyd's branches dotted every nautical mile across the Pacific Ocean in case he sinks—but he knows what's behind him if he do go down. Same with UCDA; you drop in the manure and they forks you out."

"Even if Mr Pollard canes me for tax evasion?"

"They fight for you tooth and nail. Their legal wig is allowed to interview you in jail to see if you can plead an occupational disease in mitigation, like metal fatigue or financial amnesia. Above all, he'll show the court how you're a luckless hard-working pauper. This always puts the fear of Satan up them in case you become a burden on the rates unless they let you go on working. They prefer a self-supporting pauper to a State pauper every time. I mean, they may not get any tax out of you but at least they don't have to keep you into the bargain. I think they learned their mistake with my old mate, Eddie Somers, when they put him in the workhouse while his wife was operating the motor mart under her maiden name."

"Mr Pollard intends to grill Aunt Dot about the books at her bedside, George."

"Let him. Play your cards right and you could have him up for manslaughter. Phone the *Echo,* so they can get a reporter and a photographer in the bedroom for the interview on the human interest angle—'Old Lady dies under Tax Monster's Inquisition', or 'See how State expedites Death Duties'."

" 'Weeping Nephew awarded Heavy Damages.' "

" 'Shares Same with Fellow Robin Hood.' "

" 'I'll trade on alone, says greed—stricken relative.' "

" 'Tax Axe Cracks Jack's Facts.' "

"What does that mean, George?"

"It means that the Robin Hood lawyer will tear Jack Pollard's testimony to shreds and we'll all live happily ever after."

"I'll set up the jugs again and drink to that."

George's camaraderie and infectious optimism always made me feel good, and I began to admire the way he so conducted his business that he was able to take a lunch break which almost coincided with the Flying Bull's opening hours of 10.30 to 3, then so organize his leisure to correspond to the evening hours of 6 to 11. George told me confidentially how this required considerable administrative skill, such as hanging a reversible card on his showroom door, which said on one side: OPEN, inquire next door. An arrow indicated that customers must apply to the Flying Bull on the left, not to the chemist on the right. The reverse side of the card was more frank CLOSED, inquire next door at the Flying Bull. This side also bore an arrow pointing to the left, lest customers might confuse the pub with the chemist. George had a trade card hanging in the bar of the Flying Bull inviting prospective buyers to inquire next door, but someone had written at the bottom, 'This is next door—save your feet'.

Sad-faced, taciturn Mrs Craig once told me that George's only pleasure in life was his beer, which sounded rather a defeatist remark from a wife, but she said it in such a melancholy tone that one forgot he spent nearly every waking hour in a pub. George used to declare that it was only the beer which gave him the energy to work, but lately he had stopped making this statement because there was usually someone present who asked why he didn't do any. The sole exception to George's routine was Sunday night, which he gave over to his wife. "Sunday night is Mary's night, no matter what happens," he avowed, and every Sunday evening at seven o'clock he would bring Mary into the Flying Bull, buy her a double gin and leave her while he joined his mates at the counter. Mary was a complete contrast to her husband, being dour and thin, and I could never see her without thinking she had all the makings of a widow.

Owing to the long hours worked by the motor trade, the dealers brought into the Flying Bull of a Sunday evening those ladies they had married but seldom saw during the week, that they might enjoy Ladies' Night, as they dubbed it. All the wives sat together in the parlour bar and their husbands disappeared one by one to the Gents, reappearing after a decent interval in the public bar for darts, rather than intrude upon feminine conversation. About nine o'clock a strange thing happened. If you cared to stroll into the public bar you would be surprised to find that the men playing darts there were a different group of men entirely, but if you happened to wander down the road you would see the dealers playing darts in the public bar of the Bold Forester. This arrangement never ceased to intrigue me, the men in the Bold Forester, while their wives sat in the Flying Bull.

When I asked George about this exodus to the Bold Forester he replied, "Well, Peter, the truth of the matter is that we go round to the Bold Forester because the Royal Oak is too far to walk on a Sunday night, seeing how they shuts at ten."

It was just such a Sunday evening in the Bold Forester that one of the oddest things of my life occurred. An elderly gentleman came in, and, after inquiring of the landlord, approached me to ask if I knew a Peter Pook.

"I happen to be Peter Pook, sir," I replied proudly.

He seemed to be taken aback. "Surely not! It can't be!"

I had my friends examine me and vouch for my identity, which appeared to increase his surprise. "It doesn't seem possible, young man. They warned me you were tall, with dyed hair, but I never dreamt . . . ah, excuse me for my lack of manners, allow me to introduce myself."

"Don't tell me—you're Mr Pollard," I quipped.

"No, my name is Longbothem; William Longbothem." Immediately I was on my guard. I glanced at George for signs of chicanery but he was poker-faced.

"I believe you know Hilda."

"I know Hilda, and I know her father, too, so you can't be her dad." I peered closely at the old gentleman, who looked remarkably like Hilda wearing a beard and trilby. So suspicious had I grown of late that for a fleeting moment I thought it was Hilda in disguise. I heard myself saying, "Are you Hilda?"

"I am her grandfather, young man," he replied puzzledly.

"You look suspiciously like Hilda to me, sir, except that she hasn't got a beard. Even your voice is the same."

"Perhaps that is because we are closely related. She herself told me I might find you here, but I never imagined . . . well, well, women are strange creatures. As the poet says, Then come kith me, sweet and twenty."

Hearing the word kith, I automatically looked at the old man's protruding teeth and bulging eyes. "I'll swear it's Hilda," I side-lipped to George.

"I thought Hilda was a girl," George observed through the bottom of his tankard, "but if it is, offer the old chap a stool."

"It's Hilda dressed up as a little old man, I tell you. The beard, hat and stick don't fool me."

"Order a pint and see if she goes in the Gents."

"But why should she do a thing like this?"

"All's fair in love and war."

"Then why isn't she disguised as a soldier?"

The old gentleman accepted a stool and bespoke a port and lemon.

"See, George," I whispered, "the same old port and plonk — Hilda's own passion potion for instant cold weather starting. We'll string her along and find out the score."

"The toilet test will tell, Peter," George winked confidentially.

Mr Longbothem Senior supped his port as he unfolded his story. "I'm over here visiting the Old Country to see my family before my time comes, so, gentlemen, you must forgive me if I ramble on because there is a lot to tell and much to do. As you can see, I am a very old man—you may not believe this, but I'm in my late fifties, so I'm not so spry as I used to be."

"It's affected your memory, too, sir."

"No, Peter, my memory serves me well. I recall sailing to New Zealand as a young man to make my fortune, and make it I did. I prospered in the meat trade, so Hilda shall never want. I can see it as if it were yesterday when I first set eyes on Wellington as an ambitious young shaver of eighteen."

"Don't tell me he fought at Waterloo," George nudged me as we settled back to hear the traditional success story of the early migrant who worked round the clock, purchased land cheaply because it had mountains on it, then sold it years later by the square foot when it was required for office block development.

"So you see, gentlemen, I went out poor, I return rich. But unfortunately I went out young, I return old. Therefore I must dispose of some of my wealth."

"I'll have a Scotch for a start," George laughed, perturbed at the way Mr Longbothem drove home his lesson on affluence by not standing his round. This characteristic was nothing new to us because whenever Cudford's wealthy builder, Councillor Arthur Dyke, the reputed millionaire, entered the Bold Forester to be treated we always clammed up and handed him the little net sock of coins for the blind which hung above the bar.

Embarrassed by George's bluntness I paid for the round, but Mr Longbothem merely rambled on without noticing. "Young Hilda is my favourite grand-daughter, as I am sure you can appreciate."

"She's your only grand-daughter, too," I reminded him, having been well primed on the Longbothem clan via the coloured slides.

"So my aim in life is to ensure that she never wants."

"Let's hope she don't drink then," George observed, setting up another round.

"She has told me in confidence that she loves you, Peter—that is why I was somewhat surprised when I first met you . . . what I mean is, you weren't exactly what I had pictured in my mind, although she had warned me . . . well, as the poet says, Love is blind, and women are unpredictable creatures. . . ."

"Hilda should talk," I answered indignantly. "It has been hinted in this very bar that hers is the face to sink a thousand ships. . . . "

"Only in fun," George interrupted me sharply. "Beauty is skin deep, as the poet says, and it certainly isn't everything. What really counts in marriage is compatibility and a secure financial basis. I should know because I started with neither."

"Personally, I think Hilda is a sweet, charming girl," I said. "She possesses all those qualities essential to a good wife and mother."

"And a lot more fine points aside from money, too," George added. "Such as loyalty, thrift and other things ordinary poor girls have."

"Well, Peter, it seems that Hilda has set her sights on you, my lucky lad, though I should have thought . . . but there, you can't put an old head on young shoulders. My little Hilda must have what she wants, say I . . . still, there's no accounting for tastes and one man's meat is another man's poison."

"But I happen to be engaged to another," I pointed out triumphantly. "The ladies find me extremely attractive, so there is apparently quite a demand for poison."

"Of course, I don't pretend to understand you moderns, with your dyed hair and odd faces—but for my Hilda's sake I'm going to put temptation in your way, young man. Observe my actions closely."

Mr Longbothem produced a cheque book and, leaning far back to enable his bifocals to find the range, slowly wrote a cheque on the Central Bank of New Zealand, for the sum of one thousand pounds. Then he ceremoniously handed it to me. "Accept this as a little wedding present, Peter—consider it to be the forerunner of bigger things to come."

I was too astounded to reply but George said, "You forgot to sign it, Mr Longbothem."

"Ah, but I shall—at the reception after the wedding."

I stared at the cheque in amazement. In those days a thousand pounds could buy two new houses, or nine new cars, or support two thousand Old Age Pensioners for a whole week. I heard George saying, "Can I be best man, Peter?" but I ignored it, gazing spellbound at the small fortune in my hand.

When I had recovered sufficiently to speak I looked Mr Longbothem squarely in the teeth. "I don't know if this is some kind of test on my character, sir, but I must inform you that I am a man of honour who is already betrothed, an obligation I do not hold lightly. Under the circumstances there is only one course open to me."

"Emigrate secretly to New Zealand with Hilda so Margo can't sue for breach," George suggested.

"I shall have to give your proposition long and careful consideration, sir."

"So you may have to wait till closing-time for an answer."

Mr Longbothem smiled. "Take all the time in the world, young man. I do not return to New Zealand for three months—ample time for a wedding."

George bought another round, as though he had really taken Mr Longbothem to his heart. He was saying, "Here's to the lucky couple, sir! Rely on me to do all I can to bring about the happy event. What am I thinking of? That sounds as if the bride is expecting. Never mind, that will follow in due course."

"Thank you for your support, Mr Craig. Excellent drop of port, if I may say so."

"Drink your fill, sir. We do everything possible to help our overseas visitors and make them feel at home, as you will observe from my business card." George indicated the card hanging by the bar, begging potential motorists to call next door and inspect the finest range of used cars outside London.

“I see you are connected with the motor trade, Mr Craig,” Mr Longbothem remarked, puzzled by the addenda, ‘This is next door—save your feet’.

“Good thinking, sir. It occurred to me that while you are a guest on our shores some form of luxurious transportation would not be amiss.”

“Ah, in Wellington I keep two cars—but there I am always chauffeur-driven, as befits an old-timer well into his fifties. During my brief visit to England I prefer to rely on taxis.”

George smiled his special offer smile. “A chauffeur could be laid on, sir. It would take time—say ten minutes. We have special arrangements to suit overseas visitors, you see. You purchase a car from us, use it at your pleasure, then sell back to us when your stay is ended. Our prices are highly competitive, yet we repurchase generously, enabling visitors to enjoy private motoring in this country at practically no cost to themselves. Sometimes the market so fluctuates that your investment nets you a handsome profit, believe it or not. One American tourist who patronized us was so kind as to compose this little doggerel before he sailed for home.”

George took me by surprise because he went into classical Victorian pose essential to the delivery of verse, right hand on his heart, left hand pointing irrelevantly to the ceiling, eyes focused for the distance vision necessary to perceive New York through the window of the Bold Forester, then commenced to recite in a special kind of poetry voice, alnost as if he were expiring whilst being extricated from a car crash.

“He called it St George for England, bless him:
‘Git your car from George, hard by the Flying Bull,
Then trade it back for profit—that guy must be a fool!
Ken’t figure how he does it, but George sure brought me luck,
Fer I motored up to Birming Ham and never spent a buck.
Ken’t figure how he does it, though his customers are many,
Fer I motored down to Pembroke Shire and never spent a penny!’”

"Beautiful, George—I could weep," Mr Longbothem observed unemotionally.

"I thought it would appeal to your flair for thrift, sir. All the more loot for Hilda and Peter, eh?—ha, ha, ha, ha!"

I nudged George's foot. "Don't con him, George," I hissed. "Wait till I've got the . . . well, after all, he is a guest in our country."

George talked into his tankard, as he so often did, with his eyes to starboard. "Get the thou. first, eh?"

"I love Margo more than a grand—I want to appraise the overseas dowry first."

"Check she's not a Catholic too—they don't divorce easy. I should know, I married the Vatican with an Irish accent. Keep doing the football pools and you may not have to marry anyone."

"I thought you loved your wife, George."

"I love my country, too, but that doesn't mean I must never leave it. Married love is like the silencer on a motorbike—you must have it or you'd never get any peace."

"Oh, come off it, George, where would you be without her?"

"Right now I'd be in the Flying Bull."

Mr Longbothem suggested it was time he departed, so I assured him I would give serious consideration to his proposal.

Before he left the bar George followed up his sales talk, till Mr Longbothem assured him in turn that he too would give serious consideration to George's proposal. When finally we went our separate ways each man seemed pretty satisfied with the night's work, especially me now I knew I was a lady's man at last.

NINE

I shall never forget the next time I met George in the Bold Forester, he was so changed. He glanced furtively around the bar as if someone might be planning to steal the tankard in his hand, and when he quaffed from it his eyeballs kept watch to left and right against flank attacks. I tried to be casual, like at a car auction when the only thing between you and an under-bid four and a half litre Lagonda Six is a poised hammer.

"Take a jar of kidney pickler?" George asked shortly.

"Thanks, George. Why the traffic-jam scowl—you run out of love?"

"Skip the pleasantries. When do you wed Hilda?"

"Oh, that! Frankly, George, I've done a lot of pillow wetting these past nights but I can't jilt Margo. My trouble is I'm like you—too straight. It's tempting, of course, but my word is my bond, and that's all there is to it."

"The thou. isn't high enough, eh? Won't Grandad up his offer?"

"He won't up the thou. and he won't disclose his hidden reserves out there in Lamb-land. I can't afford to end up with Hilda plus a Sunday joint."

George shook his head. "He's a sharp negotiator, that old boy. I've done something for him I've never done for anybody before."

"You let him keep enough money for a hot meal and a bed?"

"On the contrary, Peter, I sold him an as-ex-works, one-owner-nursed Merc, with a genuine low no-clock-rewind mileage."

"So, not knowing the list price, he paid you over the top, like it was a new Mercedes?"

"That's just the point—he hasn't paid me anything. I've trusted him till his funds are transferred from Wellington to London. I know you can vouch for him, but that was three weeks ago."

"Maybe his funds are coming by sea in one of the old wool-clippers. Check on the trade winds in *The Times.*"

"Don't joke about it, Peter, because on top of that I've lent him two hundred pounds so he could visit his relatives north of the border."

"The Picts or the Scots?"

"I know he's as good as gold and there's a small commission in it for me, but three weeks is a long time."

"Maybe it's time you retired, George. Once you start trusting people you're on the skids."

"But it's only till the bank transfers the cash."

"And these days that could take hours. They say the stagecoach is finished, what with this new-fangled electric telegraph."

"Oh, shut up! I know everything's O.K.; it's just that he promised to remit the money to me as he passed through London. That was three weeks ago, and so far he's bombarded me with silence."

"Maybe he isn't used to London's traffic and crash-parked the Merc in the Thames. Last year a foreigner did that in the dark and told the River Police he thought it was the North Circular Road."

"I expect you think you're cheering me up, but they had a fellow like you in the Bible called Job—so don't. By the way, when did you last see Granpa?"

"I saw him about three weeks back—about the same time as you last saw your money."

"What did Hilda say about the old chap?"

"I reckoned this was a purely personal decision, so I didn't consult her at all."

George put down his tankard heavily on the counter. "You mean to say you haven't checked on the relationship, Peter?"

"Why should I? He hid nothing from us."

"Ye gods, man!—how do we know he really is her Grandad?"

"Well, he said so and he knew all about the family. Besides, we both saw the cheque he offered me."

"I can show you an American dollar but that doesn't mean I'm George Washington. The point is that neither of us has cross-checked with the Longbothems."

"Oh, I wouldn't trust them too far anyway."

"Shut up, Peter, before you drive me off my rocker."

"If you're so worried about a Merc and two hundred quid why don't you phone the Longbothems yourself. It's Cudford 3871."

"Positive action, Peter. Will do."

"That'll set your mind at rest, George. He's probably got involved with the tribe in Scotland and overlooked your debt."

"He promised to sell the Merc back to me anyhow, so I expect he figured on making one deal of it."

"That way he would be able to see more clearly how it would have been cheaper to hire a train. Who said the Kiwis were simple sheep farmers?"

"I feel almost ashamed to suspect the man with a phone check, Peter."

"Then tell them you trust him implicitly, but do they happen to have a set of his fingerprints for your sales book."

"Or his passport would do."

"Say you always send the police round when you make a deal, as part of the after-sales service."

George's eyes darted about the bar. "I'm not panicking, am I, Peter? If not, why am I shouting?"

"You're just talking very loudly, George," I reassured him. "I've often noticed how you raise your voice when you're quietly confident and serene. I expect your mind is preoccupied with clouds and flowers."

"Then why do I keep banging the counter with my fists?"

"Actually, I hadn't noticed, George. In fact, I was only thinking how coolly you're bearing up under the strain."

"What strain? Are you insinuating that I might have taken a terrible business risk and been peeled? Where is the old devil, that's what I want to know, damn it? I'm not worried about an as-new Merc or two hundred folders—I'm merely concerned for the safety of an elderly visitor to our shores, that's all. People have been hijacked before now, you know—remember the Good

Samaritan story? Everyone passed by on the other side while he lay coshed under his tight-up Merc, stripped of his two hundred nicker. Then along came the Good Samaritan and laid on a breakdown crew to pull in the Merc. Don't you ever think about people, Peter? Does it always have to be autos or loot? Can't you worry about people for a change?"

"I do, George—I'm worrying about you now, and you count as people."

"Why worry about me? All right, suppose I was peeled for a clean run-in-only Merc plus two hundred sheets, so what?—Joyce, draw me a double brandy fast—They're not people. All I'm concerned about is where that two-faced little butcher's disappeared to. That's why I'm drinking brandy, because I care about people, not things."

"I've heard that the Salvation Army undertakes to trace missing persons, George."

"So does Scotland Yard, but the thievin' old rat isn't missing is he? We both know he's gone off and forgot to remit, that's all."

"But surely no one could possibly drive about in an AA-inspection-invited Merc for three weeks without remembering to pay for it, George, let alone the two hundred crisps."

George spilled a tiny globule of brandy. "I like you, Peter, and I'm telling you nicely, as a friend, to shut up before I glass your face. You're deliberately trying to hide the fact that letters often go astray and postal delays are quite common. Why go out of your way to conceal it from a fellow Hood? If I was in your shoes I'd help you by being quite open about it and keep talking about wrong deliveries and such."

"I read in the *Echo* how a retailer got a letter from a customer thirty years after it had been posted, George."

"I'm begging you not to overdo consoling me, Peter. Thirty years' time I shall be somebody's ancestor, not a retailer. They may not even have cars by then—though no one will ever have a faultless spot-on Merc like I did—so I won't have you worrying me about the future as well as the present."

I set up another brandy for George to tremble over. "Come on, George, just make a quick phone call and put your mind at rest," I advised.

"My mind is at rest—it's my body which is playing me up. Besides, there's no point, Peter. I trust him like a brother. What am I saying?—if he's anything like my brother I'm bubbled already. You know the Longbothems better than me—you do it without telling me, Peter. Pretend you're going to the Gents, then come back with glad tidings. Don't mention me or the Merc or the two hundred skins—just ask how, and where, their lovable old Granpa is. If it's bad news, don't tell me. Maybe I can sue Longbothem junior on the grounds of a family debt. He might settle out of court to avoid a scandal here and in New Zealand. We'll show him that phony cheque he conned you with to marry Hilda."

"But he didn't sign it, George."

"Of course he didn't sign it—but we've got a specimen of his handwriting, see?"

"When I decided not to many Hilda I tore it up, George."

"Why don't you simply waylay me outside the pub and batter me to death, Peter? That's what friends are for, aren't they? Look, give me the phone and I'll stop your little game of trying to drive me crazy. You'll eat your words when you hear them confirm my faith in that lousy little twister with the buck teeth."

When the pub phone was disengaged I hustled George to it and inserted tuppence for Cudford 3871. I insisted George made the call rather than involve me with Hilda, then I listened in as best I could. Although the squeaky noise at the other end indicated a woman, I could not catch the actual words, but this is a faithful record of what I heard.

"It's Mrs Longbothem," George told me aside. "This is George speaking, George Craig, an old friend of Mr Longbothem Senior. I was wondering if I might have a word . . . well, I am inquiring as to his present whereabouts, Mrs Longbothem. In Cudford? Oh, excellent; I thought he was in Scotland. Is he staying with you?—Everything's O.K., Peter, he's here locally—I see; could I ask where he is then? Up the cemetery? Do you think he could ring me when he gets back? He won't be back? Why, does he work up there or something? He's buried there! But that's impossible, Mrs Longbothem, I was talking to him just recently. No, I'm not a spiritualist, I'm a car dealer. Did he meet with some kind of car accident?—he did say he wasn't used to driving himself. I was persuaded against my better judgement to let him have an autobahn-burner Merc Six, hardly suitable for our English country roads. Perhaps you would be so kind as to inform me what happened to the Merc . . . I mean, to Mr Longbothem Senior—he must have crashed the Merc, Peter; already buried and not a word from the insurance. Worse still, I've nothing in writing to claim for the two hundred wrappers, let alone legal ownership of the Merc. The old chap didn't peel me, fate done it. How in hell can you claim on fate?—Did I hear aright, Mrs Longbothem, no car accident? So the Merc is undamaged? He died of natural causes? Oh, I am glad. Would I be correct to suppose that you have the Merc now? No, Mrs Longbothem, it's not a disease but a car. Actually, an as-new one-owner-nursed Mercedes Six, in ex-works immac. condition, suit enthusiast.—Oh, boy, Peter, this duchess is thicker than a Bentley half-shaft. She thinks a Merc is some kind of bug, like 'flu.

"What did he die of, George?" I queried.

"Natural causes, which don't add up like he wrecked the Merc. Natural causes is a bed job, not traffic bash. Hell, how she yaps on about nursing him. No wonder he passed away. Listen."

George held up the receiver as though we were listening to the commercials on Radio Luxembourg. "The old bat drives you right off the wire just when you're sweating on good news."

"Yes, but what's she on about, George? She's saying how she nursed him night and day for three years till he finally went to sleep in her arms."

"Probably a ruse on his part to get some peace and shuffle

round to the Bold Forester. If I can get a word in when she pauses for breath I'll check on dates. Ah, Mrs Longbothem, most interesting but would you be so kind as to inform me when my late client actually passed on to glory? No, the exact hour doesn't matter; I was more concerned with the date, like Friday week. Tuesday? Tuesday when? Nine years ago! No, don't bother to look it up because I believe we must be talking about different grandfathers. I was referring to a Mr William Longbothem. You were too?—Peter, grab me a refill brandy and rush it to me here. I'm confused at the moment but I may have been peeled by an imposter. She knows damn-all about the Merc or my two hundred snickers, and this grandad isn't our man.—Sorry, Mrs Longbothem, I was momentarily overcome. I was wondering if you have another elderly gentleman in your family by the same name who has lately returned from New Zealand? Nobody? You are Hilda's mother, aren't you? I'm sorry, let me put it another way. Does anybody in your family, or out of it, possess a grey Mercedes motor car, or used to have one, or has mentioned one, or intends to purchase one, or knows somebody who owns one? Oh! Have you personally ever heard of a make of car known as a Mercedes? No, I thought not. When I use the term 'motor car' you do understand me, of course? Yes, good."

"Check her out on Hilda," I suggested.

"Sharp thinking, Peter," George snapped, mopping his brow. "Listen to me for a change, missis—forget your old dad for ten seconds, and concentrate on my Merc. It is possible that your daughter might have a relative, such as another grandad, whom you don't know about or it slipped your memory?"

I could tell from the fruitless way George took the receiver from his ear and examined it that he had been cut off by Mrs Longbothem. "I've been peeled, Peter," he said simply. "For the first time in my life I've been gelded."

"You often told me before how you got peeled, George."

"Never. That was just pub talk. For years I've played Ali

Baba and his forty mates with some of the sweetest singers in the trade, but they never conned me. So now a nice old granpa stumps into a pub and peels me for my still-under-guarantee, no-offers Merc Six, plus two hundred rice. Back in Ealing I used to be known in the trade as the virgin villain because they couldn't shake me down."

I put my arm reassuringly around George's shoulders, under the impression he was close to tears. "Never mind, George, let's hope you've been done in the trade."

"What do you mean by that?" he demanded suspiciously.

"Well, you said yourself that don't count."

"It only don't count when it ain't you, son. Still, I know you'll stand by me and take half the knock, seeing it was you who unwittingly set me up for the peel about marrying Hilda. I'm not saying you done it on purpose, only that if you had been operating with the old man you couldn't have laid it on better. Just give me two hundred sheets and we'll say no more about it."

"How do I know you haven't set up the whole scene to con me for two hundred sheets, George? There's no proof that you did a deal with the old man—you said so yourself."

"Oh, Peter, where's your sense of loyalty? Are you going to boot me when I'm down—your best friend?"

"I'm a lousy sort of friend, George—utterly unreliable. When you need me most I quit on you. I'm ashamed of myself but a leopard doesn't change his spots. Let's face it, I'm just not worthy of you."

To prove my basic qualities I left George to his grief, and walked out of the tavern surprisingly cheerful for one who had just witnessed such human suffering.

So distraught was George's condition that it took him three days to figure out that Cudford 3871 was an unusual number, because the next time he rang it to double-check on the Longbothems, Hilda answered. She said, "Who is that speaking, please?"

"George Craig, the motor dealer. I was trying to trace your grandfather, but when I called the other day your mother didn't seem to know anything about him."

"She should do," Hilda laughed, "he's been staying here until his ship left for New Zealand yesterday."

"Yesterday! Which one of us is crazy? Did he buy a Mercedes motor car during his stay, Hilda?"

"Indeed he did. A lovely one, too. We had such fun in it. He drove us all through the. . . ."

"Never mind the itinerary—where is it now?"

"Why, he sold it, of course. He couldn't take it back to New. . . ."

"Sold it! Who to?"

"To a friend of yours—Peter."

"Peter who?"

"No, Peter Pook. Oh my!"

Hilda's exclamation jumped out because George had slammed down the phone with a special oath one hears only in the motor trade, so dreadful that even with the repeal of the Porn Laws it has not yet appeared in print. Yet he repeated it once more, within three minutes or less when he tore through the directory for my number and found it to be Cudford 3871. This coincidence so astonished him that he looked up the Longbothems, who were listed as Cudford 2871.

"Funny," George said aloud, asking the operator for 2871.

"Hilda speaking—Hilda Longbothem."

"Sorry to bother you again, Hilda, but may I ask you one further question about your grandfather?" George persisted.

"My grandfather! Who's that speaking, please?"

"George Craig again. I wondered if your grandfather left word for me before he sailed about a little loan of two hundred pounds?"

"You mean you owed him all that money?"

"No, girl—he owes me!"

"Where did he sail to then?"

"New Zealand, where else?"

"I didn't think the Boer War was in New Zealand. Daddy has always told me Granpa was killed in South Africa."

"Oh, save me from this cursed family! How many granpas do you run in your lot, girl? Haven't you got one who sailed yesterday?"

"That's silly because the Boer War ended years before I was even born. He'd be much too late."

"Listen, Hilda, I'm talking about your grandfather William Longbothem who sold the Merc to Peter."

"I didn't even know him, let alone what he sold before he joined up. Oh, here's Mother. Mother, didn't you say that Granpa was killed in the Boer War? Mr Craig is on the phone and he says Granpa owed him two hundred pounds. Yes, 1899 to 1902. I don't know—Mr Craig just asked if Granpa left word about it, when he sold something to somebody. Try who? Oh, the War Office records in London. I could fetch the family Bible and find out when Granma died. I remember her when I was a tiny little girl. Oh, my!"

"Sorry, Hilda, I shouldn't swear like that but it slipped out. Forget it. Trouble is I'm under terrible emotional stress and very confused. You see, when I ring 2871 I get you, but when I ring 3871 I get other Hildas, and whatever number I ring I get all kinds of grandfathers, dead, alive, left yesterday or killed in 1899."

"You must be in a bad way, Mr Craig. This is the first time you've phoned me."

"Sometimes I get one or other of your mothers, too."

"If you've been ringing 3871—and people often do mix them up—that's Peter's Auntie Dot. It's her bedside phone."

"Peter's Auntie Dot!"

"Yes, that's right. We're 2871. . . . Oh, my!"

Hilda rubbed her ear as the oath hit it, followed by the crash of a slammed phone.

As soon as George calmed down sufficiently to make another call, he got through to Cudford 3871. It was a call to be remembered by all the parties concerned.

"Who's speaking, please?"

"George Craig."

"Oh, this is Hilda."

"All right, you've been rumbled. I know very well who you are, you wicked old bat."

"Auntie Dot, your friendly motoring adviser, speaking. Hello and greetings, fellow Hood."

"O.K., fellow Hood, so everybody is entitled to their chuckle but now I want my Merc back, along with the two hundred skins."

Aunt Dot cackled mirthlessly. "Inquiries welcomed from the trade, of course. Substantial knock-off for cash. There's an immac. one-owner-nursed, as-ex-works grey Merc on the forecourt right now, George. Suitable connoisseur for Continental travel. Sacrifice at £500. Ten per cent knock-off to bona fide retailer. Regret no cheques or near offers. AA, RAC inspection invited. Your satisfaction is our best advertisement. Phone brings demo run to your door."

"I want that Merc back fast," George hissed.

"Of course you do, George—it's the car of the week. Give me £450 and see how fast it comes to you. Or you could buy it privately for £500."

"But you stole it from me. I was peeled in the Bold Forester."

"On the contrary, George, we have full legal entitlement to the car. We purchased it through the usual channels, so perhaps you would like to check the log book and receipt? I am given to understand that the gentleman bought it from you, which is recommend enough in all honesty. A cash deal, too, I believe—still, who am I to pry into your tax affairs?"

"But the shyster never paid me for it."

"I bet you say that to all the tax inspectors—not that we don't, too. But let us not disclose our little trade secrets over the phone, eh, George?"

"On top of that, he peeled me for two hundred sheets."

"Goodness gracious, how remiss of you, George! I must say Peter and I found him most dependable. My advice is to take your documentary evidence to a solicitor and court him for it."

"How can I when I haven't got any and don't know who he is?"

"Well, I can help you there, George. He told us he was the grandfather of Hilda Longbothem. You know the Longbothems, they're friends of Peter who live in Cudford. 2871 I think their phone number is."

"Then he must have sold you the Merc posthumously because he was shot in 1899."

"Poor man; I said to Peter at the time how poorly he looked, though little did I realize he was wounded."

"I know time means nothing to you, but he was killed in the Boer War when you were just an old woman starting out on a second life."

"Actually, George, I remember the Boer War well because Uncle Sydney created quite a stir at the siege of Ladysmith by being posted missing. Sir George White, the garrison commander, could not understand how anybody could be posted missing, in view of the fact that Ladysmith was completely surrounded by the Boer soldiers for 119 days and nobody could get in or out of the town. Also missing was the garrison's wine and spirits wagon, which wasn't something you could mislay like a glove. When Lord Roberts relieved Ladysmith in March, 1900, it was discovered that Uncle Sydney was part of the relief column which marched into the town—though Uncle Sydney himself was not marching, but lying inside a field ambulance suffering from acute Natal nephritis, or, as we call it today, alcoholic poisoning. Sir Redvers Buller himself referred to Uncle Sydney's feat of breaking through the enemy lines as the Charge of the Tight Brigade, and in his later years Uncle Sydney used to tell how Sir Redvers decorated him with the D.C.M., or Disorderly Conduct Medal, during an investiture held at the detention centre in Ladysmith, where he was promoted to the rank of private."

"How in the name of Henry Ford do I get the Boer War thrust down my throat every time I open my mouth about my as-new Merc? I lost it this month, not before it was invented. On top of that I been caned for two hundred smilers what I had put by for my funeral tomorrow."

Aunt Dot sighed deeply. "Ah, George, there are too many unscrupulous rogues about who take advantage of the honest citizen."

"There sure are, and at your age I should have thought you'd go straight—straight to jail. But I'll take Peter to court, mark my words, Little Red Riding Hood."

"Peter's under age, George."

"Then I'll take you to court, see if I don't."

"I'm over age—and the doctor says I mustn't be moved."

"So I'll take possession of my Merc by force."

"That would be stealing, George. The police wouldn't approve of that, so we've immobilized the Merc like they told us to. However, part-exchange is no robbery—we'd be prepared to trade the Merc for a Frazer Nash, like the one we lost."

"Oh! How do you mean, part-exchange?"

"Well, we could barter the Merc for the Frazer Nash plus two hundred. That sounds fair to me."

"Fair! I've already lost two hundred!"

"Not lost, George. You've merely deposited it with us as part of the deal. All we need do now is exchange cars. Oh, my, what dreadful language! For the moment I thought my dear Sydney had come back to me from the grave. Oh, why do men become so abusive when they negotiate a price? Have you rung off, George—or has my ear-trumpet gone phut again? Dear, dear, such a nasty bang. I do hope he hasn't shot himself, the silly man."

Like all good diplomatic missions, the transfer was effected without fuss or publicity. One Wednesday morning a red souped-up Frazer Nash mysteriously appeared on our forecourt, and on the Thursday morning George Craig discovered a grey as-new Mercedes parked outside his showroom, no questions asked.

When the matter was closed Aunt Dot puzzled me by declaring that the two hundred pounds was to be put into our barratry fund to cover demurrage, but as I didn't know we had a barratry fund or what demurrage was, I felt none the wiser. Aunt Dot looked at me and giggled. "When you sup with the Devil you need a long spoon," she said, quoting the motto upon which our firm was founded.

"I always thought the Devil was a man, not a lady, Aunt Dot," I giggled back. "Let's have our supper now."

TEN

You may recall that at this time Honners was going through what he himself described as his Blue Period. Up to now, he told me, he had considered himself to be like any ordinary member of the nobility, but recently he had become much more conscious of the blue blood which trickled sluggishly through the varicose veins in his little legs, before treacherously turning red upon reaching his retroussé nose.

Honners was extremely angry with his nose because, whereas the Pilkington-Goldbergs exhibited the classical Roman nose in their portraits back to the year dot which hung in the Long Gallery at Cudford Hall, his had taken the wrong turning and let down the family tradition.

"You could hardly call me the Eagle of Cudford Manor, with my bent vent the wrong way up," Honners told me, as we stood before the oil-painting of that particular ancestor in the Long Gallery. "They say it's all in the genes, Peter, so I guess my genes got buckled somewhere along the line. Worse still, all the Pilkington-Goldbergs were monsters till me—just look at their armour. I could use my great-grandfather's sword at the local sports for the pole-vault. If armour were still used today I'd have to go into battle clad from head to toe inside one leg of the Eagle's suit."

"Never mind, Honners, at least you're a little monster," I consoled him.

"Actually, I was seeking sympathy, not insult, my good fellow. However, nature always compensates—I make up for it here." Honners indicated his head.

"Your head isn't all that big, Honners, unless you're speaking figuratively."

"Brains, man, brains. You see, it has always been the tradition in our family to follow the ancient Pilkington-Goldberg motto, 'The Sooner the Better', and die young. Any male PG over the age of thirty was regarded as a coward, because we were expected to rush out of the cradle, find a war or a Crusade or start one, shriek the family war-cry, 'Come out and fight, you son-of-a-bitch', then end up stiff in the front line with a face full of arrows and battle-axes. That's how we came top in the State funeral league and runners-up to the Churchills in the medals table for assorted gongs, crosses, stars and other awards for disintegrating into handy one-ounce meat-balls under enemy fire—such as Sir Vernon Pilkington-Goldberg, who was brought home from the Battle of Inkerman in 1854 in an urn and kept on our sideboard in the breakfast-room next to the cruet."

"So you intend to be the first fully-grown Pilkington-Goldberg of the line, Honners?"

"I intend to be our first Old Age Pensioner, and draw ten bob a week like any normal coward. I'm fed up living in a world of widows. As a child I thought all my uncles dressed as women. Anyhow, you may have noticed how I've changed lately. Quiet, even-tempered, kindly and smiling. It's all part of this thing I picked up in that rag you write for, *Family Help,* on how to live graciously and avoid the box and shovel up the churchyard, called 'Life Begins at Eighty'. In fact, I wondered if you ghost-wrote it for Aunt Dot."

"But you're only about twenty, Honners."

"So I've got a head start. Already I've given up drinking, smoking, women, working, and all the other vices I had when I was popularly known as Sir Shortarse the Bold. Apparently the secret is not to do anything which makes your heart beat faster than a tortoise's tail. Notice how slowly I move here from picture to picture, and speak to you in a soft voice that won't rupture my larynx. Even when I pointed to the Eagle of Cudford Manor I raised my arm only from the elbow, then gradually rolled my eyeballs up the canvas to his family nose."

"I had noticed, Honners, but I thought you weren't well or something. Is that why you're not wearing any shoes?"

"Ah, shoes. Shoes can be a killer. Not only is it exhausting to put them on by bending down, but over a single year your poor feet lift a total of eight tons of leather, according to last week's article in *Family Help.* Of course, I've got this rotten cold as a result—but what's that compared with heartfailure?"

I had not seen my old friend Honners for some time, and the main purpose of my visit to Cudford Hall was to drum up some business, like selling him the Frazer Nash. The Pilkington-Goldbergs were an extremely wealthy family, chiefly because they never seemed to spend any money as ordinary people do. They possessed everything, but it was handed down from generation to generation until it finally fell to bits—such as clothes—or its very age turned it into a priceless heirloom—such as the paintings and practically everything else.

For example, Honners' cradle dated from 1650, and most of his childhood toys were over a hundred years old. I recall how, when Honners grew too old for whipping his top, it was carefully cleaned, re-painted and replaced in the family museum. Likewise when he began to play cricket, he puzzled us with a bat shaped like a hockey stick, which bore the legend on the brass plate let into the handle: 'Presented to Sir Thos. Pilkington-Goldberg by the Men of Hambledon, 1768.' Another incident I recall was when the rest of us were riding tricycles, Honners was sent out to play with a large iron hoop which he had to bowl along by means of an iron hook set in a wooden handle, taken straight from the Industrial Revolution section of the museum at Cudford Hall.

When we boys bought roller-skates, Honners was to be seen dancing alone round the only extant maypole in the county, and when the ice-skating craze gripped us Honners was given skates carved from whale bone by Eskimos when the Hudson Bay Company was formed in 1670.

"Don't they ever give you new toys, Honners?" I asked him one Christmas, as he tried to manipulate the first yo-yo to reach Europe from China.

"I prefer timeless toys, Peter, like these marbles I found in my stocking this morning from Ancient Greece. My forebears have received these same marbles for Christmas since time immemorial, together with this exciting game of Hoodman's Blind and this set of bells for morris dancing. Next year I shall get diabolo and our hobby-horse—possibly, if I'm very good, Pater will give me a bright new penny to add to my collection of coins."

"Doesn't he ever give you sweets or anything nice, Honners?"

"Sweets are bad for the teeth—I don't like sweets," Honners repeated mechanically. "Moreover, they cannot be preserved, so are a waste of money. Cook has been told to stop baking sweet-meats for the table because they spoil one's appetite and make one fat. I prefer something special, like the little oak tree Pater has promised me for my tenth birthday."

"An oak tree! There's hundreds on your estate already."

"Pater says he will give me one of them for my birthday present."

"But what on earth will you do with it, Honners?"

"I shall watch it grow to a big oak tree. Then, one day, when the forest has to be thinned, it will be felled and sold for hardwood."

"But how can you play with an oak tree?"

"Oh, stupid!—if I want to play I shall lose myself in the Great Maze or count the gargoyles on the East Wing of the Hall."

We boys often visited the Hall to play, but playing with Honners usually involved collecting firewood from the estate parkland, clearing weeds from the ornamental lake, or potato-picking in the vegetable gardens. Honners' father, the ninth Earl of Cudford, assured us it was capital fun and organized little competitions for us, to see who could cut most grass, or collect the most mushrooms, or clean out a stable fastest. The winner was dubbed Victor Ludorum and allowed to choose the next competition. During one game we picked the entire season's strawberry crop ready for market.

One day we arrived at the Hall to find it full of house guests, and we were invited to join in the morris dancing with them. My friend Alec looked surprised to see a game one could play without the aid of a shovel or baskets, but we took part with zest, prancing and clapping our hands for the best part of two hours in the open air. Honners' father stopped us dancing while he produced a theodolite to take measurements of the ground, then had us all dancing up one end of the area for a further hour.

"Are our boots damaging the earth?" I asked Honners as we hooked each other's arm for the circle in the centre of the dance formation.

"No, Peter, we're flattening it just right. Pater says this end is almost level now with the other end."

"Level for what?"

"Level for when we build the new barn tomorrow. We have to ensure the floor is hard-packed and level before the concrete goes down."

"Do your house guests know about this, Honners?"

"No, they're from London and think they're keeping up rural folk-lore. Pater wants to start on the barn tomorrow because they're only staying for two weeks."

"How on earth will he get them to build a barn?"

"At prayers tonight he's going to announce a demonstration of the ancient craft of thatching which has been specially laid on for them. Then he'll ask them to erect a barn so there'll be something for him to thatch. It's ever so simple and shouldn't take them more than a week."

"Will your dad thatch it himself then?"

"No, Pater will demonstrate with the first few bundles, then ask them to try their hand at the ancient craft as a special privilege because it's part of our heritage. Usually he runs it as a competition in rustic arts between the ladies and the gentlemen, and the winners are presented with buckets of creosote for the walls."

"What do the losers get?"

"They receive enough brushes for everybody. Pater emphasizes this is a friendly house party where nobody need feel out of things."

"But I thought they had come down from London for the shooting?"

"Oh, they've stopped shooting because they're sick of pigeon-pie for every meal. Only yesterday Mr Harrison had to leave the breakfast table in a hurry after his poached-egg-on-pigeon. Our butler says Mr and Mrs Kenwood have actually joined the National Bird Preservation Society since they arrived, and Mr Welch is secretly eating down at the Crown pub."

Another thing which struck me about the infant Honners was his apparel. Although always smartly dressed in his little Norfolk jacket and breeches, the suit was composed of more leather than tweed. There were leather patches at the elbows, down the edges, round the cuffs and, when Honners bent down, we observed a large all-leather bottom. Closer examination of this extremity revealed leather patches on the leather itself, one on each buttock. Furthermore, Honners was hopeless at the game of hide-and-seek because he was mounted on the stoutest pair of hobnail boots I had ever seen, giving people the impression that a platoon of soldiers was just down the street. One disadvantage of the Norfolk suit was its refusal to grow like its owner, with the result that Honners seemed to possess abnormally long arms and legs for his size, and he was never able to button up the jacket or the waist-band of the breeches, nor could he run far without becoming undressed in the most embarrassing places. In cold weather he was permitted to don a green triple-caped cloak, like highwaymen used to wear, which fitted him like a tent, having once belonged to his great-grandfather's coachman.

Honners' headgear was well-known in Cudford, consisting of a kind of cushion fitted with a button on top and a peak at the front, which he called his cap, although in summer he sported a straw boater, brown with age. During heat-waves he appeared in public wearing a General Gordon solar topee, complete with ventilation louvres and topped by a silver nob.

Thus I did not expect Honners to be a ready buyer of the Frazer

Nash, but he was one of the few prospects I knew who had the cash available. When I broached the subject to him he walked me round to the stables to view the Rolls Royce Silver Ghost of another age. He patted the bodywork affectionately as if it was a horse.

"That is a car," he informed me confidentially.

"Yes, being in the trade, I could tell," I replied.

"In the same condition as when it left the coach-builders, except that we had to renew the tyres once, and put a new wick in the rear light."

"A new wick!"

"Yes, Pater is certain the lamp was originally fitted with a faulty wick that smoked, but as the car was a gift to my grandfather from the Nawab of Shaggapore we could hardly bill him for that, so Pater made a new one from a piece of settee webbing and said no more about it."

"When did the Nawab present the car to your family, Honners?"

"Oh, way back in 1913, just before the Great Bang. It has served us faithfully ever since—apart from the war, when it became a hearse—and should certainly last out my lifetime. The engine has done around 200,000 miles, so is now practically run in. Uses no oil, of course."

My heart sank, causing me to spread out my hands in despair. "Look, Honners, I'm a motor salesman trying to make a living, not writing the history of transport. Couldn't you consider buying a second car and using it as a runabout? That way you could avoid the cost of another tyre for the Rolls when you're an old man."

Honners looked pained. "We use the Rolls for long journeys, and our two feet for short journeys. However, if the distance is in excess of five miles but less than twenty miles we use the bicycle."

"What have you got, a penny-farthing or a velocipede?"

"Actually, we possess both in the Transport section of our museum but they have become too valuable to ride. Pater won't let us use anything the moment its current market price exceeds its original cost. So we take the tandem, which seats four adults and two children on the pillion."

"And you tow a caravan behind?"

"Please don't be facetious, Peter. Whenever possible, Pater travels by horse."

"So he can visit France without using the cross-Channel ferries?"

Honners performed the difficult task of looking down his nose at me. "If more people practised thrift instead of reckless prodigality the world would be a better place, Peter."

"Except that we'd all be unemployed. For one thing, the motor industry would have shut down in 1913."

Honners smirked sanctimoniously. "My longevity course does not permit me to become ruffled in argument, Peter. So the new calm me is smiling kindly at you instead of kicking you off the premises into the moat. I say to myself, this young man is engaged so we must congratulate him; this young man will soon be married so we must rejoice; this young man must soon support a family so we should console him. . . ."

"Oh, come on, Honners, violate the family code for once and buy something," I interrupted impatiently. "Fit the Frazer Nash in between the horse and the sedan chair and astonish the peerage. Why let your mother travel to Ascot by canal barge this year? It's heart-breaking trying to sell you anything. I suppose if I was peddling pens you'd take a goose from your pocket and pluck a quill. What have you got in the toilet—a roll of dock leaves on the wall? Why don't you help me?"

Honners' nose went extremely red, but he managed to smile serenely over it. "My dear friend, I may have helped you more than you think. Follow me to the Banquet Room—leisurely, lest we exhaust ourselves—and you may be surprised."

"Why, are we going to have our dinner?" I jeered. The Banquet Room was a complete misnomer because nobody ate there. It was a magnificent spectacle of red, gold and white, with the long table for thirty diners so lavishly laid with cutlery, glass, flowers and candlesticks that there seemed no room for food. The entire area was roped off, except for a narrow alleyway through which tourists filed during the season at half-crown per head to see the splendour of the past. The mechanical discourse of the old guide at this point always intrigued me: 'This is where the Pilkington-Goldbergs last 'ad a big dinner, way back in 1897 to celebrate Queen Victoria's Diamond Jubilee. They don't 'ave big dinners no more, what with the cost of living and death duties, but this 'ere room is kept just as it was when they could afford proper dinners. It's a sad reflection on the times what we lives in, ladies and gentlemen, that the contents of this room is worth a king's ransom, yet the present Earl can't have his dinners no more.' Honners was extremely angry when he heard the guide for the first time. I remember him telling me, "I realize that elderly retainer of ours lives in a world of fish and chips, but he's spreading a rumour throughout the South of England that my family is slowly starving to death. Already a lady visitor has left two shillings in the poor box, with a note asking it to be used to buy the present Earl a hot dinner, and more humiliating still, Pater has received a food parcel from America. We'll have the Salvation Army up here next, mark my words, if that old dodderer shows many more folk round."

Honners led me through the Banquet Room to the Music Room, which, like everywhere else at the Hall, was roped off with a kind of crimson ship's cable supported on brass posts. The various musical instruments bore notices, 'Do not play', and other objects were labelled, 'Do not touch', except the chairs, which were carded, 'Do not sit in'. This last notice was reinforced by more rope stretched across the arms, possibly for those who could not read. We were also warned by cards that we were not to tread on the carpet, open the windows, light the great fire or read the music scores.

Standing by a notice forbidding us to smoke, I said to Honners, "Just as a matter of interest, what can one possibly do in this room?"

Honners appeared surprised at such a question. "One follows

the arrows and passes through, of course, What else?"

"But the arrows direct you to the library, where you're not allowed to open the glass doors of the shelves, let alone read the books. That leads into the Portrait Room, marked 'No cameras'."

"You're supposed to look at the objets d'art, not wear them out, Peter."

"But how do you manage to live in a place where everything is roped off and forbidden? What does your family do at night—eat in the corridors, then sleep on the stairs?"

This question had always puzzled me, where the Pilkington-Goldbergs actually sat down together like a normal family. Usually they were shepherding the endless queue of half-crowns through the entrance hall, round the building, then out through the rear door to the souvenir and refreshment kiosks set up in the old wash-house. If the crowds were thin, Honners' mother was always to be found pruning roses or weeding, while her husband, the ninth Earl, seemed capable of turning his hand to any task, from restoring oil paintings to clearing the drains.

Sundry relations appeared about the house and grounds from time to time, always busy about some chore which absorbed their whole attention. Nobody was idle, or even stationary, invariably telling you they would be back to see you in two ticks, then vanishing on their errand, never to return.

On this occasion Honners bade me wait for him in the Billiards Room, where the two full-size tables were roped off and carded, 'Do not play'. He disappeared through a door marked 'Private. No admittance'. I passed the time inspecting the billiard cues, locked in a frame labelled 'Do not use', then gazing down a corridor to where one of Honners' aunts was re-embroidering a Queen Anne fire-screen. Being alone, I felt a heavy sense of frustration caused by the cautionary cards on display. Happening to stand by the light switch, marked 'Do not switch on', I was gripped by an urge to disobey this particular edict. Impulsively, I flipped all six switches, yet not a single light came on.

Still Honners did not appear, and when I again looked down the corridor his aunt had vanished. I crept to the door marked 'Private. No admittance', and opened it sufficiently to peep through. The room was stacked with antique furniture protected by dust sheets, but there was no sign of Honners. I walked across the room to the main window and looked out down to the east avenue of the gardens to where a Pilkington-Goldberg uncle was trimming a large shrub to the shape of a peacock.

But what really caught my eye was the sight of Honners struggling along the avenue pushing a wheelbarrow laden with horse manure. When he drew level with the window he spotted my face and called out, "You shouldn't be in there, Peter, it's private".

"I got fed up waiting for you, Honners. Is that manure the surprise you had in store for me?"

"Oh, I'll be with you in two ticks. Pater just wants me to dump this lot by the vegetable gardens. You can help, if you like."

"No, thanks, I'll wait in the Billiards Room. Hurry up though because I only came to sell you the Frazer Nash."

Refusing to be sucked into the Pilkington-Goldberg labour schedule, I returned to the Billiards Room, standing because the chairs had tasselled cords tied across the arms. My long reverie was broken by the hum of a Hoover down the corridor, so, for want of anything better to do, I sauntered along in that direction. I was disconcerted to discover it was Honners cleaning the carpet in the Salon.

"Sorry about this, Peter," he said, without pausing as he quartered the room like mowing a football pitch, "but Mater asked me to clean up before the afternoon horde charge in. It won't take long, but if you'd lend me a hand it'll be even quicker."

"All right, what can I do?" I snapped impatiently.

"Just take the Hoover and carry on as I was. I'll nip down to the cupboard and fetch another one."

"O.K., but make it fast, Honners. Next time I'll bring my apron and mob cap."

While Honners hurried off, I continued to vacuum the great carpet of the Salon, a Persian job, I learned, reading the card: 'Presented to Sir Reginald Pilkington-Goldberg by the Shah in 1810. Do not walk on it.'

After some twenty minutes Honners had still not returned. Instead, his mother came in with a bowl of fresh flowers from the garden. "Hallo, Peter, how nice of you to help Honners," she purred. "You wouldn't know, of course, but he should have told you to remove your shoes while you clean our priceless Persian carpet."

"Where is he?" I inquired sourly.

"I haven't set eyes on him since early morning, the giddy boy. Please be a darling and flick round the furniture with this when you've finished. Vacuuming a carpet does raise the dust so."

Before I could protest, she stuffed a duster in my pocket and made off. I continued working, but when I reached the south window of the Salon I could hardly believe my eyes. There was Honners struggling up the south avenue pulling a handcart loaded with fruit from the orchard. I banged angrily on the window, whereupon Honners indicated by mime that he needed my help to pull the load up the final incline to the house.

For once I responded willingly, leaving the Salon and running out to assist him . "I thought you had gone to get another cleaner for the Salon?" I told him sharply.

Honners puffed for breath. "This is the last job, honestly, Peter. Just take this load round to the old wash-house because we sold out this morning. Meantime I'll pop back for the other cart and that's it."

"No, Honners. I'll help you take this lot to the wash-house, but you're staying put with me until I leave this stately labour camp."

Seeing I was determined, Honners accepted the offer and we trundled the barrow of assorted fruits to the wash-house for sale to the visiting public, next to the home-baked bread, cakes and souvenirs. It was not until we entered the converted wash-house that I realized the extent of the Pilkington-Goldberg's retail outlet. The place resembled an Indian bazaar on one side and Sainsbury's on the other—each stall piled high with produce and goods.

"Of course, lots of people come here for the shopping, not to view the house," Honners informed me as we unloaded the cart, "and in addition we supply several hotels in the area. For example, our sausages go all over Cudfordshire and we send our cheese as far as Canada, wholesale, too."

"But I thought you only sold the odd jam spoon stamped with the PG crest, Honners."

"Look, just polish these tomatoes as you stack them, Peter, and I'll explain. We sell everything, from postcards of Cudford Hall to a complete set of lodge gates. Every time an American buys our lodge gates Pater has another pair knocked up in the smithy. Same with the Tudor roasting-spits down in the kitchens—we export one per week on average during the season."

"Don't they spot they're new, Honners?"

"Ah, we use old iron, then leave them out in the rain to rust. Finally, we dip them in bacon fat, burn it off and rub down with goose grease. Come round one evening and we'll make one—it's great fun."

"What about my surprise, Honners? Or do I have to boil these beetroots first?"

"Ah, just help me grade the eggs while I spring the first one on you. See, three sizes, thus: Giant, Jumbo and Extra Large. Sheer psychological selling technique—the meanies purchase a dozen pullets and go home thinking they've got Extra Large. When they eat them they wonder if they've got extra large egg-cups instead. Only our Giants will fill a domestic egg-cup without rolling about inside it."

"What about my first surprise, Honners?"

"Let's finish the eggs or you may break one with shock."

"Then tell me while I'm getting the spuds up, to be on the safe side."

"Well, you know Margo?" Honners said, grading eggs all the time with machine-like rapidity."

"I ought to—I'm engaged to her."

"She wants me to be best man at the fry-up."

"Whatever for?"

"To lend a bit of class, of course. 'Titled toff honours local fry-up' will look good in the *Echo.*"

"It's all right by me, Honners. The question is can she afford you as well as choir and organ?"

"Actually, Peter, I come free with the buffet reception; we cater for all special occasions like that, so naturally Margo wants to have the reception here for snob atmosphere. Besides, we undercut the Royal at six-and-six per head, including champagne-type perry from our own orchards, followed by a glass of home-made mead for the toasts. There's stand-up snacks, too, if required."

"But Margo never mentioned this to me, Honners."

"As I said, it was a surprise. I phoned her and she jumped at the idea. She said Peter will love it, and I wasn't to tell you about it."

"But how could I love it if I didn't even know about it? Margo and I keep no secrets from each other—we tell each other everything."

"That's exactly what she said. She wanted to spring it on you as a surprise."

"When—at the altar? In any case, why did you tell me if you'd promised not to?"

"Well, Peter, we fixed it last month between us, but she is such a long time springing it on you that I got worried about the deposit. So I thought I'd better mention it to you in confidence without Margo knowing. I trust you as a friend, but unfortunately Pater is pressing me for the usual twenty per cent plonk and balance for the use of the Green Room. I didn't breathe a word to a soul except my family, and I made them promise not to tell you or let Margo know you had found out from me. So if you swear to keep it from Margo everything will be O.K., though if she does suspect you know, I'm relying on you to keep me in the clear by hinting you heard it from a third party. On the other hand, if she doesn't mention anything about it to you, play dumb and say nothing — but tip me off as soon as possible about why she keeps you in the dark.

"I am going to be married, Honners—not organizing a spy ring. Margo and I have complete trust in each other."

"Of course, Peter—that's the way it should be. But this is different because it concerns money, not trust. You'll soon become united in holy wedlock, but before that happens one of you has to pay for the reception. Unfortunately, Margo can supply everything for a happy marriage except cash. That's your side of it. She gave me the guest list so I could figure out the bill. Here it is—fifty sheets, give or take a quid, as we say in the stately homes racket, so the down plonk is ten peelers, leaving forty to come as I hand you the sword to cut the cake."

I thanked Honners for the diplomatic way he had handled such a delicate situation between lovers, and passed over two fives. He did not give me a receipt, explaining how this would only complicate the estate's financial arrangements with the National Trust and cause a lot of book-keeping difficulties at the Ministry of Works. Instead, he offered to perform the ancient family custom in such cases by cutting a vein in his sword arm and drawing blood. I hastily waived tradition by reminding him of my second surprise.

"Ah, now you're really in for a shock, Peter," he chuckled. "Let us away to the Salon for my *pièce de résistance*, or, as we say in the stately homes racket, my resident ghost."

When we returned to the Salon, Honners pointed to the Hoover I had abandoned in mid carpet. "Just finish it off, Peter, while I fetch the surprise. We don't impose on guests but they always like to muck in to preserve the way of life in our national heritage. I shan't be gone two ticks."

"That's hardly long enough for you to gather in the harvest."

"No, Peter, you have my word as a Knight of the Bedpost—Edward Three, 1349—that I'll be right back."

True to his word, Honners evaporated into the labyrinth of Cudford Hall without trace while I vacuumed the great Persian carpet. By coincidence it was not until I had just completed the last square yard that the whistle blew. It came from the speaking-tube which hung to one side of the Adam fireplace, next to the brass bell handle. One simply extracted the little wooden whistle, placed the aperture of the tube to one's ear, and listened.

At once I recognized Honners' high-pitched voice. "Sorry to be so long, Peter, but there was more to it than I had bargained for. Anyhow, while you're dusting off the furniture in the Salon I'm sending down an old friend for you to meet."

I took the tube from my ear and spoke into it. "Who is this old friend, Honners?"

"Well, it's supposed to be a surprise—but you'll recognize him at once."

"By the mop and bucket he'll be carrying?"

I could hear Honners giggling as he cut me off by replacing the little wooden whistle his end, so I did likewise. The speaking-tube communicated only with the servants' hall below stairs, making me wonder what Honners was doing down there, unless he had this new arrival decoking the ovens as a prelude to our introduction in the Salon.

But when there was a knock on the door and the visitor entered I really did start with surprise—so much so that I dropped the duster on the Louis XV escritoire I was polishing and cried, "It can't be! Fancy you having the nerve to show up round here!"

ELEVEN

The old gentleman shuffled across the Salon, extending a bent hand for me to shake. “How are you, my dear Peter? What a joy it is to see you once more before I return to New Zealand.”

“But I thought. . . .”

“Ah, I know exactly what you thought, Peter. You thought here is dear old Mr Longbothem to give me a last chance to marry Hilda and have that lovely big cheque signed, even though I am ugly and awkward.”

“But, Mr Longbothem, you defrauded George Craig of two hundred pounds with my aunt’s connivance. In fact, she refused to tell me anything about it, even when it was all over.”

“Wise woman, Peter. You see, if we were to peel Mr Craig as skilfully as he did you, it required experts—which eliminated you, of course. Why, Peter, you would have given the game away the moment I entered the bar of the Bold Forester. Aunt Dot said you couldn’t act naturally, I said you couldn’t act artificially, and we both said you couldn’t act full stop. Therefore, the best course was to keep you in the dark and hope you would help us by means of your most outstanding asset of keeping your mouth shut for a change.”

It was a mystery to me why everybody—even a stranger like Mr Longbothem—thought so lowly of my talents. When I joined the Royal Marines they tested me for perfect physical fitness, assured themselves I was ready to die for my country, trained me till I dropped exhausted, then paid me two shillings a day.

“With great respect, Mr Longbothem, I realize you find me unprepossessing to the extent that under Darwin’s law of natural selection I would become extinct in my own lifetime, but actually I’m a smartie underneath. In a sense, I’ve become a woman’s plaything, what with Hilda and Margo practically fighting over me.”

Mr Longbothem emitted that strange noise of the aged when

chuckling is accompanied by catarrh, bronchitis and loose dentures. "Hilda, poor child, did not inherit the Longbothem features, Peter."

"So things could have been worse. . . ."

"With the result that suitors have been difficult to find."

"You mean they go into hiding. . . ?"

"That is why you are on her short-list of undesirable bachelors."

"And you can't have a shorter list than one."

"Margo, on the other hand, sees you as the ideal husband because no designing females would take you from her; rather they would bring you back to her if you tried to be unfaithful."

"Could they charge me with attempted adultery?"

"No jury would convict you once they had seen you, though they might reduce it to causing a public disturbance. You'd probably be bound over to keep the peace."

"Are you saying all this to get me cheap for Hilda, Mr Longbothem?"

"I'm not saying anything like that, except don't look in that mirror over the Adam fireplace—it's a priceless Louis Quinze."

"Admittedly I'm not the local Clark Gable."

"I'm sorry if I've hurt your feelings but please don't start crying, Peter."

"I'm not crying. I'm smiling, dammit! Do I have to tell people what my face is doing? I suppose if I was laughing you'd want it in writing. And now we're being personal, Mr Longbothem, may I say how your own face wouldn't look out of place as a brass door-knocker."

Our petty altercation was interrupted by the arrival of Lady Pilkington-Goldberg dressed as a Georgian beauty on the way out. "Oh, sorry to butt in, Peter, but I've just changed into costume for the afternoon shift. Three hundred Americans are mustering in the Walled Garden for Day 5 of their Stately Homes schedule—or skedool, as they say—in their Cradles of Civilization 21-day European Coverage Tour. It has to be timed to the second because they are programmed for Hampton Court at 4.27 p.m., then Magna

Carta House before sunset."

"I was just coming," Mr Longbothem said.

"Just coming! Dressed like that! How long will it take you to change into your Regency Buck outfit?—you know full well how tight those breeches are. Get Peter to pull them on for you, then hurry down to the Vinery without delay."

"Very good, Mater."

"And find Peter a footman's livery while you're at it. Peter, darling, be an angel and help us out just this once. You don't have to say anything—just walk about regally with a silver tray and push the genuine Saxon-type mead at a dollar per goblet—six goblets for five bucks—and the venison-burgers at a dollar a time."

"Mater!" I gasped. "Surely Mr Longbothem can't be your son?"

"Oh, you know what Honners is for dressing up," Lady Pilkington-Goldberg said impatiently. "It wouldn't be so bad if he stuck to history but he's been bitten with this silly idea of portraying commoners—not that I have anything against commoners but the Americans don't want to be shown round by folks like themselves. They expect to get pomp and circumstance, not the lodger next door."

"I do not dress up," Honners emphasized coldly. "It so happens I am an actor born, but owing to my aristocratic puff it is not seemly for me to tread the boards. But for that accident of birth I should have been a top thespian and had fags named after me, like Du Maurier and De Rezke."

I still could not fully grasp the situation of Mr Longbothem turning out to be Honners in disguise. Honners was Honners, and I could not imagine anything altering the fact outside of plastic surgery. All I managed to say was, "So Aunt Dot must have known all along when she planned the operation?"

"Oh, yes, she knew, but bringing me into the plot was Margo's idea . . . please forget I said that, Peter—it slipped out. I promised Margo I wouldn't tell you."

"But Margo tells me everything."

"Naturally. She wanted to surprise you herself; that's why I had to promise not to tell a living soul, didn't I, Mater?"

"Of course, dear. It was vital that the secret should not leak out—those were my husband's very words when Honners told us you weren't to know."

"Don't you mean it was vital that the secret shouldn't leak out of the county?" I demanded. "Why wasn't I to know?"

"Aunt Dot said it would be better to tell George Craig than you, Peter," Honners explained. "That's why she had to tip Hilda off in case you met her about the cheque, but keeping that dark from Margo because she might have been jealous. That would have ruined the whole scheme, what with Margo blabbing to you about Hilda, and so you finding out about me. Then the secret would have been out."

"And I would have known it like everybody else. What beats me is the way Margo treats me, Honners. We're engaged and share all our confidences."

Honners chuckled smugly. "Women are strange creatures, Peter. They say now we're in love we'll hide nothing from each other; whereupon you tell them everything, for hours, like a sinner at the confession box in a church. They listen all ears, storing it up for the years ahead when they can play it back to you word for word like a repeat radio show, or use it at your trial. Eventually your voice starts to go, so you say now you tell me everything, darling."

"So then they do?"

"Of course, Peter. They tell you everything you've just told them, to make sure they've got it straight and not forgotten anything. Then they say isn't it wonderful to be in love and to feel we know every single thing about each other. Later, when you're married, they share your money on the same basis."

"But Margo says that everything she has is mine, Honners."

"Don't accept them—make her pay her own bills. That's why my family still operate the dowry system. It's covered by that beautiful part of the marriage service which always brings a tear to my eyes, when the bride says to our side, 'With all my worldly goods I thee endow'."

"I thought the groom said that, Honners."

"Only if he's marrying into our family. It's known as the PG Endowment Clause, obtained under special dispensation by Sir Hector Pilkington-Goldberg from Henry Eight in 1529 as a reward for being the first family in the land to switch religions and go Protestant the moment Henry quarrelled with Rome over Anne Boleyn. We've been staunch Protestants ever since, except for that difficult period under Charles One when we belonged to both Churches while Charles was trying to make his mind up one way or another. Sir Vernon Pilkington-Goldberg wrote in his diary for 1630 that he spent all his Sundays inside cathedrals, minsters and churches until he retired to bed in a confused state. However, this uncertainty ended with the defeat of Charles at Naseby in 1645, when Sir Vernon became a Roundhead under Cromwell."

"But there's that gorgeous painting of Sir Vernon in the Long Gallery dressed as a Cavalier," I reminded him.

"Ah, that was painted by Van Dyck in 1641—it's known as Van Dyck's Free Period because he died in the December of that year before we could pay him for it. But Sir Vernon was a Royalist at heart, as you can see in the subsequent work where he is portrayed at the Coronation of Charles Two, dated 1660, dressed as Master of the Revels."

"What has all this got to do with Margo and me?" I demanded, peeved at the way any conversation with Honners got bogged down in his family history. On one occasion I had merely asked him the time, with the result that I spent the rest of the morning climbing round the Pilkington-Goldberg clock-tower with him.

"Well, quite a bit really, Peter. You see, Margo is writing one of those historical sex novels."

"How do you know about that, yet I don't?"

"Naturally, I assumed you knew. I'm simply helping her with the research in our family archives, that's all. Anybody could do the same, provided he had historical records stretching back to the year dot. Obviously I don't go around saying to Margo have you told Peter about this because, after all, he is your fiancé, who might get jealous?"

"Maybe she wanted it to be another surprise for me, eh?"

"You'll certainly get a surprise when you read it," Honners smirked. "Margo sees herself as an orphaned ruff-starcher in Drury Lane. Starched ruffs becoming unfashionable, she finds herself unemployed and driven to take lover after lover until she meets the Earl of Cudford, who takes her as his mistress. The ageing Earl, ignoring the advice of his physician, wrecks the honeymoon by dying on it. However, so great is her love for the family, that she transfers her affection to the Earl's son, who, for her sixteenth birthday present, gives her a child, then presents her at the court of King Charles."

"Where all ruff-starchers end up."

"Charles falls in love with her, so she becomes one of his mistresses."

"Row five, next to Lucy Walters."

"Then her amours really start, so that even King Charles is shocked."

"She opens Parliament in the nude?"

"Even worse, Peter— she is the only lady at court who is not attended by maids."

"What's so terrible about that?"

"She's attended by footmen instead. The King exclaims, 'My court is so full of flunkeys I may have to move out!' Margo figures this kind of historical umph has come to stay. She's planning to do another one, only going right back to the Pharoahs. She's going to call it *Porn in Egypt.*"

"You really mean to say my Margo writes this sort of Merry Monarch whodunher yarns?"

"Yes, indeed—under the delightful pen-name of Polly Andry, the closest we could get to many husbands, see?"

"But she never said a word about all this to me, Honners."

"Ah, how she considers you, Peter—probably didn't want to shock you."

"Any chance of you coming on the honeymoon with us so I can be kept in the picture about what's going on between Margo and me?"

"No, thanks, Peter. Remember the old Ramsami wedding adage: Two's company, three's none—four or more is really fun."

"But how come you seem to know so much about my affairs?"

Honners looked down and up his nose. "I keep my eyes open, I put my ear to the ground, I piece two and two together, I listen to the little birds, I ask a question here and there, I talk to the servants. . . ."

"Steam open the mail, listen in on the phone, look through keyholes."

"Oh, no, no, Peter. Mind you, if I were the busybody type I must admit I could do quite well, but the fact is I'm just not interested. All I ask of life is to sit under a tree with a book, a jug of wine and. . . ."

"A pair of field-glasses."

"You are unkind, Peter, but I do not blame you. It is the fault of your breeding, not you. Nevertheless, there is something important I do not know, therefore cannot tell you. I wish I could because it concerns your marriage to Margo."

"Then don't ask me—I'd be the last person to know."

"There is a rumour which I didn't hear, you understand? If an echo of it reached me I have forgotten it, see? I discount all gossip, so I didn't even bother to listen. The few words that drifted my way I promptly dismissed from my mind because they were for your ears, not mine."

"All right, Honners, so who else in Cudford doesn't know besides me?" I demanded impatiently.

Honners looked alarmed. "Nobody knows, Peter, I swear it. How could they know when there is nothing to know? And how could I tell anybody what I haven't heard myself? In fact, if Margo tells you, let me know at once."

"Supposing even she doesn't know?"

"It's about her so she must know. Actually, the only thing I'm sure of is that she does know and you don't. Anyway, let's hope it's not true, for your sake."

"What do you mean by a snide remark like that, Honners?"

"Well, suppose it was the other way round—I was engaged and you had heard a rumour which might wreck my whole life."

"Like a visitor had slipped into the Hall without paying?"

"Be serious, Peter. You'd want the girl to tell me with her own lips, now wouldn't you? You wouldn't wish me to hear it from a third party."

"In your case I'd make sure you heard it from everybody's lips."

"Joking aside, you should ask Margo about this one next time she's telling you everything because it's too hot to wait—but don't let her know I suggested it."

"I'll use the tactful approach—I'll hint that I'm psychic. I'll say darling, I have a strange premonition that you're hiding something from me that Honners ought to know in more detail."

Honners looked extremely worried. "Don't play with it, Peter. She'll kill me—she made me swear not to tell you."

"Why did she tell you in the first place then?"

"I happened to be in the next room when she was on the phone to London and accidentally overheard her conversation. Actually I was merely checking that she wasn't using our phone for a trunk call, that's all."

"How did she discover you were listening?"

"I heard her say, 'All right then, Bonnie, I'll hold on this end while you look up the address.' Everything went quiet, and I thought she was still on the line, when suddenly I realized she was peering into my eye through the fanlight over the door. It was most embarrassing, Peter. She demanded to know what I had heard, so

I said I'd heard nothing. It just happened that Pater had asked me to fix the catch on the fanlight. Then she made me swear I wouldn't repeat a word of what I hadn't heard to you, or she would kill me for Christmas, as if I were a turkey or something. She had the nerve to accuse me of eavesdropping in my own house, if you ever heard such nausea, but I guess that's what lack of breeding does for a woman. Anyhow, I'm the last person to pry into your affairs, Peter, but I advise you to tackle her on this one the very next time she's pouring her heart out to you."

"Is there another man involved, Honners—apart from you, I mean?" I asked anxiously.

"Yes, but if we can keep it down to only one we won't be doing too badly. These days you don't have to worry unless there's a build-up."

"Say ten or more?"

"What I'm getting at, Peter, is that nowadays it's not wildly immoral if a girl has one or two men friends. I mean, a girl like Margo is bound to have the odd admirer. Look at the Mayor of Cudford—he thinks the world of her and there's a strong rumour in the air that she's to be made a Freeman of the town."

"She never told me that, Honners."

"I don't suppose she knows herself—the Mayor asked me to regard it as sub judice the moment I suggested it."

"So she'll be entitled to march through the town with fixed bayonets." I made this remark to conceal my chagrin about Margo and to stop my friend revealing even more of my love life to me. At the same time I made a mental note to have an urgent chat with Margo without the benefit of Honners' presence—such as while riding a motorbike with her on the pillion behind me.

"Would you like me to act as intermediary?" Honners inquired, as though sensing my intention.

"There's not room for three on a motorbike," I replied absent-mindedly, "and nowhere for you to hide either."

TWELVE

My customary rendezvous with Margo was Saturday afternoon when she came down from London. Unable to find anywhere to park near the flat I left the car in another street and walked round. Margo answered the door, flinging her arms round me in the lobby before I could open my mouth.

"Och, you've come at last, you wicked boy!" she exclaimed, kissing me as though I was a year or so late. "Oh, how I love your wee bristly chin—you're all man!"

"I haven't changed much since last week, Margo."

"Och, how could you leave me so long alone?"

"Actually I'm two or three minutes early, dear."

Margo ran her hands over me like an octopus checking a new rock. "You look weary, darling. Would you be wanting to go to bed the noo'?"

"But it's only tea-time, Margo. . . ."

"We don't have to stay in bed, yew daftie."

"But it sounds as if you have company in the flat."

"Och, just a friend or two. You see, Peter, I've been so worried about us that I daren't be alone. I must surround myself with one or two friends to stop me thinking."

"Thinking what, Margo?"

"Thinking about you, Peter. If I think about you any more I'll go mad—mad, d'ye hear?"

I wondered which of my personal qualities drove women insane, but I stopped wondering because Margo ran her hands passionately through my red hair until the pain in my scalp brought tears to my eyes.

"You're crying, Peter," she exclaimed in surprise. "Surely you haven't guessed what has happened?"

"I didn't need to guess—I can feel the roots coming out."

"I mean about us. Can you imagine how I feel about it, Peter?"

"I'm positive I feel it more than you do."

Margo pulled me so close to her that my face warped under the pressure of her own beautiful features, one of her high cheek bones flattening my right eyeball in its socket. "I am a woman, Peter," she informed me confidentially, in case I thought I was caught between automatic doors, "and sometimes I feel more than a woman."

"Your mother was expecting triplets?" I suggested.

"So I do not try to hide my sex, you understand?"

"That would be like trying to hush up the *Queen Mary* when she sails into New York."

"Nor do I conceal the fact that I like men's company."

"It sounds as if the flat is full of them," I observed. Now I knew why I couldn't find a parking space in this street.

"Oh, those! My darlings are just trying to help me forget."

"Judging by the racket in there I should have thought they were helping you to remember."

"Now, Peter, we've got to sort this thing out dispassionately before it ruins both our lives. So what is the next step?"

"Ask some of them to leave so we can get in?"

"No, we must have a serious tête-à-tête right now."

"But I don't even know what the trouble is, Margo."

"You don't! Can't you guess, Peter?"

"You need a bigger flat perhaps?"

"Och, you poor boy—Honners hasn't told you!"

"I suspect he wants to marry you—but don't they all?"

Margo lowered her black lashes modestly. "Oh, darling, that's gorgeous, though it does sound a wee bit like you don't trust me. Yew're the only man for me, you know that. I don't even look at another fellow. Let me tell you all about it. . . ."

Margo's confession was interrupted by the opening of the door by the Mayor of Cudford, backed by several of his aldermen from the local Council. "Ah, there you are, Margo!" he cried, throwing out his arms. "How can we start the dance without you?"

"Dance!" I exclaimed. Over his head I glimpsed Paul, Marcus

and several other members from the club.

"Hallo, there, Peter," the Mayor enthused. "Come inside and have yourself a dance, boy!"

"Just excuse me a second, Peter," Margo whispered, kissing me farewell. "I did promise the Mayor the first dance."

Attracted by the gramophone music I entered the flat to dance, but although I searched the place I couldn't locate a girl to ask. I said to Paul, "Where are the women then?"

Without taking his eyes off Margo he replied, "Oh, Bonnie will be back soon with some more Scotch . . . ah, just watch me cut in on the Mayor."

It seemed the quick-step ration with Margo was two paces before someone jumped forward and excuse-me'd, except when Marcus refused to give her up, causing Paul and Alec to dance together in the confusion. Seizing the opportunity I strode over boldly and cut in on Marcus. "Make way for the lucky bridegroom!" I said, and everybody laughed. For the first time in my life I found myself dancing with Margo and eight men, traversing the floor in a solid block of rhythm.

"The darlings are helping me to forget, Peter," she called to me over the heads of her partners as I was ousted to the periphery of the group.

"Yet you still remember my name," I called back.

Margo sighed madonna like. "The doctor said I need company; I mustn't be left alone till the shock is over."

"You'll be all right next Saturday—I'll take you to Highbury and we'll watch Arsenal. They expect a gate of fifty thousand—nearly all men."

"Oh, lovely! I haven't been so spoiled since Cudford Rugby Club took me on their French tour as their mascot."

"I can guess who won," I retorted sourly. Retiring from the fray I took up position by the door, ready to pounce on Bonnie the minute she returned. There were five men standing near the door, most of whom I recognized, and they told me to move to the end of the queue because they also were waiting for Bonnie. I explained how I was leaving, not waiting for Bonnie, so they let me out. I figured it would be smart to meet Bonnie in the lobby, but there were two men tossing a coin by the main entrance, apparently to decide who should dance with Bonnie first, so I explained how I was leaving the party. I figured it would be smart to meet Bonnie in the street, but outside I bumped into the Town Clerk. I asked him if he was leaving the party and he said no, he was waiting for Bonnie and trusted I was shoving off home.

I said I was, because my alert mind figured Bonnie would be returning from the off-licence with the Scotch, so I set off in that direction. Outside the off-licence I found three Justices of the Peace, who informed me I was fifth on Bonnie's dance card, the winner being inside the shop paying for the booze Bonnie was collecting for the party. I paused until he had paid the bill, then glided into the shop and stood behind Bonnie.

"I don't want the next dance," I said simply, in case she thought I was the head of the queue from the flat to the off licence. "Just tell me what Margo's trouble is, Bonnie. Is it another man—or another men?"

Bonnie looked into my eyes sadly. "Hasn't she told you, my poor Peter?"

"You have deduced correctly, dear, with feminine intuition. I am asking you because Margo has not told me."

"Oh, dear! Why hasn't she told you there is another man?"

"Because I cannot force my way through the men in her life to hear about one of them in particular. All I know is that she has suffered a shock and must not be left alone, rather like Joan of Arc surrounded by the French Army. She says they are helping her to forget."

"Forget what, Peter?"

"Forget there are other women in Britain, I guess."

Bonnie sighed. "I still think it would be best that she breaks the news to you herself, Peter. But I want you always to remember this, darling—you still have me by your side. I am lonely, too, you know."

"Does lonely have a different meaning in Scotland, Bonnie? At the last count there's over a dozen men waiting for you—three of them outside this shop and one right here with his arm round you, praying for me to disappear."

Bonnie lowered her eyes bashfully. "Och, Peter, men! Any girl can get a man—but can any girl get you?"

"They sure can if they'd only mention it to me. I'm hard to get because nobody seems to want me." I said this merely for time to work out the implication of Bonnie's last remark. Last year I had joined the Lonely Hearts' Dance Club, and when the organizer saw I was the only member not dancing during the Ladies' Choice Waltz she gave me a kettle and told me to make the tea for the intermission. Later, when I stood up right in front ready for the Ladies' Invitation Foxtrot, the same lady came across to me and said she would allow me to break the club rule the following week by bringing my own partner to the dance. This concession struck me as odd because you could only join the Lonely Hearts if you didn't have a partner. When I pointed this out to her she as good as hinted that if I turned up next week unaccompanied I wouldn't get in. Next day I asked Hilda if she would come with me so I would be admitted, but when she learned it was the Lonely Hearts Dance she slammed the phone down.

With regard to my problem of Margo I decided to sleep on it, which was our family motto for both love and business, first adopted by an uncle of mine who made mattresses. I still had a trump card to play in the Margo stakes, contained in a bottle of Bronzo and labelled The Golden Tan of Aussie-Land, as used by Stars of Stage and Screen. Although this product was advertised in *Family Help* as Liquid Allure for Men and referred to in the text as Bottled Sunshine, many of the ladies used it on their legs in place of stockings.

Before applying the lotion I extracted the wadding from a bottle of aspirins and packed it up my left nostril in order to support that side of my nose which had collapsed following my fight with Bugler Bleach of the Royal Artillery six months earlier. The press said of me at the time that I was always most dangerous in combat when I had my back to the floor, as the soldier discovered to his cost when I regained my feet and broke his right hand with my nose.

Then I moulded the cottonwool by gently pressing my nose, at the same time gradually encouraging it to centralize itself on my face. The result was quite satisfactory, the wadding shoring up the left side of the nose and enabling me to breathe through the right nostril.

The next task in my beauty treatment was to apply Bronzo to my face, ears and neck with the tiny paint-brush supplied by the makers. The lotion went on like thin emulsion paint, pleasantly cool and quick drying. In the light of my bedroom my countenance appeared to be more yellow than bronzed, so I applied a second coat to deepen the hue, as recommended in the instructions for those seeking a tropical tan. The mirror revealed that the new face clashed badly with my red hair, but apart from that I was pleased with the results, even if I did wish for more sunburn and less of the buttery yellow.

Finally, I donned a white shirt for contrast, then my new cream Bondi Beach suit. Consulting the leaflet, I observed the bronzed Adonis therein surrounded by adoring girls as he debonairly stepped from his plane into the blizzard enveloping Croydon airport. Despite the snow he was clad in khaki tropical kit, permitting us to perceive that he had used Bronzo on his knees too. Furthermore, he sported sun-glasses, but whether as protection from the tropical sun or snow blindness was not clear.

I suffered two setbacks before repairing to Margo's flat in my glamorous new make-up. The first was when I daringly dabbed *Napoleon's Secret,* the irresistible after-shave, on my jaw and observed my countenance turn white from the nose downwards as the after-shave acted like paint-stripper on a door. The effect was quite alarming until I re-painted that region of my face with two coats to match up with the rest of my features, and skilfully eradicated the join with my finger.

The second shock came when, pleased with the overall impression, I winked at myself in the mirror. The eye I had closed flashed white, like an indicator on a switchboard. I winked the other eye with the same result, but soon put the matter aright by painting Bronzo on my lids. At last I was satisfied with my appearance, so, giving a final adjustment to my nose for centre, I strode confidently from the building to take Margo by storm.

Although it was twenty-four hours since my last call on Margo, I still could not park in her street, and once again the mayoral Daimler was standing outside her house. Parking two blocks away I walked round and knocked on the door of the flat. I was somewhat taken aback to be greeted by Honners, and Honners seemed somewhat taken aback to see me. Recovering his wits he said, "Where's your banjo then?"

"What do you mean, where's my banjo?" I demanded.

"I thought you were a Kentucky Minstrel, Peter. It is Peter, isn't it?"

"Of course it's me."

"Come in then and say you're the cabaret for the party."

"What party?"

"Oh, Margo's throwing a party for the Mayor and Council."

"But she had a party yesterday."

"Yes, this is the same one. I'm on the evening shift today. Come inside and I'll introduce you."

"You can start by introducing me to Margo."

"Ah, Margo is under the doctor and can't stand a shock. I'll warn her you're here and have changed colour—all you need now is a turban. Just between ourselves, Peter, why did you come in disguise tonight?"

"Actually, I am not in disguise. I merely put on the glam to fight the competition. I'm not the sort to lose Margo without a struggle.

"Well, you'd better struggle first with Paul. The man's so infatuated with her that we've had to pull him off her twice already. Follow me."

Honners introduced me to the nearest group, where Doctor Evans, the town's Medical Officer of Health, seemed to greet me more as an epidemic than a guest, inquiring if I was suffering from yellow jaundice.

"Sunburn," I told him coldly. "I've just returned from an expedition to Skegness."

"Hallo, dere, Massa Bones," Marcus cried with his silly giggle. "Your name came up at lunch today."

"Then our lunch followed suit," Honners smirked.

"Actually we were discussing how you were taking the bad news."

"I'm taking it very well considering I'm the only one who hasn't heard it."

"Oh, tactless me! Still, Doctor Evans here will give you a sedative on the house when you do. That's women for you—off with the new love and on with the old."

"Surely it's not the Mayor?"

"I think Margo should break it to you herself, Peter, alone."

"Like when she's in the bath?"

"But don't take it too much to heart. Remember what the song says—Somewhere, someone is waiting for you."

"They must have written that song for buses, not me."

At that moment I caught sight of Margo waving to me over the crowd, so I pushed my way through to her with an anxious heart. Women are usually so fussy about clothes that it struck me as odd how Margo's never seemed to fit properly. She had to be continually hitching up her off-the-shoulder blouse one side, then re-parking her hair behind her left ear, until the next movement of her body or turn of her head brought the entire ensemble down again.

Moreover, she bought skirts which were apparently designed for standing up only, splitting open when she walked and disappearing completely when she sat down. If she dropped anything she could only pick it up by slowly kneeling down as if to pray. When she laughed—which was often—she had to hold herself together, then re-button the blouse and pull it down to meet the skirt.

"My poor darling, what have they done to you?" she cried dramatically, falling to pieces in the process. "Have you been in a terrible fire, Peter?"

"I am sunburnt," I explained wearily. "Maybe I should wear a placard on my chest marked 'Business as usual during alterations'."

"But your poor nose, darling! What has happened to it?"

"It's come up for air, that's all. I've propped it up from inside, like a tent. If I could stretch a guy-rope to my right ear I could get it dead centre."

"But I liked it flat and bent, Peter. It made you different."

"It also made me extremely unpopular with ordinary folks. Apart from you, nobody else regarded it as a kind of beauty spot. There was nothing in the glossy magazines about having your nose flattened for a romantic summer cruise this year."

"Och, with a man it doesn't matter!"

"I know. It doesn't matter till he meets girls. The silly creatures give the game away by screaming with terror."

"I never screamed, darling."

"With great respect, Margo, you wouldn't scream if I had a third eye and wore glasses to match. Anyway, enough of this love talk. I must speak to you alone, dear."

"Yes, of course, darling. Come into my bedroom where it won't be so noisy."'

It was much quieter in Margo's bedroom, away from the music. With only the Mayor and his alderman to break the silence, we were able to converse in peace. Margo whispered in my ear that she could hardly turn them out because there was not room in the lounge for them, so she made them promise not to listen. She sat on the bed and immediately her skirt disappeared, leaving her long bare legs to dominate the room by dividing it in two, like a Continental check-point barrier.

Before we could begin, the Mayor insisted on Scotch all round for a toast to Beauty, whereupon everybody drank to Margo, then looked pointedly at my face as though silently adding the Beast to complete the phrase. Margo acknowledged the compliment by holding both my hands and drawing me very close to her bust.

"Prepare yourself for the worst, darling," she whispered, letting her hair fall forward into my face.

"Surely not in front of the Council, Margo?" I protested.

"I mean about us. To cut a long story short, Peter, I can't marry you. It's not just you—I can't marry anyone."

"But you didn't tell me you'd been to the doctor, sweetheart."

"No, no, Peter, you don't understand. It's wee Harold."

"His memory is too strong in your mind?"

"He's been found, darling."

"So you're a widow?"

"He's alive! He was found in the mountains by the Kinetis, the legendary Lost Tribe of Borneo."

"But I thought they were still lost, Margo."

"They didn't know they were lost until they found Harold. He told them. He said he was lost, too, but at least he realized it."

"How do you know all this if it's true?"

"Well, it took Harold over two years to convince them that they were lost, just as much as he was. Their argument was that they knew the route back to Brunei on the coast, whereas Harold did not. He had tried many times to find it on his own but on each occasion the Kinetis had to rescue him, either lowering him down from the mountains or hauling him up from the valleys. Once he climbed so far that he actually glimpsed the coast and the Macassar Strait on the horizon, but this was the barren east coast, not the west coast where Brunei is, and but for the Kinetis finding him he would have starved to death. Eventually the Kineti headman agreed to send Harold back to Brunei under escort rather than having to keep rescuing him, saying something like 'You lost, we lost—now get lost!"

I shrugged my shoulders resignedly. "So, provided wee Harold can find his way back to England, it's all off, Margo?"

"I can't marry you, Peter, but we can still be good friends," she replied, flattening me across the bed on my back and kissing me as good friends do, until I had to cry for mercy, being in immediate danger of asphyxiation.

"Whatever have I done to your nose, darling?" Margo asked tenderly, kissing that organ where it had buckled under pressure.

I tried to keep up a semblance of romance while I extracted the wadding from the left nostril so I could breathe once more. By looking downwards I could no longer see any nose with my right eye, whereas there appeared a lot of it under my left eye. Hurriedly secreting the cotton-wool in my pocket I smiled winsomely at Margo. "Sorry, darling," I whispered lovingly. "Your kiss caught me unawares and my nose collapsed under the strain. My fault for not testing it before I came here."

"Oh, my poor wee boy, why don't you try plastic surgery?"

I lay there in Margo's arms silently cursing my inability to make love like other men without this endless discussion about my features and how to remedy my face. How, I asked myself, could I ever engender that romantic atmosphere of the film lovers when one's sweetheart kissed you so passionately that your nose collapsed in a heap and she suggested plastic surgery? To add to my discomfiture I was alarmed to see small blotches of yellow disfiguring Margo's soft mouth where she had kissed me. Surely I had not started to run like a badly painted watercolour under the heat of my embarrassment?

Margo seemed to sense my concern with feminine intuition. "Please don't worry about your face, darling," she consoled me. "It only makes you miserable—you never laugh nowadays like you used to."

This remark hit home because I had not laughed for three weeks, ever since two of my front teeth had been knocked out playing rugby for Cudford, who were so permanently at the bottom of the league table that every match was like a battle for life itself. Moreover, I was determined not to laugh until the dentist had fixed me up. Meantime, I had practised the difficult technique of laughing with my mouth shut or burying my head in my hands in a paroxysm of mirth.

"My advice to you is to stop trying to pretty yourself, Peter. I like you for what you are."

"Hideous?"

"No, darling, don't listen to people who call you hideous. You're manly and rugged. Women don't want their men to be pretty."

"Well, they can never accuse me of that, Margo. Hilda even went so far as to call me pretty ugly."

"I don't think you're ugly, darling, nor does Bonnie."

"I'm beginning to think your family would consider a rhinoceros as the ideal household pet."

"So for goodness sake stop being self-conscious about your teeth."

"You noticed?"

"Only when we kiss—your lips sag. But I like that."

"What about when I smile?"

"I find that romantic—it reminds me of Traitor's Gate at the Tower of London."

I decided to change the subject before my confidence waned completely. "Listen, darling; your news has been a bitter blow to me, naturally, but I'd like to make the most of the time left before wee Harold returns from the Far East. How much longer have we together?"

I was puzzled by the way Margo consulted her watch in connection with my question, because I knew the dial did not contain a date box. "About ten minutes, honey," she replied.

"About ten minutes! But it takes weeks from Borneo."

"Not on these flying-boats. He's due here at five o'clock. That's the whole idea of the party. Fancy having my husband and my fiancé in the flat together!"

"If wee Jock turned up we'd have a full house," I observed sourly. This world of husbands, fiancés and lovers in which Margo lived was beginning to tell on my nerves, especially now I had to bid farewell to her in the bedroom, surrounded by Cudford Town Council.

Margo sensed my distress. "Don't bother about the Mayor and the Aldermen, darling. Just let's have one last fling together."

"This is hardly the time to dance, dear, even if there was room."

"Oh, Peter, you know what I mean—the traditional Skagh farewell. Don't be shy—carry on like when there's just the two of us alone."

"But we've never been alone, Margo. There's always just you and me, plus half of Cudford playing gooseberry. The only time I got you on my own was when I took you into Woolworths so we could be surrounded by strangers who didn't know you."

Margo enveloped me with arms and hair. "Och, my poor Peter, let me make up for it now. . . ."

Her threat was mercifully thwarted by the door bells chiming in the lobby. "That must be wee Harold at last, Margo, so let Peter get up," the Mayor announced, as though refereeing a bout.

Margo made lightning pantomime of tidying herself for the return of her husband, then hurried excitedly forth as the cry went up that wee Harold was indeed on the threshold.

I watched the reunion across the room with a heavy heart, marvelling how anyone could have made a failure of his life at such an early stage of it. Now that I was back on the shelf again, it did not boost my morale to reflect that I was banned from the Lonely Hearts' Dance Club, and when I visited Cudford Palais de Dance I always sat there surrounded by empty chairs as if I carried a death-ray gun which swept my immediate area. Last year's

Halloween Ball was still fresh in my mind, where the M.C. insisted I remove my mask at midnight despite my protestations that I had already done so. One particularly inebriated reveller kept shouting, "Unmask! Unmask!" and tried to snatch my face off.

Unexpectedly, a small voice beside me whispered, "You've lost her, Peter."

Glancing around I saw it was Bonnie. "The moral is don't fool around with married women," I jested sadly.

Bonnie looked at the floor shyly. "You've always got me, Peter. I can help you forget."

With my finger under her chin I lifted up her face. It was incredibly soft and feminine, like women should be who are about to help you forget—so much so that I kissed her gently on both cheeks. "By the way things are going, Bonnie, it looks like you've always got me, too," I whispered in her ear.

"Let's say we've always got each other, darling."

I smiled bravely through my tears, which welled up in the left eye only owing to a recent injury in training. "Every cloud has a silver lining," I replied. In love situations one has to use clichés for romantic effect, otherwise one sounds insincere. As a writer I was well equipped in this art, being quite prepared to walk hand in hand together into the sunset if necessary.

"I want you to know I love you for what you are, Peter, not for what you look like. I don't think you're ugly."

"That's like telling an elephant you don't think he's big."

"All things are relative, Peter."

"But I have to compete with other men, not elephants."

Bonnie kissed the stricken area firmly. "Just you listen to me, Peter. I'm going to fix you up. Your hair has already turned pink where it's growing out, so that will cure itself. The doctor says your right eye will open within a fortnight, and you've already asked the dentist to replace your front teeth. As for this yellow stuff on your face, that's going already in places and should be clear by tomorrow. That only leaves your nose."

"Honners says it looks like a train ran through and flattened the level-crossing gates."

"Never mind what Honner's says—Daddy says he knows a man in London who can lift it for you and re-centre it."

"With a breakdown crane?"

"No, with plastic surgery; he's a specialist."

"But you said just now that I wasn't ugly."

"You're not ugly, dear—you're handsome underneath but you're unlucky at sport and games, that's all. Give up boxing and rugby for a little while."

"Say ten years or so?"

"Only for a season. You'll never regret it."

"O.K., Bonnie, but there's just one stipulation I'd like to make about all this. I don't want to end up pretty. Girls should be pretty, not men."

"I shouldn't worry too much on that score darling. I promise not to make you pretty. They can do wonderful things these days but not miracles."

"I should like to be just debonairly fascinating—the irresistible charmer. People will whisper there goes Beau Pook, the handsome devil—so attractive with an eye each side of his nose, and his mouth underneath containing teeth. Just look how he can open both eyes at the same time."

"He's a plastic surgeon, dear, not a magician. I was speaking to Daddy the other day about your face, and he believes with any luck Dr Laski may be able to shorten your mouth that end where it was torn, so that when your nose is recentred there'll be the same amount of lips each side of it."

"You positive I won't look effeminate, Bonnie? I wouldn't want folks thinking I was a matinée idol or something."

"I promise, darling."

"And you'll love me just the same as when I was plain?"

"Even more. I shall be possessively jealous of you."

"You needn't worry about me, dear—I'm not just a woman's

plaything. Bruce Bold taught me how to overcome it by physical culture, so I don't have to bother about other girls any more, provided I take the tablets every two hours."

Bonnie laughed and made to kiss me, so I turned my head slightly to the left where I had more lips available and hoped she wouldn't notice the onset of muscle-flutter in my pectoralis major as we embraced. Then we walked hand in hand together into the sunset.

Not easy from a flat—but fortunately love is blind.

END

If you enjoyed reading
"Beau Pook Proposes",
you can follow more of Pook's adventures in
"Pook's Curiosity Shop".

An extract follows.

POOK'S CURIOSITY SHOP

So many readers requested a sequel to *Pook in Business* that *Pook's Curiosity Shop* was a must.

This time Pook enters the high class antique world in partnership with the beautiful Olga, and financed by Honners. At once we plunge into the antique dealer's life of auctions, private buying and other means of unearthing the treasures essential to this unique trade.

Set against Pook's accurate background of business practice we see our hero encounter the hazards of the profession in the shape of eccentric dealers, awkward customers and difficult situations. In his search for success Pook meets the girl of his dreams, the lovely female Viking called Tora, while Olga is wooed by Yosseff, a wealthy Arab prince.

The resultant havoc is a hilarious romance, but the book will have an additional appeal to everybody who has paused by the window of an old curiosity shop.

POOK'S CURIOSITY SHOP

ONE

When a big operator like me goes into business he needs premises in the heart of the city among the commercial giants along High Street. With my kind of capital there is only one way to do this. You select a site between Tesco and Boots, then during each evening you wheel your hot chestnuts barrow there and park it to catch the cinema trade.

But you can't conduct an antiques' gallery from a barrow, so you find a shop as near High Street as possible without having to visit Tesco by bus. I found Mortimer's Hairdressing Salon midway down London Road—a business thoroughfare aptly named because it led to London when one left Cudford, and as Mortimer's was number 975 I gained the impression that it was nearer London than Cudford. London Road actually started from High Street—'Adjacent Main Multiple Shopping Area' the advert stated, but what it did not state was that London Road was one of the longest streets in Britain, like a motorway with shops, and to reach number 975 I walked as far as I could, then boarded a bus.

Another interesting point about Mortimer's was the ancient red-tiled roof and walls above the shop. I discovered later that these dated back to 1700, when the building had been a farmhouse in the village of Half Horseball Norton on the turnpike road to London, before being swallowed up by Cudford.

The shop was vacant because Mr Mortimer had died at an advanced age, though rumour had it that he had drowned. Drowned very slowly over a period of some sixty years in the public bar of the Flying Bull Inn, an ordeal which had given him a nose similar to a mandarin orange. Hence I was able to purchase the premises freehold for what would appear to be a ridiculous price today of £2,100—'inc. goodwill, fix. & fittings'.

Both goodwill and fixtures were to give me considerable problems in the months ahead when I was struggling to convert the premises from a barber-shop to an antique gallery. Although I had painted over the facia-board my new trade name of *Nostalgia*, customers still entered demanding a short-back-and-sides, shampoo and singe. Another aspect of the goodwill took the form of customers who insisted they should escort me next door to the Flying Bull for a hair tonic, as they phrased it. Some of them who had already visited the Flying Bull called me Harold and inquired how my gout was, or asked if my old woman was still at it.

The fittings and fixtures were a big stumbling block, being in the main irremovable. The five great shampoo basins might have come from Ancient Rome, let into solid blocks of white marble which apparently held up that side of the building. I feared that any attempt to remove them would lead to the collapse of the party wall I shared with the butcher next door. The walls themselves were decorated with massive Edwardian plate-glass mirrors inscribed with gold Gothic lettering exhorting us to use

Parker's Pomade in our fight against dandruff, baldness and grey hair. I proved by experiment that these mirrors were also irremovable, being welded to the walls by huge plugs, as though the craftsmen of the Edwardian era feared that one day Cudford would be the centre of an earthquake zone and consequently we must needs trade from retail forts.

Another prominent snag was the barber's pole outside the shop on the right hand side, painted in the traditional red and-white spiral to inform the passing carriage folk that here they could have their wigs combed and powdered. This nine foot pole left me weak and trembling in my efforts to remove it. The securing bolts had long since rusted into the damps, making me feel I was struggling to remove the bowsprit from HMS *Victory* single-handed. Nor could I saw it into sections, for time and weather seemed to have fossilized the wood into a kind of bog-oak. Eventually I solved the problem by affixing a metal plate to the pole which bore the legend: 'Rare example of Medieval Maypole, *circa* A.D. 1400, originally set up at Half Horseball Norton's annual Maid-and-Shepherds Fair, 1297-1836.'

Oddly enough, this exhibit was to become such a success that I could have sold it time and again to the American market if only I could have wrenched it from the building. However, necessity being the mother of invention, I arranged for our local carpenter, Gus Piper, to supply me with medieval maypoles which he constructed from as many old boat masts as I could lay hands on.

As you may remember from *Pook in Business,* I had served a hard apprenticeship to the trade of some nine years, starting off without knowing a thing about it, yet staving off bankruptcy until my premises had become so valuable because of regional development that I was able to make a profit at last by selling the shop itself.

This time Olga was determined I should make good, so she began reforming me right from the start. I don't know if you have ever experienced women trouble, and I don't know if you have ever suffered business problems, but if you've ever had them both together you have my sympathy. Olga's current campaign was to stop me smoking so we could meet the mortgage payments and keep me fitter for work. I assured her that smoking was the only vice left to me; that without it I should be unbearable. She thought this was strange because I was unbearable with it. I assured her that it was perfectly normal in our English climate to have a cough from November to May—in fact, foreigners dubbed it the English malaise. I showed her how smoking did actually stop coughing if she would let me have a cigarette—as it did for a full ten minutes.

But Olga was adamant that I give it up completely. To this end she took me to church with a mouth full of boiled sweets in order to strengthen my resolve and to put the Archbishop of Canterbury between me and tobacco. In my pocket reposed a packet of twenty, supplied by Olga so that I should never feel completely cut off from the habit. Unfortunately I had smoked them the moment her back was turned.

"No need to worry any more, Peter," Olga informed me as we sang *Fight the Good Fight.* "Always remember there's the sealed packet of twenty in your pocket to boost your morale, and the boiled sweets will take away the craving."

I smiled gratefully at Olga over the hymn-book, thinking how handy the altar candles would be to light up from. I felt guilty as only a smoker can, standing there with the empty packet in my pocket, a half empty packet hidden in my waistband, a box of matches secreted in a handkerchief and six panatella cigars lodged in the top of my right sock. Also about my person was a tiny box of snuff and a deodorant aerosol for my mouth.

"Thank you for helping me give it up, love," I mumbled, wondering if her sensitive nostrils would smell the tobacco warehouse standing next to her. My sense of guilt was so strong in this religious environment that I momentarily feared I might be punished by bursting into flames, like the burning bush.

"Smell the incense, Peter—that's all the smoke you should ever inhale," Olga smiled, sucking her share of it through her lovely nostrils.

I had already noted the censer with interest, a figured brass objet d'art circa Late Georgian that would look well in my shop. Throughout the hymn and the Lesson about driving the money-changers from the Temple it dawned on me more and more how this beautiful old church resembled a high-class Antiques' Gallery with music. The bronze Lectern and the silver candlesticks particularly caught my eye, so I made a mental note to call on the

Vicar as soon as possible.

Where I had gone wrong on my last venture in this field was my inability to resist the junk side of the business. Most of the junk came with the good pieces, especially at auction sales, so that one prize of a Victorian brass lantern clock with a French movement would be knocked down to you with its accompanying retinue of fairground china, bamboo pot-stand, Edwardian multi-knife-polisher, trousers-press and twelve rolls of wall-paper. Junk came in even larger quantities when you cleared a house, right from the perks in the parlour to the mops in the scullery.

Junk sells fast but unfortunately it ruins the classy side of the business, like selling crashed car components in a Rolls showroom. So I had brought Olga into the business to keep it strictly haut monde, uncluttered by the push-chairs, jelly moulds and assorted magazines of the general dealer. She was an excellent salesgirl, having long replaced the dog as man's best friend, and, wearing her little black dress, as she always phrased it, could certainly handle the male clients.

"Peter, meet Yosseff," she said, soon after we had opened. "Yosseff is studying over here. He is a prince."

Yosseff held up his beringed hands. "Not a prince, my pretty one, please. In my country I am nothing, just a mere princeling. But for our oil I should be poor."

"Does he intend buying anything?" I whispered urgently, taken aback by this handsome student with the white teeth.

"Wants to buy me!" Olga hissed with wide eyes.

"What did he offer?"

"He's rich. Will buy the shop plus stock if I go with it."

"How rich?"

"Well, I don't know what sort of a grant he gets for college, but his private income is £1,327,480 per annum, tax free. It's the oil, you know."

"Is he at Cudford University, Olga?"

"Yes, darling. Says he is learning so much there about geology that he would like to buy the place at the end of the course and take it back home with him. Isn't he ridiculously dishy, Peter, even in European clothes!"

"And no camel."

"Don't be jealous, Peter, just because he says I'm the most ravishing creature he has ever met."

"Pretty quiet in the desert, dear. Maybe you're the first woman he's seen."

"Oh, he's so incredibly romantic and dreamy—I could give myself to him over the counter."

"Move the glass and china clear first, Olga."

I did not worry over much because Olga could always handle the fellows, and she certainly attracted business. Sometimes she seemed to think I was not the world's greatest lover, but as I told her, the highest romance of all was the thrill of commerce. With feminine meticulousness Olga was stocking only good class merchandise, which she catalogued and ticketed as if we were Bond Street. The trash she threw out ruthlessly, often directly into my lap if small enough, or into the yard when I carted home double-beds and picture-frames.

"Price your space, Peter, and stop crying over the junk," she counselled me. "You have to choose between a thirty bob pram and an Edwardian inlaid mahogany china cabinet at sixty guineas."

"But the pram cost us nothing, Olga. They threw it in so I could carry away all these potted plants, free."

"Those plants died soon after you were born. Now you've got eight sticks of fossilized wood embedded in concrete."

"We can still sell the pots, Olga—tanner a time."

Olga sighed. "Why don't you go the whole hog and set up as a rag-and-bone man with a barrow? We could fill the windows with scrap-iron and jam jars."

"You're so right, Olga."

She was right, of course, but the waste appalled me. I took all the junk I could manage round to my general dealer friends, like Eddie Flaxmon who sold everything from a bath with geyser still attached to it, down to old copies of John Bull magazine. They did not pay me a fortune but at least it kept me in petrol for my station-wagon. This vehicle was surmounted by a huge roof-rack, seven feet long by four feet wide, that would carry anything up to a three-piece suite—the two armchairs cradled in the settee. Behind I towed my trailer, converted from a horse-box, so I had virtually a one-man pantechnicon. This ensured us cheap speedy transport available at all times, so essential in this business.

Olga transformed the showroom, as she now called our shop, by having me decorate the place with three coats of emulsion paint. Her colour scheme consisted of

Egyptian Gold Walls, white woodwork and wine red drapes—real classy effect when completed. I solved the problem of the marble basins by boarding them over to form a long display counter down one side of the showroom.

The worst expense was the deep wine carpet, wall to wall, upon which began to appear familiar objets d'art ticketed with very unfamiliar names. In fact I had never heard of them. For instance, a Victorian ebonized sideboard with glazed ends was now listed as a Period Credenza, and an Edwardian inlaid mahogany china cabinet turned out to be a Superb Vitrine. An Edwardian inlaid rosewood writing-table with inset leather top proved to be a Lady's Bonheur du Jour.

"How on earth were you in the trade so long, yet learned so little, Peter?" Olga demanded, hearing my exclamations of "Fancy that!" and "You could have fooled me!" as I walked round the exhibits.

"That is a trade secret, darling," I jested.

"I'll tell you why. Because you suffered from junk on the brain, that's why. You were so engrossed in selling sixpenny gas-brackets and flock mattresses that you went bust."

"And I didn't have your exquisite taste, Olga. I bought all wrong, then chased the pennies instead of the pounds. I was my own worst enemy. The miracle was I lasted so long. I should be thankful I've got you behind me now—as you know I am."

Agreeing wholeheartedly with Olga on everything not only saved time and energy but also took her mind off one's shortcomings. Otherwise she was liable to drag up smoking when she wasn't with me to act as chaperon between myself and the Devil. Personally, I found it pretty tough being a man and having to cope with tobacco, drink, horses and women, none of which bothered Olga at all.

"How do you like the decor of the showroom, now, Peter?"

"Just can't recognize the place, dear. A fantastic job. Flowers too. Let's only hope we can sell the stuff and pay Honners his interest."

My old friends Honners—the Hon. Lesley Pilkington-Goldberg—had put up all the cash for our venture, and he called every day to ensure that his money was safe or at least being properly used.

"You have to speculate before you can accumulate, Peter. Don't expect a fortune overnight."

"The awful thing about establishing a business is the outlay, dear. Nothing coming in, yet money pouring out in every direction. At least when I was broke there was practically no expenditure."

Olga smiled her beautiful smile which was to become familiar to me as her successful sales smile. "The tide has turned already, Peter. I have made our first sale. Remember Item 7, late Victorian Samovar in Burnished Copper which I purchased for £10? Well, I have sold same for twenty-five guineas!"

"Collapse of stout partner! Brilliant! Who bought it, dear?"

"Yosseff. He has decided to collect special pieces to take back to his palace when he finally leaves Britain."

"Good work, honey, but isn't that an awful lot of profit?"

"In our business one charges what the market will pay. I went to great trouble buying that samovar, and you spent nearly half a day polishing it up from black with Brillo pads, so our profit is not excessive. You go out and buy the right goods at the right prices, then leave me to sell them to our best advantage."

I looked at Olga with new admiration. We were trading in the happy days before Value Added Tax, and before those excellent television programmes had popularized antiques to the extent that nothing was sacred any more, prices rocketed and bargains became almost non-existent. The days when dealers were still breaking up Victorian washstands as useless and throwing out brass bedsteads for scrap. But best of all they were the days when exciting finds could be made for next to nothing, even at the auction sales. By today's standards we bought ridiculously cheap and sold ridiculously cheap, but there was a worthwhile profit in between. In my previous business I grossed three pounds for every pound I spent, but as the job was labour-intensive I certainly earned it—bargaining, transporting, repairing, cleaning and polishing.

Just to make your mouth water—and a dealer's heart bleed—we were buying walnut canterburys and dumbwaiters for thirty shillings, mahogany knee-hole desks for seven pounds, tub chairs for two pounds, brass fire-irons for a pound or less, and rosewood sideboards for three pounds. On the other hand, you could still rent a shop for two pounds a week and if you could net a thousand a year you felt like a millionaire.

"Now, Peter, your job is to supply me with stock—I'll do the vending," Olga told me at our Daily Orders meeting. "Don't waste time in the Bold Forester because those layabouts in there are a bad influence on you."

"Birds of a feather flock together, Olga," I agreed.

"Go straight to Mellon's Auction Galleries and bid for the items I have marked, but don't get carried away and pay more than I have pencilled in, understand?"

"A fool and his money are soon parted, Olga."

"Mind you're early so you can get a good position right underneath Mr Mellon's nose on the rostrum."

"The early bird catches the worm, Olga."

"And the late bird catches the woodworm, Peter, and we don't want any of that—it's the trade's worst nightmare. The porters know about that, so ask their advice but remember to tip them."

"A bob a nod is the rate for the job, Olga."

"Yes, and if something is going ridiculously cheap catch the porter's eye and perhaps have a little flutter."

"Cast your bread upon the waters, Olga."

"Don't gossip to the other dealers, Peter; concentrate on the bidding every second—even if you're not in it just then."

"He who hesitates is lost, Olga."

"But have inexhaustible patience, then come in with your bid bang on the psychological moment."

"Rome wasn't built in a day, Olga—strike while the iron is hot."

"Now, if the bidding is too keen force yourself to withdraw."

"He who bids and runs away lives to bid another day. If in doubt drop out, Olga."

"And don't make your old mistake of arguing with Mr Mellon if he beats you to it with his hammer."

"Never complain, never explain, Olga."

"So keep your temper and be polite to Mr Mellon at all times."

"A civil tongue costs nothing, Olga."

"But when you do land a prize don't go boasting to the other dealers around you, Peter."

"An empty kettle makes most noise, Olga. A still tongue in a wise head. Don't make other people as wise as yourself, Olga."

Olga regarded me quizzically. "Peter, you sound more like a parrot every day. In fact you're beginning to look like one."

"Who's a pretty boy now then?" I squawked. Olga counselled me thus daily, and experience had taught me that it paid to reply with the wisdom of the ages because that is the one thing difficult for anybody to contradict.

"Finally, Peter, don't you dare smoke while you're out of my sight, understand? I shall know it if you do."

"Smoke in that dangerous place, Olga! That's how the Great Fire of London started. Why, it would be like striking a match in a coalmine. So there's No Smoking signs round the walls."

"I am well aware how those other dealers smoke on the quiet behind piles of furniture, Peter. That Wally

Tate is the worst offender—I saw him puffing away inside a huge Edwardian wardrobe once."

"Mr Mellon even has a No Smoking sign pinned to his rostrum."

"Solely to stop those blessed dealers setting fire to him as they bid, Peter. As it is it's a wonder he can see through the fug to take bids from the rear of the hall. I can't understand it; smoking strictly prohibited yet the place is blue up to the ceiling. Mark my words, one day that lot will go up like a torch and everybody will be trapped inside."

"Always use a long spoon when you sup with the Devil, Olga."

"I can't help feeling, Peter, that lately your conversation has lost some of its sparkle. Sometimes I wonder if I am speaking to some kind of calendar with a tear-off motto for each day."

"Never judge a sausage by its skin, dear."

"So you're a talking sausage after all. Still, I expect giving up cigarettes is a strain on your nerves, eh?"

"If nerves can have hernia that's what they've got, Olga. My head feels as if it may implode at any moment, like a busted television tube. Then I get dizzy spells followed by hot flushes and nausea."

"So in actual fact you're pregnant. For goodness sake be a man and face up to life, Peter."

"I could face up to it much better if I could have a fag, Olga. Doctors recommend the gradual withdrawal method to prevent addicts like me going potty. Wally Tate is on it and now he's cut right down to forty a day.

Only he can't use matches any more because he shakes them all over the shop when he opens the box."

"But you're not a weakling like Wally Tate, Peter."

"I'm taller than he is too."

"I mean will power, Peter. You're a man of iron resolution, as you've told me so often. You laugh at temptation."

"Ha-ha-ha-ha! Now can I have a fag, Olga? Just one to strengthen my will power—please?"

"Peter—stop that nonsense! Where are your boiled sweets?"

"One more boiled sweet and I shall throw up, Olga. They're hinting in the Bold Forester that my presence turns the beer off."

"Then don't go in there, as I told you before. Now hurry along to the sale-room and concentrate on the day's business."

Leaving Olga to polish a Late Victorian mahogany shaving stand with boxwood inlay and shield mirror, I fled to the car. Safely round the block I lit up skilfully with one hand, then drove to the Mellon Auction Galleries better prepared for the battle of the bids against my fellow bandits. . . .

. . . . Continued in "Pook's Curiosity Shop", which can be ordered from all good bookshops or direct from Emissary Publishing.